S. N. A. F. U.

H. P. Oliver

MYSTERIES IN HISTORY

HPO Productions
8698 Elk Grove Boulevard, Suite 1-271
Elk Grove, California 95624

Cover art and book design by Steve Eitzen

Printed in the United States of America

ISBN-10: 0-9888331-9-0
ISBN-13: 978-0-9888331-9-7

DEDICATION

Respectfully dedicated to those who served on the home front
during WWII and helped make victory in Japan and Europe
possible.

AUTHOR WEBSITE

You are cordially invited to visit the author's website at
http://www.hpoliver.com for many free features related to this
and other H. P. Oliver books. These include a unique visualization
section providing illustrated quotes from S.N.A.F.U. that will
increase your reading enjoyment by allowing you to "see" parts of
the story. (use link below.)

http://www.HPOliver.com/BOOKS/SNAFU/VISUALIZATIONS/INDEX.html

ACKNOWLEDGMENTS

The author gratefully acknowledges the following research sources used in the writing of this book: Moffett Field Historical Society, United States Coast Guard, MilitaryAuthority.com, Pan Am Historical Foundation, PearlHarbor.org, Biltmore Santa Barbara, Golden Gate National Parks Conservancy, Los Angeles Public Library, San Francisco Public Library, the California State Military Museums, the Goodyear Tire & Rubber Company, and the Wikimedia Foundation. In addition, thanks to Gary Weisenberger for his assistance in maintaining authenticity and continuity.

PLEASE NOTE

This novel occasionally refers to individuals and groups with terms that are considered disrespectful and inappropriate in today's society. These terms, however, were in common usage during the historical period in which this story is set and are included here solely for the purpose of accurately depicting the attitudes and customs of the day.

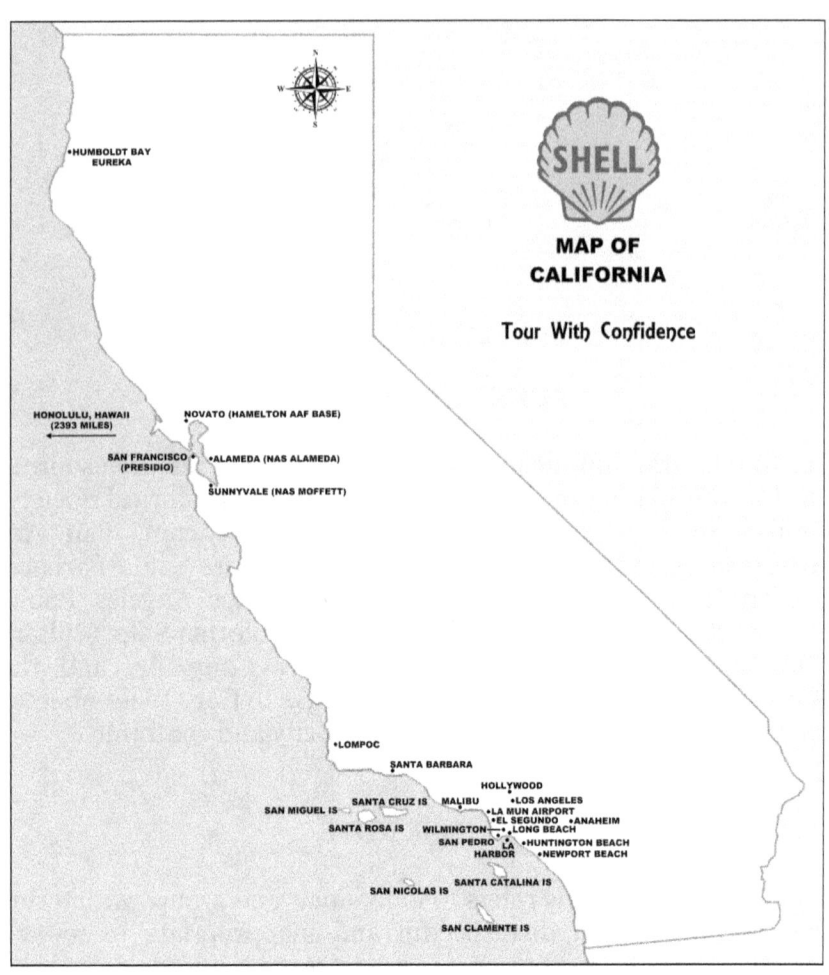

MAP OF
CALIFORNIA

Tour With Confidence

OFFICER RANKS

ARMY/MARINES	NAVY/COAST GUARD
Second Lieutenant	Ensign
First Lieutenant	Lieutenant Junior Grade
Captain	Lieutenant
Major	Lieutenant Commander
Lieutenant Colonel	Commander
Colonel	Captain
Brigadier General	Rear Admiral (1 star)
Major General	Rear Admiral (2 star)
Lieutenant General	Vice Admiral
General	Admiral

One

Hangar One – Moffett NAS – Sunnyvale, California

Three brilliant yellow-orange splotches flared in the blackness overhead. FLASH, FLASH, . . . FLASH. Those muzzle flashes were accompanied by corresponding pops echoing through the darkness. POP, POP, . . . POP. All that commotion was followed a split second later by the whining of three slugs ricocheting off of the concrete floor.

Having someone aiming to kill you is generally a worrisome thing, but at the moment I was more concerned about the guy hitting me by accident than with a well-aimed shot. I estimated the distance between us at around 350 feet, and from the sound of it, he was shooting a Colt forty-five semiautomatic, which has an effective range of about 50 yards. My long-barrel thirty-eight caliber Smith and Wesson revolver had a little more range, but not enough to matter. In other words, we could shoot up a lot of ammo without much risk of doing any damage to each other unless somebody got very lucky.

All this long-distance shooting was taking place inside Moffett Naval Air Station's Hangar One and the place is huge. It had to be because it was designed to accommodate the dirigible Macon. The hangar measures more than eleven-hundred feet in length, roughly 300 feet in width, and nearly 200 feet in height, The building is so big it even has its own weather system with patches of fog occasionally forming up near the curved roof.

The Macon, however, was no longer in residence because it crashed five years ago, helping bring an end to the Navy's enthusiasm for dirigibles. Now the battleship boys are all excited about blimps, which are lighter-than-air ships of much smaller proportions. In fact, they can park nine blimps in less space than one dirigible. The Navy's current interest in blimps is part of a scheme for patrolling the California coast in case some enemy tries to attack us from that direction.

So until the blimps arrived, Hangar One was empty—empty, that is, except for me and one Japanese espionage agent. The Military Intelligence Division in which I was currently serving spotted this guy a while back and was just waiting for an opportunity to put him out of business.

He was a crafty character, though, so when he didn't offer any such opportunities they set a trap for him. The plan was to lure him into a deserted location—Hangar One—for the purpose of stealing a gadget the Navy called an occuscope—a top secret bombsight device supposedly stored in the hangar for use on the top secret blimps to come. In truth there wasn't an occuscope, top secret or otherwise, within a hundred miles, and for all I knew, occuscopes might not even exist.

My part in the scheme was to spring the trap and catch the mouse if he went after the cheese. The orders I'd been given specifically said, "by whatever means available," but my boss, Colonel Si Peterson, did mention it would be preferable to take the guy alive if possible. At the moment that prospect was looking less and less likely.

Despite my arriving promptly at the appointed hour, the Japanese agent was already there. I spotted him in the light from outside when I came in through one of the small doors along the side of the hangar. He also spotted me and decided to get while the getting was good. We were just inside the north end of the hangar and the guy headed for the nearest high ground—one of the longitudinal catwalks mounted way up on the hangar wall. To make matters even more difficult, he was on the east side of the hangar and I was on the west side, putting us well out of each other's range, and even if we had been within range, we couldn't see each other in the pitch black hangar.

To catch this mouse I had to get a whole lot closer and shed some light on the subject. I knew there was an electrical control panel below his position on the east wall. If I could get across the hangar to that panel, I would have the light I needed and I would be within killing range. So would he.

About a minute passed since his last shots, and I knew if I was going to nail the guy before he found a way out of the hangar, I had to get moving. Looking across the floor, I noticed something I hadn't seen before; a dim orange light. I was pretty sure it was an indicator of some kind on the electrical panel over there. That put a small advantage on my side of the ledger because I could see my destination, but there was no chance he could see the tiny light from where he was.

Thinking, "Now or never," I took off across the hangar floor running a broken field pattern like a UCLA halfback. And like that halfback, I had a hundred yards to cover if I was going to score.

The guy heard me and unleashed another volley of shots. They flashed and echoed throughout the hangar again like Fourth of July fireworks. I heard one slug smack into the concrete floor a few feet behind me and found the energy for a little more speed.

When I thought I was close enough, I changed sports and dove for the floor like a baserunner stealing home. I smacked into the electrical panel head first, and reached for a row of red switches above my head. I flipped them up two and three at a time. Hangar One lit up like a motion picture sound stage.

Looking up from the electrical panel, I couldn't see my opponent, but I heard him. Fixing the position of the sound, I scuttled out onto the hangar floor and looked for the guy. The sound I heard was him moving the locking levers for a maintenance hatch in wall.

I was directly below him and in plain view. If he turned and saw me, he had me. I decided this particular spy was not going to be taken alive. I put him squarely in my sights and squeezed the trigger twice. He staggered a few steps along the catwalk before he collapsed and rolled off the walk. It seemed like a very long time before he hit the ground with a sort of dull smack.

With my Smith & Wesson still in hand, I walked over to look at the guy. The term "ragdoll" hardly did him justice. My mind was busy reciting the litany of rationalizations befitting the moment . . . he was an enemy of my country . . . he'd been trying to kill me . . . we both knew the risks. To hell with that. I had no feelings of remorse and I was damned glad it was him on floor of Hangar One instead of me. My orders were to put a spy out of business and I'd carried out those orders. How I came by those orders is another story.

Two

First National Bank Building, Hollywood

Two days later I found myself standing in another empty, although considerably smaller, space. My reason for being in a vacant downtown Hollywood office was a mild case of what my mother would've described as nostalgia-itis. For an uninhabited space though, suite number 213 in the First National Bank Building still had a lot of stuff in it.

Besides me, the only other physical thing in the room was a telephone on the floor where a desk once stood. Not long ago you could call that phone, HOllywood-two-seven-seven-two, and if nobody was in the office you could leave a message with Rosie at Rosie's Professional Telephone Exchange Service. Not anymore.

The office walls were covered with pale blue paint lovingly applied by a lady trombone player who now sings with a popular big band in San Francisco. If you lean just the right way while looking out the two windows in the west wall, you can see Hollywood Boulevard to the south, the throbbing main artery of an imaginary city constructed of dreams.

Looking straight out those same windows, you get a terrific overhead view of traffic on Highland Boulevard. If you leave town in that direction, you will eventually travel over the Cahuenga Pass into the San Fernando Valley and the realms of Warner Bros.-First National Pictures, Uncle Carl's Universal Studios, Fox, Disney, and a few other moviemakers, and from there, on into the unscripted real world.

Despite needing to be repainted for some time, you can still read the name on the frosted glass window in the office door of suite 213. It says, "Jonathon A. Spicer Investigation Agency," but don't bother coming in. Johnny isn't here anymore; he's off protecting the USA from the Japanese, Nazis, Italians, and everyone else who thinks they have a better system for running our country than democracy. I know that's what he's doing because I'm him . . . Johnny Spicer, at your service.

In all honesty, those aren't exactly the words I would use to describe my role in the current world situation, but I'm pretty sure it's what the brass hats in the Army Military Intelligence Division were imagining when they sent me a letter politely explaining they were changing my Army reserve status from inactive to active. Effective immediately, I was Spicer, Jonathon A., Major, US Army, serial number 0392788721.

It's the sort of letter every able-bodied male expects to receive when there's a war to be fought. The only trouble is the US isn't fighting any wars at the moment. True, most of the rest of the world's countries are trading shots across their borders, but FDR is staying a course of neutrality, despite Winston Churchill's pleas for our military involvement.

That being the case, I suspected the Army brass was responding to their idea of the next best thing to thing to a world war—an imminent world war. Now, you might think predicting imminent world wars is tricky business, and for most it is, but remember my outfit is the Military Intelligence Division—folks who spend their lives watching and listening to what's going on, and then translating what they observe into probable outcomes.

The relatively small group of men and women in MID are observers, translators, historians, spies, and code-breakers, especially code-breakers. These days countries wanting to communicate secretly translate their words into a secret code before they transmit the message. Theoretically, this means only someone else who knows the code can read the message. You might say the MID folks are specialists in maintaining this theoretical illusion.

Although I've always been fascinated by encoding and decryption, my job with MID has little to do with secret codes. I am connected to what's known as the counter-intelligence group. Our job is eliminating or neutralizing known espionage threats. My trip to Moffett Field NAS day before yesterday is a good example of the chores my group handles.

Anyway, judging by my sudden recall to duty and various other clues anyone can find by looking for what isn't in the newspapers, I suspected MID was expecting something big imminently—something very big.

Be all that as it may be, you might imagine my life changed significantly when that letter from the United States Army General Staff, Military Intelligence Division showed up in the mail. Boy, did it ever!

After first making sure the letter wasn't some jerk's idea of a very bad joke, I found myself in the Los Angeles Federal Building shoveling my way through enough paperwork to sink a battleship. Then came the uniforms—officers provide their own uniforms in our cheapskate Army—and all the other paraphernalia required to do whatever the brass thought I was going to be doing.

I have to admit, though, the Army did kick in one item that pleased me. It seems the brass thinks I'll be doing a lot of highway travel up and down the west coast, so they provided a vehicle with which to do that traveling, a brand new 1941 Dodge Club Coupe.

I was told the Dodge would be an unmarked undercover car instead of another olive drab Army vehicle with white stars and numbers stenciled all over it. Well, the motor pool guys got it partly right. The spritely and rugged little Dodge had no stars or numbers on it, but can you guess what color they told Dodge to paint the car? Yup, it is a factory color so close to Army olive drab you'd have to park 'em next to each other to see the difference. Now, that's military intelligence.

Next came the personal bits and pieces of a major life change: closing my business, address changes, packing and moving everything I own into a Bekins storage warehouse. While all that was going on, I was also busy saying goodbye to associates, people I've known for years and who've become friends.

Most of this preparation was accomplished in less than a month. After that I went immediately to work getting up to speed on operational changes and my expected assignments.

Now I had a few more days off to wrap up the loose ends of my life. Most important of all and far from just being a loose end, was Susan Jackson. Susan and I share a relationship that slowly evolved from a fun, kicky romance to a love so deep we felt incomplete when we were apart.

We were just coming to terms with those feelings and what we were going to do about them when my letter from the Army arrived. That meant the plans we were thinking about making needed to be postponed before they were even made. Now we had temporary plans instead of permanent ones, and in a few hours I would be in Santa Barbara with Susan working out the new details of our lives.

On that thought, I sighed goodbye to the Jonathon A. Spicer

"Well, you've eaten enough of our kosher food to be Jewish, even if you weren't born that way. What's it going to be today?"

I knew what I wanted, but as a matter of pride, I had to order it just right using the proper protocols. Most people don't know it, but there are several kinds of Reuben sandwiches and the first thing you need to know is that all true Reubens are made with corned beef. There is also a thing called a "Pastrami Reuben" which is sometimes made with coleslaw instead of kraut. To a connoisseur, however, this sandwich is not a true Reuben.

Eli is a purest. All of his Reuben sandwiches include corned beef, Swiss cheese, sauerkraut, and the family's secret recipe Russian dressing grilled between two thick slices of rye bread. That's Eli's standard Reuben.

For those who can't be satisfied with just a good, honest sandwich, however, Eli offers one other Reuben, the Fancy-Schmancy Hollywood Reuben, so named by Danny's mother. Two modifications turn Eli's standard Reuben into a Hollywood Reuben. First, a thin slather of yellow mustard is added to the stack for a little extra tang, and second, it is made on marbled rye bread, but, here again there are secrets true rye bread gourmets must know.

Traditional marbled rye is made from dough created by mixing two different rye flours—one light in color and texture with one heavier and darker. Another way of marbling rye bread is to use only one type of rye flour and adding cocoa powder to half of it for the marbled coloring. And finally, we have the aristocrat of marbled rye bread made with a combination of Russian rye and German pumpernickel flours. This is the only marbled rye Eli will use in his Fancy-Schmancy Hollywood Reuben.

Now we come to choosing a side dish to go with our sandwich. All Eli's sandwiches come with a crunchy dill pickle spear and a side dish. Since it would take an entire lunch hour just to list all of the sides, I'll simplify this part of the lesson with a tip: go for the warm German potato salad. You can't beat it.

So, with the air of an expert, I answered Danny's question, saying, "I'll have a Fancy-Schmancy Hollywood Reuben mit heißen deutschen kartoffelsalat bitte."

Danny laughed out loud. "Johnny, if the Army sends you to Germany, keep your mouth shut and use sign language."

I feigned a hurt expression. "Hey, I thought that sounded pretty authentic."

"I'll give you an E for effort."

While Danny got busy on my sandwich, I asked, "Where's

your dad? I wanted to say goodbye to him while I was here."

"He's home, Johnny."

"I hope he's not feeling poorly."

"Oh, no. It's nothing like that. He's worried about some of our family in Austria."

I nodded. "I would be, too."

"Papa is writing letters to family members, trying to get as many of them to move here while they still can, if they still can." Danny frowned. "Things just keep getting worse over there. We just found out that fellow, Hitler, made a new law that says all Jewish people have to wear a large six-pointed star made of yellow cloth to show they are Jewish."

"I heard that. Hitler is making no effort to hide his anti-Semitic views, and that's making him pretty unpopular in this part of the world. That film Warner Brothers made a couple of years ago, Confessions of a Nazi Spy, with Edward G. Robinson is a good example. Remember, Danny, this is where they make the movies the rest of the world watches, and most of the studios are owned by descendants of European Jews. They can be very influential."

"I know, Johnny, but that's not enough. Somebody has to stop that man now before he kills every Jew in Europe."

"I understand how you feel, Danny—at least I think I do—but I have no idea how things will go in the coming months. I can tell you this, though; the US is headed for a war, maybe two wars, and they aren't far away. The best advice I can offer is learn as much as you can about what's really happening in Europe, and if you believe this country should be involved in the fighting over there, write letters to let everybody from FDR on down know what you think. Just remember, if the US does go to war, a lot of Americans are going to die. It will be hard to convince some of them Europe's problems are good causes to die for."

Setting my sandwich on the table, Danny said, "Johnny, what do you think? Is fighting against what guys like Hitler are doing worth dying for?"

"Absolutely, Danny, and I'll tell you why. Right now Hitler doesn't happen to like folks named Cohen and Levy, but tomorrow he might just as easily add everybody named Spicer to the list. No individual or political party ought to have the power to turn an entire country against any group or race. That's what a lot of people have a hard time seeing. If any of us are vulnerable, we are all vulnerable."

"You've got a good way of saying it, Johnny. I'm gonna try to remember the way you put that. I'm glad we Jews have some good gentile friends like you. We're gonna need all the friends we can get."

"Danny, when it comes to friends, I make my decisions based on the person, not the race or color. First and foremost, you're my friend. That you and I have different religions just gives us more to learn from each other."

I thought Danny looked like he was getting a little choked up, but before I could say anything, he gave me a pat on the back and said, "Eat your Reuben before it gets cold. I need to get busy behind the counter." He glanced out the front window and added, "I see hungry customers heading our way."

As if on cue, the little bell over Eli's door tinkled and hungry voices came into the deli. We shook hands and Danny said, "You take good care of yourself, Johnny. I hope to see you again soon."

"You take care, too, Danny. At least for the time being it looks like I'll be working on the west coast, so keep the corned beef warm . . . I'll be back for another Reuben before we know it."

As I enjoyed my sandwich, Eli's little shop quickly filled to overflowing. By the time I was done, two young women were edging their way in my direction with the obvious intention of grabbing my table as soon as it became vacant.

As I walked to the door, I caught Danny's eye. Knee-deep in sandwiches, he gave me a big smile and a wave. I gave him the same back. Then I was out the door and it swung closed behind me. A few minutes later I pointed the Army's Dodge toward Santa Barbara and headed out of Hollywood.

Four

Hollywood to Santa Barbara – US Route 10

I don't think I ever really understood the true meaning of "bittersweet" until that moment. In my rearview mirror the First National Bank Building—site of so many of my life's successes and disappointments—faded into the hazy, indistinct Hollywood skyline. At the same time my windshield was full of US Route 101, showing me the way ahead to new challenges and whatever the future held in store. For me that moment will always define bittersweet.

Picking up US 101 in Hollywood, you travel over the Cahuenga pass before swinging west through the citrus groves and dairy farms of the San Fernando Valley. Eventually the route winds through the coastal hills to the seaside town of Ventura. From there, US 101 turns northwest, following the coastline to Santa Barbara. The total distance is about a hundred miles and weekday afternoons are the best time to make the trip because the only traffic consists of farm trucks on their way to and from the produce markets. The trucks are slow, but there are plenty of places to pass.

Despite it being the end of November, the air blowing through the open car window was pleasantly warm, and as I traveled through the peaceful rural countryside under a cloudless sky, I thought about where I was going—not my physical destination so much as where my personal choices would take me in the future. At the center of those thoughts was the woman I call Angel.

Her real name is Susan Jackson and she is the Director of Nursing at a small private hospital in Santa Barbara. I met her there while recovering from a gunshot wound. I call her Angel because I first laid eyes on her as I regained consciousness after surgery and the lighting from a window behind her gave Susan an ethereal glow that to my blurry eyes looked like a halo. It turned out she had a personality to match that halo, so the name stuck.

Susan is around five-four, slender, and fair-skinned with enchanting emerald green eyes. Her hair, usually worn shoulder length, is the color of rich mahogany with highlights that glisten when the light catches them.

It takes no more than a few minutes with Susan to realize you are in the company of a unique person; someone a little above and beyond the average. She's smart as a whip, clever, and quick, dangerous qualities in a woman who loves to tease and can take it just as well as she dishes it out. Among her other qualities I admire most are a natural curiosity about the world around her and a way of seeing things from a perspective all her own.

Susan's immediate family consists of a large orange and white tabby named Mister Whiskers and an older brother named Jack. He's a Coast Guard Lieutenant currently stationed in Santa Barbara and one of the nicest guys you'd ever care to meet. Unfortunately, Jack hasn't always had reason to think as highly of me.

Not long ago, while Susan and I were enjoying a weekend at the Santa Barbara Hyatt House Hotel, we invited Jack up to our room for a room service dinner with a great view of the harbor. We were just sitting down to eat when a suspect in the case I was working took a long-range rifle shot at me from the street below. Unfortunately, he mistook Jack for me.

After a few weeks at the Navy's Port Hueneme base hospital, Jack was as good as new and now we joke about the incident, but at the time it was no laughing matter. I figure any guy who can survive an introduction like that and still laugh about it is someone I want for a friend.

One less significant outcome of that night was Susan and I sort of lost interest in the Santa Barbara Hyatt House. The shooting certainly wasn't the hotel's fault, but the surroundings just weren't as appealing as they were before. Since then we've taken to staying at the Santa Barbara Biltmore.

The Biltmore is two or three years older than the Hyatt—both were built in the 1920s—and it has the same great ocean and beach views, plus it's a little closer to the downtown area. With romantic Spanish architecture, luxurious appointments, and first class service, the Biltmore is a great place to forget the cares of the word for a few days.

How, you might wonder, can a Hollywood gumshoe afford luxury hotels in classy vacation spots? If it's anybody's business, I've had the good fortune to attract the attention of some Hollywood bigwigs who are willing to pay top dollar when they got themselves into jams they could have avoided if they were smart instead of rich. I stay at places like the Biltmore when I'm on an expense account or when I need to recharge my batteries for a few days. I've also stayed in more than my share of cockroach infested rat holes.

My seemingly extravagant spending habits have occasionally put Susan and I at odds because she was brought up in a frugal home. I've finally managed to convince her that I am building a nest egg for the future, so she's relaxed a little on that subject, but I can tell it still worries her at times.

Besides spending a few days together before I have to go back to work for my Uncle Sam, this trip is an opportunity for us to make sure we have all of our paperwork straight. With no immediate family around that I'm aware of, I asked Susan to take care of my mail, banking, and so on while I'm away on assignments. My personal affairs are mostly simple and straight forward, but Susan takes her responsibilities seriously, so I knew she'd want to go through the whole works one more time.

It was almost three when I pulled into the Biltmore's circular drive and parked the Dodge in front of their entrance. Inside the hotel's richly appointed and comfortable lobby, a fellow I recognized as the hotel manager welcomed me like long-lost family.

"Good afternoon, Major Spicer. Welcome back to the Santa Barbara Biltmore."

"Thank you, Mister Dekker, I'm glad to be here."

"I reserved the suite you requested, Major Spicer, number 2101 on the second floor at the front of this building. Personally, I think it's the accommodation with the best ocean view in the hotel."

I agreed, and signing the registration card, I said, "I have two suitcases in the trunk of my car. Please have a bell boy take them up to our suite."

Tapping the button on top of the silver bell on his counter, he said, "Certainly. Would you care to have one of our valets to park the car for you?"

"No, thanks. I'm driving an Army vehicle today, so I'll have to park it myself."

"Of course, Major Spicer. Is there anything else we can do for you?"

"No, thanks, Mister Dekker. I think we're all set."

"Very good, enjoy your stay at the Santa Barbara Biltmore."

Outside, I opened the Dodge's trunk so the bellboy could grab my bags and take them up to our room with a fifty-cent tip in his pocket. After parking the car in the hotel's lot, I glanced around to see if anyone was paying attention to me. They weren't, so I took advantage of the moment to lift the trunk mat and make sure the compartment below it was securely locked. The compartment was added by the motor pool as a relatively safe place in which to transport anything I didn't want in plain sight, like weapons and such. It was locked and I left it that way. I didn't anticipate getting into any skirmishes at the Biltmore.

Five

When I saw Susan's '38 Pontiac Eight convertible, a graduation gift from her folks, turn into the hotel drive, I pulled the bill of my cap down so she wouldn't recognize me right away and, as she stepped down from the driver's seat, I gave her an appreciative wolf whistle.

Susan shot a sidelong glance in my direction as if she was loathe to acknowledge such crude behavior, and then she did a classic double take right out of the movies. "Johnny!"

Two seconds later she was in my arms. "Gosh, it's so good to see you! You look swell in your soldier suit."

"Don't get to liking it too much. This uniform is a pain in the neck and I'm not wearing it one more minute than I have to."

She gave me a smile. "That's good. I won't have to worry about all those women who go gaga over men in uniform."

"You most certainly won't." Susan was looking pretty swell herself in a short-sleeve black dress that fit like it was made for her. "On the other hand, if you're gonna run around looking all swanky-sexy like that, I'm the one who's gonna be worried."

She gave me a wink. "Then you'd best be taking good care of your lady."

A bell boy who knew our routine of arriving in separate cars was standing nearby, apparently getting a kick out of our bantering. I looked in his direction with a smile and said, "Well, what are we waiting for, Jimmy? Let's get the lady's bags up to our suite."

"Yes sir, Major Spicer. Shall I have 'em park the car?"

"Yes, please." I gave Susan another admiring look and added,

"I don't think we'll be needing it tonight."

While Jimmy got busy taking care of the bags and car, Susan slipped her arm through mine and we walked into the lobby. As we did, she said softly, "Won't be needing the car tonight, huh? That sounds promising."

"I thought so."

The Biltmore had an elevator, but I steered us toward a circular staircase that offered both views of the grand lobby and of the grounds through arched windows in the outside wall. On the second floor we were just steps away from suite 2101.

Having taken the elevator up, Jimmy was already there and had the door open for us. He set Susan's bag on a folding suitcase stand and I tipped him appropriately. Then he was gone and I took Susan in my arms.

"Angel, I know it's only been a couple of weeks and we've talked on the telephone, but I've missed you."

"I know, Johnny. I've missed you like crazy. I wish the darned Army would go just go away and leave us alone."

We kissed again, and then just held each other. Finally, I said, "How 'bout we get room service to send up a couple of libations and something to munch on until dinner?"

Susan nodded enthusiastically. "Good idea. We can sit out on our patio and enjoy the ocean breezes."

"All right, Angel, what would you like?"

After making a show of giving the question a great deal of thought, she said, "Something with rum and fruit—lots of fruit. Fruit is good for you."

I called room service and ordered a Mai Tai, a double Scotch and soda, and some salted nuts. Fifteen minutes later we were toasting the Pacific Ocean on our balcony overlooking the beach.

Susan leaned back on her chaise, closed her eyes, and said, "I think this is just about as close to paradise as a person can get."

"You'll get no argument from me on that score. Seems like this is the first break I've taken in a month. I need to catch up on all the latest news. How's my pal, Mister Whiskers?"

Grinning, she said, "Quite well. In fact he sends his regards and suggests that, as long as we were at the ocean, we ought to bring him a fish."

"What a character! I suspect, however, he would actually prefer the variety of fish that comes in a can. How's that other character in your life?"

"I assume you mean dear brother Jack?"

"None other."

Susan seemed to think about my question for a moment. "I guess he's okay. He just got back from some business or other in San Diego, and he's behaving . . . well, oddly."

I looked over and asked, "How so?"

"I'm not sure what it is. He seems worried or concerned about something, but when I ask him, he says nothing's wrong."

I nodded. "Angel, I don't know if this is it or not, but I'm seeing a lot of signs that something big—I mean world-wide big—is coming. One of those signs is the fact that the Military Intelligence Division is calling guys like me back to duty. Jack may be seeing some of the same signs and has come to the same conclusion."

Susan looked at me over the miniature pink umbrella in her Mai Tai. "That scares me, Johnny. It scares me for him and for you. I don't know what I'd do if anything happened to either of you."

"I know, Angel, and I don't mean to make light of the situation, but I've had a little experience with this sort of thing and Jack can handle himself. I don't think you need to be too concerned right now. Besides, from the look of things, it seems like I'll be doing my job right here on the west coast, at least for the near future."

Susan's face brightened. "Really?"

"That's how it looks. MID has newer people with recent experience in Europe and the Orient. They've got the latest training, like languages and customs. My new boss, Colonel Peterson, seems to be of the opinion I'll be of the most use in my home territory. There's a lot of defense industry on the west coast and he wants me where I can deal promptly with any issues that come up." Images of Moffett NAS Hanger One popped into my mind, but I kept them to myself.

"That would be wonderful, Johnny. We might be able to see each other more often."

"I hope so, but the tricky part is, if I'm working undercover, I have to be careful not to let the subject connect me with you. That's the last thing we want to have happen. We'll just have to see how things go and play it by ear."

Susan was looking a little less cheery, but she gave me a smile. "We'll do whatever you think is best. Just so long as you can let me know you're all right once in a while if we have to be apart for a long stretch."

Giving her what I hoped was a reassuring smile, I said, "Count on it." Then, wanting to redirect the subject a little, I asked, "Has Jack given you any hints about his assignment?"

She nodded. "Yes. He thinks he'll be right here. I'll be glad if things work out that way."

About that time the sun finished its descent into distant fog bank and the air turned cool. Susan shivered and I said, "Ready to go in for dinner?"

She gave me a sleepy-eyed look. "Well . . . I'm ready to go in."

Two hours and some change later the warm body in my arms stirred. "I think I'm ready for dinner now."

Six

Santa Barbara Biltmore Hotel

Friday flew by much too quickly. As expected, we spent most of the day going over the arrangements we'd made for Susan to act in my behalf while I was unable to take care of personal business myself.

Nearly everything I owned was in the Santa Barbara Bekins Van and Storage warehouse and Susan had access to all of it, including my car. She was signatory to my checking and saving accounts with First National Bank, plus she had the key to a safe deposit box at the Santa Barbara branch where I stashed a few minor valuables. Susan was also the executer of my will and the beneficiary of my Army life insurance policy.

At one point Susan looked at the paperwork spread out on the table and shook her head. I said, "What's the matter, Angel, am I piling too much on you here?"

Shaking her head, she said, "No, it isn't that. It's just . . . well, I've just never had this kind of responsibility for anyone else before."

"Angel, if I can't trust you, who can I trust? If something happens to me, you get just about everything I own, anyway."

Susan gripped my arm. "Don't even say that! I don't want what you have, I want who you are."

Grinning, I said, "I'll do my best to save you the burden of inheriting my colossal estate."

I could see my attempt at humor hadn't eased her concerns, but she gave me a smile and said, "Please do."

It was around five when we finished dotting I's and crossing T's. We had a date to meet Jack at one of the hotel restaurants for dinner at six. That left us a little time to relax, so we retired to our balcony.

Susan was wearing her white shorts, which hadn't made keeping my mind on business any easier. I was just banishing that thought from my mind, at least for the time being, when she said, "What do you think, Johnny? Did we cover everything to your satisfaction?"

"Hell, we had everything covered to my satisfaction a couple of weeks ago. Today was just to put your mind at ease."

She smiled, "That's kind of what I thought. Thanks for indulging me. It's really important to me that I get this right."

"I appreciate that, Angel." Then a thought occurred to me. Standing, I said, "I did forget one thing, though. I'll be right back."

When I returned to the balcony my little door alarm bell from the office was hanging from my right hand. I gave it a shake and it jingled. Susan stared at the gadget. "What on earth is that?"

"That, Angel, is the alarm bell I rigged at the office so I'd know when someone came into the outer office."

Looking a little confused, Susan asked, "Why is it here?"

"I felt sad about leaving it behind, so I took it down and brought it along." I handed her the bell. "Please take good care of this until we have another door to hang it on."

Susan laughed. "You nut. Okay, I'll take good care of it." After a short, thoughtful pause, she added, "I know, I'll hang it in my apartment where Mister Whiskers can give it a ring from time to time. Is that all right?"

"It's positively brilliant."

"Thank you, sir. Now that we have the work done, what is our agenda for tomorrow?"

"I thought we'd take it easy and just enjoy being together."

She smiled. "I like that agenda." Glancing at her watch, Susan added, "Oh gosh, it's getting late. We'd better get ready."

"If we must."

"Johnny?"

"Yes, Angel?"

"Would you please wear your uniform to dinner? Jack will be wearing his and I think having dinner with two handsome men in uniform would be great fun."

I glared in her direction, but a pair of emerald green eyes won the argument. Sighing, I said, "Okay, Angel, but just this once."

Susan grinned. "Thanks, Johnny!"

We were to meet Jack at the Biltmore's Terrace Restaurant, an outdoor establishment overlooking the beach with concrete fire pits scattered about to keep patrons from shivering on chilly nights. As an added bonus, the food was even pretty good.

Jack was waiting for us near the maître d' podium. He gave Susan a hug and a kiss, and then snapped to attention and saluted me, saying, "Good evening, Major Spicer."

I returned his salute, saying, Good evening, Lieutenant Jackson. Now, let's make that the end of the soldier-sailor stuff. We're here to have fun, not make war."

He chuckled and said, "Yes, sir, as you wish, sir."

The maître d' showed us to a table with a great view of the lights in the harbor and a fire pit close by. A cocktail waitress took our drink orders and Jack said, "So how do you like being back in harness, Johnny?"

"Honestly, I'm not overjoyed about it. I was forced to shut down a profitable business and move my entire life into a Bekins warehouse on some brass hat's whim."

There was no humor in Jack's expression when he said, "I have a bad feeling there's more than a whim behind all this."

I nodded. "Yeah, Jack, you're right. I was just blowing off a little steam."

"Well, you're the military intelligence genius, so tell me when to duck, will ya?"

"Don't depend on what I know. The only thing they tell me is where to go when they need someone to put out a fire."

Tilting his head in curiosity, Jack said, "Been putting out a lot of fires lately?" Then he immediately realized his mistake and added, "Don't answer that, Johnny. I don't want you to haul me off to the slammer as a spy for asking the wrong kind of questions."

While dealing with the Japanese espionage agent two days ago certainly qualified as putting out a fire and it wouldn't have been giving away any top secret information for Jack to know the general details of the incident, I didn't especially want Susan knowing about it. She was already on edge about me being back in the service, I didn't want to make things worse.

I laughed. "Not much chance of that. Angel would have my hide if I did. As for fires, let's just say in times like these there will always be a conflagration or two that need extinguishing."

Jack nodded and went back to studying the menu. Susan, however, was still watching me with a peculiar expression on her face. I'd taken too long to answer Jack's question and the answer I'd come up with wasn't convincing. I suspected Susan sensed I was avoiding the question. She's good at picking up subtleties like that.

The rest of the evening was pleasant enough, but something was definitely bothering Susan. When we got back to our suite she went out onto our balcony and stood watching the lights in the harbor. I stood behind her and gently put my hands on her waist. "What's on your mind, Angel?"

She turned and put her arms on my shoulders. "I'm sorry, Johnny. It's just . . . that conversation you and Jack had about putting out fires . . . well, I just got the idea there's something you aren't telling me. Is there, Johnny?"

I kissed her on the forehead and said, "Nothing important, Angel. It's just routine work stuff . . ."

Susan stared into my eyes as if she was reading something there. "They're already sending you out on assignments, aren't they? And you've already had a close call, haven't you? Tell me, Johnny."

Maybe she really could read something in my eyes. I sighed and said, "Yes, Angel, I had an assignment two days ago, but it went off without a hitch; no problems."

She put her arms around me and held on tight. "Johnny, I know there are reasons you can't tell me a lot about what you do now, but don't hold back on what you can tell me just because you don't want to scare me. I'd much rather be a little scared and worried about you than have no idea what you're doing and fearing the worst. Do you understand what I'm saying, Johnny?"

"All right, fair enough. Yes, I've already been on an assignment. It involved catching a Japanese espionage agent at a military base. I was successful. Does that make you feel any better?"

With her arms still around me, Susan said, "Yes . . . yes it really does."

"Okay, from now on you get all I can tell you, both the good and the bad."

Susan stepped back so she could look up into my face. "Thank you, Johnny. I don't mean to be a problem for you, but I'm counting on a future that includes us being together. So far most of what we've talked about is business, and I know you've been very busy, but sometime soon we need to talk about us."

I gently pushed her back and said, "Okay, wait here a minute."

Inside, I got a small black box out of my civvies bag. Back on the balcony I said, "I was going to save this for tomorrow, but now seems like an especially appropriate time."

She was looking at me with the hint of a smile on her face.

There was no surprising this girl. I sat her down on one of the chaise lounges and, as is the custom, I got down on one knee. "Angel, for two years now you've brought more happiness into my life than I ever expected to find there. Would you consider taking that job permanently?"

With that I opened the little box so she could see my mother's engagement ring—a one carat round diamond in a simple, elegant gold setting. There were tears in Susan's eyes.

"Yes, Johnny, yes! Nothing in the world would make me happier."

Mom's ring fit perfectly. I took Susan's hand and held it up so the light made the diamond sparkle. "This was my mother's engagement ring. If the style is too old fashioned, we could have the stone mounted in a more modern setting."

"Oh, no, Johnny. The ring is beautiful, and I love that it was your mom's. I wouldn't change the setting for the world. I can't wait to show it off."

Seven

Presidio – San Francisco

Susan and I spent Saturday doing the kinds of things people in love do when it's likely they won't see each other for a while. We walked on the beach, ate clam chowder at Stearns Wharf, drove out to the Coast Guard station so Susan could show Jack her ring, and discussed plans for the wedding.

Susan favored a small ceremony in Santa Barbara, maybe on the wooded grounds of Casa Sobre El Mar, the clinic where Susan works, all of which sounded fine to me. We left the date open because we had no idea when our time would be our own again. We agreed it should be soon, though.

Early Sunday morning we got up, packed, and checked out. After breakfast at the Terrace, we said our goodbyes and I pointed the Army's Dodge north on US 101. Eight hours and some change later I pulled up to the San Francisco Presidio's main gate.

The Presidio Army base occupies about two-and-a-half square miles of mostly undeveloped wilderness at the extreme northwestern tip of San Francisco near the southern anchorage of the Golden Gate Bridge. The area was first established as a military post in 1776 by Spaniards settling in Alta California. It later became a Mexican fortification and eventually the Presidio was commandeered by the United States in 1848.

Today the Presidio serves as headquarters for the Army's Western Defense Command, as well as home to the Military Intelligence Division's Japanese Language School. The Presidio is also MID's west coast command center supporting the main headquarters in Fort Belvoir, Virginia. That was my reason for being there.

The Army's offices, barracks, officers' quarters, Letterman Hospital, and other sundry buildings only occupy a small portion of the Presidio. The biggest part of the base is rugged undeveloped country in which numerous large coastal artillery guns are concealed to protect the entrance to San Francisco Bay. Some of the big gun emplacements date all the way back to the turn of the century. Beginning during the World War, though, more modern artillery pieces replaced the original cannons. Some of the newest 12-inch guns are capable of lobbing thousand pound projectiles up to fifteen miles.

Most of the buildings in the Presidio date back to the Civil War and are constructed of red brick in what the Army describes as the "Georgian" style. My new home away from home was in one of these Civil War era structures. The combined Bachelor Officer and Visiting Officer Quarters were located in a three-story building at one end of "Officers' Row" near the parade ground.

I lugged my bags up to the raised porch and into the lobby, where a colored staff sergeant manned the registration desk. In addition to checking me in, he also had a message. It was from my boss, Colonel Simon Peterson, suggesting that, if I arrived in time, we meet at the Officers Club for dinner. Peterson had permanent quarters on the base and the staff sergeant provided the Colonel's telephone number. Once in my room, I called Peterson and agreed to meet him in the O-Club at 1800 hours.

My room at the VOQ was furnished with the necessities, a bed, chest of drawers, a couple of wooden chairs, a small writing desk, and an armoire, all of which had been around a while, but were still quite serviceable. The bathroom was down the hall. My window looked out to the northeast and gave me a picturesque view of the Golden Gate Bridge. It wasn't the Biltmore, but I'd certainly stayed in worst places.

I got my bags unpacked and my gear stowed, and then I went back downstairs to use one of the public telephones lined up just outside the B/VOQ lobby. The phones in the rooms were for use within the confines of the Presidio. Getting an outside line, especially to make a long-distance call required an act of congress.

The operator connected my collect call to Susan's home telephone in Santa Barbara. After Susan accepted the charges, she said, "Johnny! Did you make it San Francisco all right?"

"I sure did. I just checked into the Visiting Officers Quarters."

With a grin in her voice, Susan said, "Good. How are the accommodations? Better than the Biltmore?"

"Well, I wouldn't exactly say that, but they aren't bad. I even have a view of the Golden Gate Bridge out my window. How are things there?"

"About the only thing I have to report is Mister Whiskers whole-heartedly approves of your door-bell thing. I hung it near his food bowl and he gives it a jingle with his tail every time he walks under it."

"Maybe he's trying to train you to fill the food bowl when he rings the bell."

"I wouldn't put it past him." In a softer voice, Susan said, "Johnny?"

"Yeah, Angel?

"I'm already missing you."

"That's only fair because I miss you, too. I'm having dinner with my boss tonight. He might give me some idea what to expect during the next few weeks. I'll let you know when I can get free again as soon as I know."

"Good. You know, the light keeps flashing off my new ring and catching my eye, and every time it does, I think of you. It's the most beautiful ring I've ever seen."

"I'm glad you like it. I hoped it wasn't too old fashioned."

"Johnny, darling, it's the old fashioned design that makes it so charming. I can't wait to show it off at work tomorrow."

"Just keep thinking of me when the light catches that diamond."

"That's automatic. Johnny, do you have any idea how much I love you?"

"If it's as much as I love you, it's a whole bunch."

"It is, Johnny. It really and truly is."

When we finished our conversation, I went back up to my room and changed into my uniform. I didn't need it to get into the Officer's Club, but I thought it might make a good impression on the boss. Peterson is always in uniform.

It's a short three block walk from the B/VOQ to the Officer's Club at the northeast end of the parade grounds. The club itself looks a little out place because when the building was restored some time back, it was remodeled in the Spanish style with a red tile roof. Inside it looks like just about every other O-Club I've ever seen—nothing fancy, but pleasant, and it has some nice views out the windows on the east and north sides of the building.

Lieutenant Colonel Peterson, a tall slender man in his fifties with white hair and a pleasant expression, walked up to the entrance just as I got there. I tossed him a salute and we shook hands. He said, "Johnny, I appreciate you trying to fit in with the military traditions here, but don't be too concerned about them. We are, for the most part, professionals first and soldiers second. In fact, less than half of the MID crew are even military. So a salute is appropriate for formal situations, but the rest of the time a handshake will do the job."

"All right, sir."

He grinned. "The same goes for that 'sir' business. My first name is Simon, so most of the officers call me Si. Feel free to do the same."

"Thank you, Si."

A uniformed maître d' seated us and we put in our drink orders. Then Si said, "I'm glad you got here in time for us to have dinner. We haven't had much time to get acquainted and I like to know the people I work with. Most of what I know about you comes from a recent background check we did. According to it, you've made quite a name for yourself in law enforcement circles since you left the service."

I couldn't tell whether he was being sarcastic or sincere, so I proceeded cautiously. "I've always tried to cooperative."

"That's what the FBI tells me. The Los Angeles supervising agent says you've helped them out on two occasions, one a counter-espionage case, with good results."

I pictured Tom Kendall sitting across my desk unjustly balling me out for getting one of their double agents killed. J. Edger's boys screwed that one up. The same was true of another case I inherited from the G-men, one involving a Chinese diplomat up here in San Francisco. That one turned out all right, but only because I figured out the FBI was running a double cross in time to keep it from ending up in the sewer. No, I couldn't picture Tom Kendall heaping praise on me, but it seems he had.

"The Los Angeles police think highly of you, too. We talked to officers in two precincts who've worked with you. Again they both gave you high marks. It also seems you have some celebrity clients who speak highly of you. We talked to people at Warner Brothers Studios and the praise there goes right up to the top. So now maybe you can see why I was so anxious to get you up here."

"Well, I hope I can do you some good because this little escapade is costing me a lot, including a profitable business."

"I understand that, Johnny, but I think you'll soon see our reasons for calling you back. In fact, I'd like to meet with you tomorrow morning at oh-eight-hundred to discuss exactly why you were recalled and to talk about your next assignment."

Listening to Si Peterson I still wasn't sure if I was getting the straight story or if he was just leading me down the garden path. I found myself hoping he was on the level because I was starting to like the guy.

After dinner I used the B/VOQ's laundry facilities to wash and dry the contents of my dirty clothes bag. It was something I did whenever I had a free moment. I never know when I'll have to pull up stakes and get on the road.

Eight

MID West Coast Command HQ – Building 100, Presidio

The Military Intelligence Division's west coast headquarters is housed in Building 100, a two-story brick structure next to the Presidio commissary. Upon signing in and having my identification verified, I was directed to Lieutenant Colonel Si Peterson's office at the back of the first floor. Si said we were waiting for another man before beginning the briefing.

The missing man arrived about five minutes late and the three of us walked to a conference room at the southwest corner of Building 100. You didn't need to be a genius to see there was something very odd about the space in which we were meeting.

For one thing, the room had an entryway consisting of two heavy doors with an empty three-foot hallway between them. Inside it was clear the walls and ceiling enclosed a space considerably smaller than the outside dimensions of the room. The explanation for these oddities was we were in MID's soundproof security conference room, an experimental design that cost taxpayers a lot more than it was worth. We could have achieved the same degree of security by taking a walk down to the beach.

When we were all seated and a noisy ventilation fan was turned on, Si introduced me to the third man in the room. "Johnny, I'd like you to meet Lieutenant Commander Edward Nugent of the Navy's Airship Training, Development, and Operations Command in Lakehurst, New Jersey. Ed, meet Major Johnny Spicer, MID counter-espionage agent."

Nugent and I shook hands while Peterson continued his preface to the meeting. "Johnny, your next assignment involves blimps again and Lieutenant Commander Nugent is here because he knows more about lighter-than-air-ships than just about anyone. Ed, how about giving us the lowdown on blimps?"

Sounding like he was addressing a class of fifth-graders, Nugent said, "I'd be happy to, Colonel Peterson. Describing airships in the simplest way, we have two types: rigid and non-rigid. Rigid airships are also known as dirigibles and they are described as rigid because the bags containing their lifting gas, usually helium or hydrogen, are contained within a metal framework. Non-rigid airships, or blimps as they are most commonly called, have no frame and rely mostly on the gas bag for their shape.

"Both blimps and dirigibles carry their passengers in control cars or gondolas attached to the bottom of their gasbags. Both types of ships rely on gasoline powered aircraft engines with propellers to move through the air. Typically, the blimps we're concerned with are a good deal smaller than dirigibles. Are you with me so far?"

I nodded, wishing Lieutenant Commander Know-It-All would hurry up and get to the point.

"Very good. As Colonel Peterson explained, our assignment concerns blimps, specifically the Goodyear type K blimp. The K-Class is slightly less than 250 feet in length, is flown by a crew of ten, has a cruising speed of 58 miles per hour, and a maximum speed of 78 miles per hour. Typically a K can stay aloft for about 38 hours and has a range of roughly 2,200 miles. The current versions of the K-class blimps are powered by two Pratt-Whitney aircraft engines developing about 425 horsepower each.

"The reason the Navy is interested in blimps is that we feel the blimp is the best aircraft for patrolling our country's 12,000 miles of coastline to intercept enemy submarines and surface ships." He paused a moment, then quickly added, "That is, of course, in the event of war."

I asked, "Are these blimps armed so they can do something about it they encounter an enemy submarine or surface ship. In the event of war, of course."

Nugent smiled, although I'm not sure he knew what he was smiling about. "The prototypes are equipped with a .50 caliber Browning M2 machine gun and four 350 pound Mark 47 depth charges."

"You said 'prototypes.' How many K-class blimps do you actually have?"

"We currently have six variants we're using for testing and

training."

"I gather you are expecting more?"

Nugent nodded. "Yes. Back in June of '40 congress passed a law authorizing the construction of 10,000 military aircraft, 48 of which are to be blimps. Goodyear was awarded the contract and they're already at work on the next batch."

Peterson asked the next question. "Ed, I assume some of those blimps are slated for the west coast. Do you know where they'll be stationed?"

"Tentatively we expect blimps to be stationed at a field in Tillamook, Oregon, which hasn't been built yet; Moffett Field here in California; and at the Marine Air Station at Tustin in southern California, which is under construction." He paused, looked at me and said, "I think that pretty much covers the basics on blimps. Any more questions?"

Si Peterson also looked in my direction and I shook my head vigorously. He said, "Okay, then. Let's move on to the mission itself. Johnny, do you remember what we used for bait in catching that Japanese espionage agent at Moffett Field?"

"If I'm remembering correctly it was some cockamamie top secret gadget you called an occuscope."

"That's correct, only it isn't cockamamie. There really is an occuscope and it's a device the Navy is hoping will greatly increase the effectiveness of their coastal blimp patrols. Ed, please tell us what you can about the occuscope."

Like a kid doing show and tell at school, Lieutenant Commander Know-It-All held up a black and white photograph. The photo was of something that looked like two camera lenses attached perpendicularly to opposite points of a vertical cylinder. "For scale, the occuscope in this photo is about thirty inches in height and 20 inches wide at the lenses. The best way to describe what it does is to compare the device to a submarine periscope.

"As you can imagine, a 250-foot blimp makes a pretty tempting target, especially at low altitudes. The occuscope reduces the risk of being shot down by a ship or a submarine on the surface. When there are clouds or a fogbank present, the blimp can remain concealed and lower the occuscope to look for enemy vessels. Essentially it is an upside down periscope.

"In addition to relaying visual images, the occuscope uses a new invention called a magnetic anomaly detector, or MAD. The MAD has the ability to detect a disturbance in the earth's magnetic field caused by a ship, even a ship under water. Scientists also tell us they believe it will be possible to add infrared detectors in the near future to make the occuscope even more effective at night.

"In addition, the occuscope serves as a remote aiming device for the blimp's gun and depth charges. So the occuscope provides images and magnetic anomaly information to help blimp crews find and destroy targets without exposing themselves to the risk of surface fire."

I added, "Assuming there's a convenient cloud for the blimp to hide in."

Nugent looked at me and nodded. "We recognize that drawback, but there are almost always clouds over the north Atlantic. I understand storms and cloud cover are less prevalent along the west coast, but we still think the occuscope can still save American lives and help sink enemy ships off our coasts."

Peterson said, "Johnny, you sound skeptical and I don't blame you, but it doesn't matter what we think as long as Japan thinks this thing—they've given it the code name 'snow goose'—is a threat. Based on decoded transmissions, that is exactly what they think. So your mission is to prevent Japanese agents from getting one of these things so their scientists can tear it apart and see what makes it tick."

Nodding, I turned to Nugent. "How many of these occuscopes do you have and where are they?"

"We have six back a Lakehurst. They're being used for development and training."

Si Peterson said, "Those aren't our problem. The Navy is responsible for keeping them safe. Needless to say, the Nazis are also very interested in the occuscope."

"Okay, how many on the west coast?"

Nugent said, "Quite a few, I'm afraid. The plant that makes them is in El Segundo. That's just south of the Los Angeles airport."

"And how is their security?"

"It seems fairly tight. It's a small company known as Optitronics. They're located in a manufacturing and warehouse facility with a secure vault—like a bank vault—they use to store the completed occuscopes. Unfortunately, they are producing occuscopes a lot faster than Goodyear is producing blimps."

I said, "Wouldn't it make a lot sense to store the gizmos at Lakehurst or some facility where they can be protected by military security?"

"It would, but Optitronics' contract with the government is a pay-on-delivery deal, and the government doesn't want to take delivery until they have blimps to put the scopes in so they don't have to lay out the money before it's necessary."

I mumbled, "And around and around the merry-go-round spins."

Si Peterson stood and said, "Okay, Johnny, I want you to drive down to El Segundo and stay there until we have confidence in this outfit's ability to keep the occuscopes safe or you come up with a better way of protecting them. Lieutenant Commander Nugent will ride down with you as an advisor. He'll stick around for as long as you think you need him. Fair enough?"

"Fair enough." Turning to Nugent, I said, "Any chance I can get a copy of that occuscope photo you showed us?"

Si answered for him, "Here, I've got a couple of copies. You can have one of mine."

I took the photo and slid it into a dispatch case I'd brought with me. To Nugent I said, "We've got about a ten hour drive ahead of us. How soon can you be ready to leave?"

"I shouldn't need more than half an hour to get my gear together."

Checking my wristwatch, I said, "Good, I'll meet you in front of the VOQ at 1030 hours."

Nugent gave me a nod and, "I'll be there."

Si Peterson and I were walking back to his office together when he said, "What do you think, Johnny?"

I shrugged. "I'll be a lot better able to answer that question when I've seen what this place looks like and how they operate."

"All right. Keep in touch." To Pauline Ashley, MID's office manager, Si said, "Draw two hundred from pretty cash for Johnny. He might be away a while."

Nine

The drive from the Presidio to El Segundo lasted ten hours and fifteen minutes, and it was the quietest motor trip I've ever made with another person in the car. I'm pretty sure Lieutenant Commander Nugent didn't say more than a dozen words the whole time we were on the road.

Since I couldn't recall anything I'd done to hack him off that badly, I guessed his attitude might be a result of the fact that Nugent is a career military type and I'm only a reservist on active duty. Vowing not to let the man's personal problems keep me awake, I pulled into a new motor inn called Patmar's Motel just south of the Los Angeles Airport. We rented a couple of rooms and agreed to meet in the joint's coffee shop at 0700 hours the next morning.

I was halfway through my first cup of coffee by the time Nugent strolled in almost fifteen minutes late. In addition to being a moody cuss, he also seemed to have difficulty telling time. His tardiness this morning didn't particularly matter, but showing up late under different circumstances might matter a lot.

Nugent joined me at my table and ordered coffee and a glass of orange juice. After that, he proceeded to sit there looking around the room without saying a word.

Finally I'd had enough of his lousy attitude. "Nugent, here's how I want to do this. We'll drive down to Optitronics' plant and you will introduce me to the people I need to know. After that I'll take a look at the plant—where they store the raw materials, where they make the gizmos, where they store the finished products, and how they keep all of that secure. I'll decide how to proceed from there when we reach that point."

The Lieutenant wasn't enjoying taking orders from a lowly reservist who outranked him, but at least I got a few words out of him: "All right, Spicer."

"While we're on the subject, what's the top dog's name at Optitronics?"

Nugent reached into the inside pocket of his blue uniform jacket and removed a notebook. After looking through it twice, he finally answered, "The fellow's name is Frank Demas. According to his business card, he's Optitronics' president and chief engineer."

"Just out of curiosity, have you met Demas or been to Optitronics' plant?"

He nodded slowly. "I've never met Demas, but I visited the plant about two years ago when they were awarded the occuscope development contract. I understand, though, that they redesigned the facility when the occuscope went into production."

For some reason the word "worthless" flashed in my mind every time I looked at Nugent. It seemed very likely I wouldn't be needing the guy around after today, if that long.

Optitronics occupies a two-story wood frame building a block east of Sepulveda on Mariposa. While the second story is well endowed with windows, the ground floor front of the building has no windows at all, only a recessed entryway with a small sign saying "Optitronics Mfg." An alleyway down the east side of the building gives access to a loading dock with three roll-up doors. The doors were all wide open and there was nobody in sight. That seemed like a good place to start checking Optitronics' security, or lack of it.

I pulled up next to the loading dock and was climbing out of the Dodge when Nugent said, "Where are you going? The entrance is around front."

"Yeah, but going in this way is sure to be more interesting."

Nugent climbed out and jogged up the loading dock stairs behind me as I got my MID photo ID case out and ready for when someone challenged us. That is, IF anyone challenged us.

The interior of the loading dock is two stories high and amounts to a small warehouse containing stacks of cardboard boxes arranged by the company names on the shipping cases. There appeared to be two ways to get from the loading dock into the rest of the facility—a ground floor door toward the front of the building and a second floor door farther back at the top of a wooden staircase. I chose the latter door.

As I started up the staircase, Nugent said, "Spicer, someone is going to get very upset with us for coming in here like a couple of burglars."

"They aren't going to be half as upset as MID will be when they find out we could sneak in here like a couple of burglars."

At the top of the stairs I encountered a door with a wire mesh safety glass window. Through the window I saw a hallway and, beyond that, several glass-walled manufacturing rooms. I gave the doorknob a tentative try. It turned, so bold as brass, I stepped into the hall and strolled along toward the front of the building observing the various activities going on in the assembly rooms to my right. Along the way we were passed by a young woman carrying a tray of what appeared to be optical lenses. She didn't give us a second glance.

When we reached the front of the building, I followed a stairway down to the lobby area. That was when someone finally took notice of our presence. An older fellow in a threadbare security guard uniform was standing next to the entrance door chatting with the receptionist behind a glass brick and chrome counter.

The receptionist, a well stacked blonde in a V-necked top that left no doubt as to the authenticity of her figure, looked up, saw me coming in her direction, and said, "May I help you, sir?"

Taking stock of the situation and seeing that Lieutenant Commander Nugent didn't seem to have the slightest idea what was going on or what to do next, I showed the receptionist my MID ID. She looked kind of puzzled, so I said, "Do you understand what you're looking at and who I am?"

Looking up at me with an anxious to please expression, she said, "Sort of. Are you with the government?"

I sighed. "Well, that's a start. Please get Frank Demas in here."

Now the receptionist came to the party. She even seemed proud of herself for figuring out what to say next. "Oh, no sir, I can't do that. He's in an important conference."

"Sister, it will be his last conference if you don't get him down here and on the double."

A frown clouded her pretty face for a moment, but she bounced back quickly and said, "Yes, sir, I'll call his secretary."

About that time it dawned on the security guard he'd screwed the pooch and he decided he should do something security guard-ish to redeem himself. Walking up behind me, he grabbed my shoulder and tried to spin me around. "Just who the hell do you think you are barging in here like this?"

I easily slapped his hand away from my shoulder and resisted a strong temptation to knock him into the middle of next week. Instead, I shoved my MID ID in his face so close he went cross-eyed trying to read it. "I'm the guy who is going to insure your early retirement. Now go sit down over there and keep your mouth shut."

That less than pleasant exchange finally prompted Nugent into action. Stepping closer to me he said in a low voice, "You're being awfully hard on these folks. Take it easy."

"Whose side are you on, Nugent? Ours or the enemy's? These folks are practically inviting espionage agents to stroll in here and walk out with the crown jewels."

Nugent said nothing and took a step backward. At the same time a commotion was making its way down the stairs. It was led by a slender balding fellow who was trying to make up for the lack of hair on top of his head by growing a beard. A yellow pencil was stuck over his right ear.

He shouted, "What the hell is going on down here?" Then, looking at me he said, "Who the hell are you?"

My badge case was getting a workout. I held it up for his perusal and said, "If you're Frank Demas, you and I need to have a talk, preferably someplace that isn't as wide open as this plant."

Demas glowered and opened his mouth to say something, but I beat him to it. "Now."

An hour later I'd given Frank Demas his marching orders. The instructions I gave him were to lock up the loading dock and to put three security guards who weren't already receiving pensions on an around-the-clock schedule.

There were other things that needed doing, but before I got to them I wanted to do some thinking about how to fix the lousy situation facing me at Optitronics. First, however, I needed to lose some weight—about a hundred and sixty pounds of worthless Navy officer.

I drove over to the military hanger at the LA airport, where I told Nugent I wouldn't be needing him any further and to get his butt back to Lakehurst, New Jersey the best way he could. He didn't seem overly upset about leaving sunny California.

Ten

Gilmore Service Station – N. Sepulveda & E. Walnut, El Segundo

After dropping Nugent off I made for the first public telephone I saw, which was at a Gilmore Service Station on the south side of the airport at Sepulveda and Walnut. I called Colonel Peterson person-to-person collect. It took a few minutes for his secretary to track him down, but she found him.

Explaining the situation at Optitronics required some time because I had to make it sound like I was talking about something—anything—other than what we were actually discussing. The message I ultimately conveyed to him in such a roundabout manner was that Optitronics appeared wide open and ripe for an espionage attack. I also told him I ordered a few changes made to tighten security there, but much more needed to be done.

Peterson let it all sink in for a few seconds, and then said, "Go ahead and make a list of additional security measures you think need to be taken, but make sure nothing goes wrong in the meantime. Keep in mind, also, we have the authority to confiscate all the materials in question and impound them if it comes to that, although I hope it won't."

"Understood. I'll try to have a working scheme before the end of the day. Will you be available?"

"Yes. Use number 96. Okay?"

"Will do. Talk with you then."

"Number 96" was a code referring to one of many randomly numbered pay telephones scattered around San Francisco. Peterson would drive to the location of number 96 and wait for my call at the time specified by an easy to remember encoding system

39

involving the day's date, in this case, 6:00 p.m. Even if someone was listening to our conversation now, they would have no idea what number I would call this evening or when I would be calling it. The beauty of the plan is we both use unmonitored telephone lines and can speak in the open without worrying about who might be listening. The only drawback is one or the other of the callers has to stand around at a payphone waiting for the call. Still, it's a simple and slick solution to a serious communications problem.

After a hamburger and French fries at a drive-in joint called Rod's on Sepulveda, I made my way back to Optitronics. A quick drive around the building confirmed at least one of my instructions had been carried out. The loading dock doors were now closed.

Walking through the entrance, I found out they followed another of my instructions. A security guard who looked as if he might actually be able to stay awake through an entire eight-hour shift confronted me demanding, somewhat politely, to see my identification.

I showed him my MID ID and he went to work laboriously copying my name, rank and service number on a form clamped to his clipboard. That done, he returned my ID and said, "What is your business at Optitronics today?"

"I'm conducting an informal security inspection."

That confused him so I rephrased my answer. "MID has concerns regarding the security measures here. My job is to determine how effective those measures are and how they could be improved."

The security guard stared at me uncomprehendingly for a few seconds, and then said, "I think that's something that needs to be approved by Mister Demas." Turning to the blonde behind the reception counter, he said, "Elinor, please call Mister Demas and find out if Major Spicer here has authority to inspect the plant."

I could have told him I had authority to do any damned thing I pleased at the plant, but he was just doing the job I demanded he be there to do. I made a note in my notebook, though, to see about military guards instead of a private security company. Teaching a bunch of barely literate security guards who's who and what's what would take too long and leave way too much room for error.

A moment later Elinor asked, "Major Spicer, Mister Demas wants to know if you need him there while you conduct your inspection."

I gave the security guard my best smart-aleck smile and said to Elinor, "No, but I do need someone who is familiar with your inventory of parts and completed products."

She repeated that into the telephone, listened for a minute, and then said, "Mister Demas is sending Miss Bishop down to help you. She's our Assistant Manager and has the inventory information you need."

Miss Bishop, or Annie as she introduced herself, was showing a little gray around the edges of her brown hair and she wore a very plain pair of wire-frame glasses that gave her a definite no nonsense appearance. With a pleasant expression on her no nonsense face, Annie said, "I understand you and I are conducting some sort of inventory. Is that right?"

I smiled my friendly smile. "We're conducting an inventory, but one of a slightly different nature. I'm interested in Optitronics' security measures and making sure that no one has already taken advantage of the poor security I witnessed earlier this morning."

"I hope not. Where would you like to start?"

"I'm told you have a vault on the premises in which finished occuscopes are stored. How 'bout we start there?"

"All right. The vault is just through this door."

We walked from the lobby into a hallway with a gray metal finish on the wall to our left. Annie said, "This is actually the vault wall." She gave it a wrap with her knuckles and got a very solid "thunk" in response.

A few steps further down the hallway, we passed a door on our right with a pair of heavy duty deadbolts. I asked, "Is this the first floor door to the loading dock?"

"Yes. That's why it has those big locks."

Pulling my notebook out again, I said, "Unfortunately, a plain old key lock would do just as good a job of preventing anyone from opening this door."

Annie looked surprised. "How can that be? Those deadbolts are an inch thick."

"The deadbolts are fine. The problem is the way they're installed. Their brackets are screwed to the door frame using woodscrews. They need to be installed with long, round-headed, case-hardened bolts that go all the way through the doorframe. One good kick from the other side of this door would rip these deadbolts right off the frame."

Quietly, Annie said, "That doesn't sound good."

"It isn't."

A moment later we came to another hallway that met ours at a right angle from the left. We took it and about ten feet later stopped in front of a large bank vault door with an electronic combination lock. She said, "Here's the vault entrance. I take it you would like to go inside?"

"Yes. I'll turn my back while you dial the combination."

"Oh, you don't have to do that. The vault isn't locked until the end of the day." She took one look at my expression and said, "Not good again?"

"Not good. Unless it's necessary for employees to be entering and leaving the vault frequently, there's no reason not to lock it. Leaving it unlocked is just inviting trouble."

Together we swung the heavy door open and Annie flipped a light switch just inside the vault. Then we stepped into a space that looked to be about twenty feet square. The floor was solid concrete. The vault was sturdy steel gray, shiny polished chromium, and impressive enough to make Fort Knox jealous.

A waist-high counter ran around the inside walls of the vault, and on it were stacked brown cardboard boxes measuring roughly ten inches high by three feet deep by two-and-a-half feet wide. Each cardboard box bore a set of markings including a ten digit number, two sets of initials, and the designation OCU002B, which I guessed might be a model number. Empty boxes were stored below the counter.

"Annie, how many of these boxes should be in here?"

She consulted her clipboard and said, "We have manufactured 51 occuscopes, six of which are in Lakehurst, New Jersey. That means there should be 45 in the vault."

"Are there?"

"I'm counting."

As she counted, I walked around looking at the boxes. As I was doing that, I stepped on something very small. I could feel it roll between the sole of my shoe and the concrete floor. Looking down, I found a small fine-threaded machine screw no more than a quarter of an inch in length. Since the floor of the vault was otherwise clean as a whistle the screw deserved further attention.

There were three cardboard occuscope boxes in a stack on the counter above where I stepped on the screw. I lifted the top one in the stack and looked inside. The contents appeared identical to what I'd seen in a box on the other side of the vault.

I could tell we were in trouble the minute I lifted the second box in the stack. It rattled. All of the occuscopes were well padded with cardboard bracing and wood wool. There was nothing in them that should be rattling.

Annie heard the rattle, too and looked across the vault. I said, "You'd better come over here to witness the opening of this box."

Nodding grimly, she walked over to where I was standing. I held the box out and said, "Go ahead, lift the lid." She did and we found ourselves looking into a box of loose parts, including several tiny screws like the one I'd found on the floor.

She stated the obvious. "That's not right."

"How about the box itself?"

Annie checked the markings on the box and, after consulting her clipboard, said, "Yes the initials are right and the serial number checks with one of the earlier prototype scopes, an OCUoo1A model."

"That means somebody used a different box to remove the occuscope and left this one full of junk to cover up the theft." I looked around the room and said, "All right, get us some help in here and let's find out the extent of the damage."

While she went to get another pair of hands or two, I wrote the serial number of the missing occuscope in my notebook. Then I set the box full of junk at the far end of the counter.

When Annie returned, she was the second person in a short parade of four Optitronics employees. Frank Demas led the parade. He looked at me, and without saying a word, I pointed to the junk box.

After looking inside, Demas said, "How the hell did this happen?"

I almost laughed, but it wasn't that funny. "Mister Demas, remember those instructions I gave you this morning?"

He nodded glumly. "Well, I'm afraid you closed the gate after the horse left the corral. Now I'd like to know if any other occuscopes are missing."

He nodded again and walked out of the vault. The two women Annie brought with her made quick work of checking the remaining boxes against the master inventory. Annie looked more relieved than the situation deserved when she said, "That's it. The one you found is the only box in the vault that doesn't contain an assembled occuscope."

One missing occuscope was more than enough. I glanced at my watch. It was quarter to two. I used the time I had left before calling Colonel Peterson to finish my tour of the plant and to finalize my list security problems. I also arranged for a list of Optitronics' employees and their addresses.

Eleven

Shell Service Station – 6000 W. Manchester Ave., Westchester

Just for variety's sake, I drove north of the airport this time and made my call to Si Peterson from a Shell service station at Manchester and Truxton. I got a few bucks in change from the station attendant and stepped into the payphone booth a few minutes before six.

By the time I finished feeding coins into the telephone for the long distance operator my watch said it was precisely six o'clock. Si answered on the first ring.

"Good evening, Johnny."

"Hi, Si, but I'm afraid that's a poor choice of words. There is absolutely nothing good about this evening."

"Oh?"

"Yeah. It seems we closed the barn door a little too late on Optitronics. An inventory of their vault adds up to one occuscope short."

"Damn! Now we've really in the soup. Do you have anything to go on?"

"Nothing to speak of. I have an employee list, and I'll question them tomorrow to see if somebody saw anything that will help, but with the lack of security in that place, you and I could have marched out with an occuscope to the accompaniment of the US Army band playing the Star Spangled Banner and no one would have noticed a thing."

Si sighed. "Okay, Johnny. Sounds like we're faced with two problems to resolve here. First, I understand the horse has left the barn, but what are your recommendations for tightening Optitronics' security so we don't lose any more of their damned scopes?"

"The only surefire answer is to impound the finished scopes and stash 'em someplace where we can keep them safe."

After a moment of silence, Si said, "All right. I'll discuss that with General Davis, but even if he goes for the idea, impounding the scopes will take some time. Any ideas what we should do in the meantime?"

"Yes, I've got a list. The first thing would be to get a security team down here to replace the private security guards Optitronics is using. They're just about worthless and we need to clamp a lid on the place so tight a fly can't get it. Any chance of pulling that off?"

"Definitely. I'll assemble a team and put them on a plane for LA tomorrow morning. They'll be down there by early afternoon. How many men per shift?"

I thought about his question for a moment. "For the day shift, one at the front entrance, another keeping an eye on the vault and work areas, and a third man roaming outside. We're in an industrial area here so there won't be much activity in the neighborhood after normal working hours. I think two men each for the remaining shifts should be sufficient."

"That adds up to a crew of at least seven. You think their presence should be obvious or low key?"

"I can't think of any reason to keep their presence a secret. Our objective is preventing any further losses and a show of added security wouldn't hurt."

"All right, Johnny, unless you hear otherwise, that will be our immediate plan. I'll discuss impounding the completed occuscopes with Davis and see what he says. As for our second problem, what are your thoughts recovering the occuscope that's already missing?"

"Hell, the thing might be in pieces on a workbench in Tokyo by now. If I can find out when the scope went missing, I'll know better what the odds of recovering it are. No matter when it was taken, the guy we're looking for had to know the combination of the vault or he arranged for the vault to be left unlocked. As far as getting into the Optitronics plant is concerned, my Aunt Tilley could break into that place with her damned buttonhook. I'll work with those assumptions and see if I can turn up a lead of some kind. If I can't, I don't know what other options we have."

"There aren't many. I'll alert our people here to the situation and tell crypto to keep an ear open for any radio traffic referring to Snow Goose. If they catch anything or something else turns up, I'll pass it along to you as fast as I can."

"All right, Si. I'll be at Optitronics most of the day tomorrow, unless I trip over a hot lead. Nights I'm at Patmar's Motel— telephone EAstgate 7123, room 12. Also, tell the leader of the security team you're sending I'll probably be at Optitronics to meet them, but if I'm not, their orders are to take charge of the security situation. I'll tell the head man there to expect them."

"Okay, Johnny, talk with you Thursday at this same time if not before. Use number 19."

I hung up and thought about my next step. I considered driving back to the motel for some dinner and a call to Susan. However, being a firm believer in an ounce of prevention, I decided to call Susan from right where I was.

I dialed the operator and placed a long distance collect call to Susan's home number. She could use a check from my checkbook to pay the bill. A minute later, my Angel came on the line.

"Hi, darling. It's wonderful to hear from you!"

"I decided it was high time I checked up on you to be sure you aren't out running around town in that sexy black dress."

Susan laughed. "You don't have anything to worry about. That black dress is in the closet and it stays there until I can wear it for you again."

"Good for me and too bad for the male population of Santa Barbara."

She laughed again. "Gee, Johnny, we've got a great connection. You sound like you're right next door."

"Almost. I don't think I'm giving away any state secrets by telling you I'm near the Los Angeles Airport. I've got an assignment down here for at least the next couple of days."

"Good. You're not so far away then."

"Nope, and with some luck and a couple of breaks, I might be able to sneak in a visit at the end of the week, but don't put that on your calendar yet. It's not a sure thing at this point."

"All right, Johnny, but is it okay if I keep my fingers crossed?"

"I'm already doing that for both of us. How's Jack? Any news from him?"

"Jack is okay. So far it seems like business as usual for him."

"How 'bout my pal, Mister Whiskers?"

"He's just fine, but he's about to drive me nuts with that darn bell."

"That's because I told him to keep jingling it so you won't forget me."

Susan laughed again. It felt good to hear the laughter in her voice.

"Oh, speaking of forgetting, I almost forgot to tell you I showed off my ring at the clinic yesterday and everyone loves it. They all think I've got myself a great catch."

"I knew there was a reason I liked those gals."

"You stay away from those gals unless I'm with you. Now that I've got you, I'm not takin' any chances."

"Okay, Angel, I'll try to avoid any foreign entanglements at the Casa Sobre El Mar."

"You're a quick learner." After a short pause, Susan said, "Johnny?"

"Yes, Angel."

"I know you have other things you need to do, but I want you to know just hearing your voice and knowing you're okay means everything to me. Thank you for calling."

"And thank you for answering. This would have been a pretty dull conversation if you hadn't."

"Oh, you goof. I was being serious."

"I know you were, Angel. Talking with you means a hell of a lot to me, too. Just take good care of yourself and I'll see you as soon as I can get there."

"I'm counting on it. Goodnight, darling."

"Goodnight, Angel."

By ten o'clock I'd had myself a pretty decent chicken fried steak at the motel coffee shop and spent some time staring at the Optitronics' employee roster. If it contained any clues as to who made off with the occuscope, I sure didn't see them. It was just a list of about thirty names and addresses. There were no Japanese names on the roster and no names with asterisks identifying them as spies.

I refolded the list and slipped it back into my inside jacket pocket. Maybe talking to each of them in the flesh would accomplish more, but I wasn't counting on any revelations.

Twelve

Optitronics, Inc. – 2001 E. Mariposa Avenue, El Segundo

When I peeked through the half-open door of Frank Demas' office the things I noticed first were his rumpled suit and an overflowing ashtray, sure signs of a man who'd been at his desk—or in this case, his drafting table—all night. I knocked lightly on the doorframe.

Looking up, Demas saw me and scowled. "Oh, it's you. What bad news do you have for me today?"

Walking into the office, I stood near the drawing table, but carefully avoided looking at whatever he was working on. "No bad news. Actually, depending on your point of view, it might be good news."

"I sincerely doubt that, but go ahead, say what you came to say."

I told him MID was sending an Army security team that would arrive after lunch to take over for his rented security guards. Still scowling, Demas asked, "How is that good news?"

"For one thing, you'll have the best possible security for your plant. Also, having the Army do it will save you the cost of the private guards you've been hiring, and it will show MID that you are anxious to cooperate. That won't make up for losing an occuscope, but it might help a little."

When Frank Demas nodded, but didn't say anything, I said, "Today I'm going to interview some of your employees to see if anyone saw something that might help us identify whoever took the occuscope and when they took it. That Jake with you?"

Demas nodded again and I added, "Before I begin the interviews, though, I'd like to ask you a few questions. Okay?"

48

"Do I have any choice?" Before I could answer that, he waved the question away and said, "Go ahead. What do you want to know?"

"Let's say the guy who ends up with that missing occuscope is a pretty smart engineer with a background in optics and electronics. If he disassembled the device, could he figure out how it works and make one like it?"

Demas shook his head. "If he was really sharp, he might figure out the principles on which the scope's various parts operate, but it would be impossible to build a copy without the occuscope schematics."

"You mean the plans? Why would he need them if he has the real thing?"

"Because, the way the occuscope is assembled, he couldn't identify the electrical values of the components. Those values are critical to the operation of the scope."

"I see. Where are these schematics?"

"In a safe I had built into the wall over there behind that calendar."

"Would you please take a look and make sure those schematics are still safe and sound?"

He dragged himself up off his stool at the drawing board as if doing so required the last of his strength. After closing the office door, he took the calendar down and turned the combination dial to unlock the wall safe. He removed some papers and unfolded them.

Holding them up so I could see they were schematics, Demas said, "They're here, right where they should be."

Of course, I couldn't tell if they were the right plans, so I had to take his word for that. "Good. Go ahead and lock 'em up again."

When he returned to his stool at the drawing board, I asked, "Can you be more specific about why a guy trying to duplicate the occuscope needs those schematics if he has the real thing in front of him?"

Demas' scowl was back at full volume. "Because the occuscope incorporates three black boxes of my own design."

"What is a black box?"

He sighed with exasperation at my ignorance or my persistence or both. "Put simply so even you can understand it, a black box is the result of a process I designed by which a group of electrical components, when wired together, are dipped into a mold filled with a mixture of hot Lucite and black dye. When the plastic cools, it hardens, resulting in a polyhedron with a plug-in base something like a vacuum tube has. The black dye makes it impossible to see what electrical components—resisters, capacitators, triodes, etcetera—are inside the box or to read their values."

"And you designed these black boxes for security reasons—so it would be difficult to copy an occuscope?"

Demas shook his head. "No. That's merely a side benefit. I designed the black boxes to make assembling the occuscopes faster and easier."

"Assuming, then, the guy who has the missing occuscope doesn't know what's in the black boxes, is there a way he could find out?"

He thought about that for a moment. "If it were me, I would use a fine-toothed saw to cut the boxes into slices, and then try to read the color codes or printing on the components. That would be tricky, though, because you would have to cut extremely thin slices in order not to destroy the markings inside, plus the components are not all aligned in the same direction, so no matter how the cuts were made, some of them would still be unreadable. Also, the black box would be worthless once it was sliced up, so the occuscope could not be used until a new and identical black box was installed."

I nodded. Demas had convinced me he was right. Without the schematics it would be impossible, or very nearly so, to find out what was inside the boxes.

"Frank, who else knows what's in those black boxes besides you?"

"Nobody."

"Don't you have someone assembling them for you?"

"No. When the occuscope's development reached the point where I was certain the basic design would work, I figured out how I could use the black boxes and built more than two hundred sets of them by myself at home." He sounded quite proud of himself as he added, "I got to the point where I could make eight or ten a night."

"So, if you've built 51 occuscopes as of yesterday, there must be about one-hundred-fifty-some unused black boxes stored away somewhere. Is that right?"

"Actually, I think there are 169 unused sets, all tested and ready to be installed or shipped as needed for replacement parts. Also, there are three black boxes in each occuscope, so that's a total of 660 pieces. We used 153 of them in the first 51 occuscopes, so that leaves 507 individual unused boxes."

I held my breath for the answer to the $64 question. "Where are they, Frank?"

Frank Demas glared at me for a long moment. "How do I know you can be trusted with that secret of secrets?"

"Because the United States government says I can. Frank, we're dealing with espionage here. Some unauthorized person already has an occuscope. My immediate assignments are to find out who that person is and somehow recover the occuscope or make it useless to whoever has it. Knowing the whereabouts of those black boxes is essential to carrying out those orders."

After glaring at me for several more seconds, Demas sighed and said, "I guess you do need to know where they are."

He walked to the office door and twisted the little knob that locked it. Next he moved a stepladder out from behind his desk and set it squarely in the center of the room. Finally, he stepped up on the ladder and lifted a two-by-two foot ceiling panel out of its frame and asked me to take it. Its weight surprised me until I saw that it was actually a sandwich of two tiles with a space between them.

Demas climbed down the stepladder and took the ceiling tile to his desk. He removed six hardware pieces that held the two tiles together and lifted the top one clear. Grooves were built into the bottom tile and each groove contained a row of black plastic shapes. The boxes were sorted into groups of three—a long rectangular box, a shorter rectangular box and a round cylinder in each group.

"There you are, Major Spicer. This asbestos tile and those on either side of it contain the remaining 507 black boxes. When a set is needed, the head assembler calls Annie Bishop, she calls me, and I take the boxes to the assembly room. Annie and I, and now you, are the only ones who know where the black boxes are."

I nodded. "Let's count them."

He looked at me as if he was going to argue they didn't need to be counted, but gave up before he began and returned to his stepladder. As he removed the tiles, I did some arithmetic. Each ceiling tile held 60 black boxes. To hold all of the boxes he built, he must have rigged eleven of his double-tile hiding places.

All told, Demas removed nine tiles, four from the row on one side of the first one and four from the other side. One by one we opened the tiles and counted black boxes. I breathed a deep sigh of relief when the count reached 507. Finally, we resealed the tiles and returned them to their positions in the ceiling grid.

From a security point of view, hiding valuable items above removable ceiling tiles wasn't very safe. On the other hand, these ceiling tiles were made of asbestos, which provided some protection from fire. The vault might have been a better place to store the black boxes, but the vault was already compromised. I decided the ceiling tiles were as good a hiding place as any until MID figured out what they were going to do with Optitronics.

Thirteen

Optitronics, Inc. – 2001 E. Mariposa Avenue, El Segundo

Walking out of Frank Demas' office I felt a little more positive about the situation. I hadn't counted on his black boxes providing an extra layer of security. I hoped whoever had the missing occuscope didn't figure on them either.

However, the occuscope schematics in Demas' safe had exactly the opposite effect on my mood. Given five minutes I could open his cracker box safe, take the schematics out, photograph them, and put 'em back where they came from without anyone being the wiser. You win some and you lose some.

There were three executive offices across the front of Optitronics' second floor. Demas' office was on the west side of the building overlooking El Segundo. Annie Bishop's office was on the east side with an interior window overlooking the stairway to the lobby. The middle office had no name on the door and was locked up tight. On the opposite side of the hall were two glassed-in assembly rooms. The one on the east side bore a sign with big red letters saying, "CLEAN – Stay Out!"

Behind these was another hallway and two more assembly rooms. Those four rooms seemed to be all the space required to make occuscopes.

I knocked on Annie Bishop's door. "Good morning, Major Spicer. I've been expecting you. When I got here they said you were already in talking to Mister Demas."

"Hello, Annie. Can you spare me a little time for a few questions? If this is a bad time . . ."

"Not at all, Major Spicer. Please sit down and tell me what you'd like to know."

I sat in a comfortable wingback chair opposite her desk and removed the notebook from my inside jacket pocket. "Annie, who has the responsibility for making sure the vault is locked at the end of the day?"

"That's me. I leave promptly at six every night to catch the bus out on Sepulveda. I lock the vault and double check it on my way out."

I jotted that in my book and said, "And you go through that routine every night?"

"I do. Major Spicer, are you wondering if I might have forgotten to lock the vault door one night?"

I shook my head. "Annie, you strike me as someone who takes her responsibilities seriously. That's an unlikely mistake for you to make. I just want to make sure I have the routine straight in my mind. What's involved in locking the vault?"

She looked at me as if trying to decide whether or not I really meant what I said about taking her responsibilities seriously. "Locking the vault is really simple. First you swing the door shut and pull the latching handle down. Then you spin the combination dial a time or two and watch the lights above the vault door. If the door is locked securely, the green light goes out and the red light comes on. I never leave before I see the red light. That's my go signal."

I jotted the procedure in my notebook. "Okay, supposing someone was accidently locked in the vault. Is there an override that allows the door to be opened from inside?"

Annie nodded vigorously. "Absolutely. Thank God nobody's ever been locked in, but the vault installers demonstrated the system for us. There's a large red handle on the inside of the vault door. If you pull it, the vault door automatically opens.

"But if the handle is pulled, it also sets off alarm bells and notifies the police. The bells just keep ringing and ringing until the shut off procedure is followed, and that requires using the vault combination."

"And nothing like that has happened recently?"

"Absolutely not. If the alarm goes off, the police come. It's an automatic thing."

"Annie, can you think of any way for someone to hide in the vault or get into it after you've locked the door?"

"Not without knowing the combination, and Mister Demas and I are the only ones who know it. I've thought about that a lot, Major Spicer. The vault scares the heck out of me. Even when we were in there yesterday I was nervous about turning my back on the door in case someone sneaked up and locked us in."

I was tempted to smile, but I kept a straight face. Annie had a serious phobia about the vault and laughing at her sure wasn't going to help her get over it. Instead I changed the subject.

"There are several offices on the first floor behind the vault. Who uses those offices?"

"The people who handle the business end of Optitronics . . . payroll, shipping, procurement, clerical . . . like that."

Nodding my understanding, I said, "If someone walked out of the vault with an occuscope under their arm during working hours, would any of those people notice?"

"Oh yes! Everyone knows what's in those cardboard boxes. I'm sure someone would have said something if they saw anyone carrying an occuscope box out of the vault, especially if it was someone they didn't know."

Slipping my notebook back into my jacket pocket, I said, "Do you have any objections if I talk with those people to see if they've noticed anything out of the ordinary recently? Maybe something they didn't bother to mention because it didn't seem important?"

"Not at all. If you'd like, I'll make the rounds with you just so they know you're on the up and up."

I wasn't sure I needed her help, but she was going out of her way to cooperate and that was something I wanted to encourage. "Okay, Annie, if you have the time, I would appreciate that."

She stood, saying, "Sure. Let me tell Mister Demas where I'll be."

While Annie went in to see Demas, I stood in the hall staring at the closed door on the wall between their offices. For some reason it kept attracting my attention, and then the light dawned. The middle office was directly over the vault.

When she returned, I said, "Annie who has the key to this middle office?"

"There's a key in the key cabinet downstairs behind the reception desk. Nobody uses the office because it doesn't have an outside window and it's so dark inside."

"Let's go get the key. I need to see inside that office."

Looking at me like I was nuts, Annie said, "Okay, Major Spicer. You can wait here if you'd like. I'll run downstairs and find the key."

She was back in less than five minutes with a key in her hand. "I think I found it."

"All right, let's give it a try."

The door opened and, as we walked in, Annie flipped a light

switch just inside the door. I went to the center of the room and did a slow turn. There was nothing unusual about the office except all the furniture—the desk, chairs, filing cabinets, and so on—was stacked against the wall to the right of the door. The stuff might have been put there when the office floor was cleaned, but the linoleum showed scratch marks indicating the desk had been moved at least twice.

I moved the desk yet again, sliding it out from the wall. I also moved a couple of chairs so I could see the entire floor. As I slid one of the chairs out of the way, its leg caught on a piece of loose linoleum. Curious how the linoleum got loose, I slipped my pocketknife blade into the crack and discovered I could remove an entire three-foot by three-foot section of the flooring someone cut out, and then carefully replaced.

Through the hole I could see the steel top of the vault beyond the floor joists. I also saw something else down there—something that didn't look like it belonged there. Dropping to my hands and knees for a closer look, I saw a bundle of wires strung across the top of the vault. Even more interesting was a spot where the outer insulation was stripped away from the bundle exposing eight or ten wires inside and where new connections were made using short jumper wires with alligator clips.

Annie was watching over my shoulder. I looked up. "How far away is the company that installed this vault?"

"Not far. It's Guardian Safe & Lock Company down on El Segundo Boulevard."

"Good. Call them and say you have an emergency. You need a knowledgeable technician out here immediately. Tell 'em you've got a government agent ready to shut down the entire operation. That ought to get them here quickly."

Annie looked shocked and ran to her office and made the call. The vault company didn't spare the horses getting there, but even so I had an audience out in the hall by the time the guy from Guardian arrived.

The technician—John according to the name on his jacket—walked in, took one look under the flooring, and said, "Oh, oh."

I said, "'Oh, oh' doesn't begin to cover it. I want to know exactly what the wires in that bundle are for and what the jumpers are doing there."

"Okay, okay. Keep your shirt on, Mack. I need to do some looking before I can give you your answer."

I stepped back out of the way. "Have at it."

After poking around under the floor joists and consulting a

couple of wiring diagrams from his jacket pocket, the technician stood up and said, "There's no use denying it, what we have here is a major installation foul-up that some smart guy figured out how to use to his advantage."

"Explain."

"Well, in the first place, the wire bundle going across the top of the vault shouldn't be there, but those bundles are a pain in the butt to thread through the space provided by the vault manufacturer, so somebody got lazy and simply ran the wires over the vault."

"All right, what's with the jumpers?"

"That's the bad part, or the clever part depending on your point of view. The way the jumper wires are arranged, if contact is made between the green wire and the white wire, the vault door unlocks just like someone inside pulled the emergency lever inside, except the guy figured out how to bypass the automatic alarm system."

"That means by using this circuitry the vault can be opened without the combination or setting off the alarm system?"

Nodding as he looked down into the hole, the technician said, "That pretty well sums it up."

"But it doesn't begin to sum up the consequences. I want a complete written report explaining how that bundle of wires ended up where it is and how the jumpers were used to open the vault. I also want the report to include the names and addresses of the employees who installed the vault, and I want it all before you leave here."

That upset John no end. Turning toward the door, he announced loudly, "Hey, pal, you got no right to keep me here against my will!"

A second later the barrel of my Smith & Wesson was in his face and my MID ID was right next to it. The crowd out in the hall let out a collective gasp. "The hell I don't, pal. You are being held as an uncooperative witness to a federal crime. Your options are to get cooperative, get taken to the nearest federal lock-up, or push the matter and get dead right here and now." Turning to Annie, I said, "Please have the security guard come up here to make sure John cooperates."

John grumbled, but made no more attempts to leave. When the guard arrived I gave him his instructions and the key Annie used to unlock the office. I told him to lock up when they were done and bring me the key along with the technician's report.

Out in the hall, Frank Demas ordered everyone back to work

and I looked out the window to be sure we were still in El Segundo. As fouled up as this place was, a Japanese agent wouldn't have much trouble stealing the whole damned building.

Fourteen

Optitronics, Inc. – 2001 E. Mariposa Avenue, El Segundo

Annie Bishop was going out to a neighborhood deli for lunch and asked if she could bring me anything. I gave her a couple of bucks and asked for a Reuben. I knew it wouldn't compare to Eli's Reuben, but I was feeling a little homesick. That realization made me wonder how the hell I could be homesick when I was less than 20 miles from the place I've called home most of my life. I wrote the condition off to some psychological flaw I wouldn't understand anyway and got back to thinking about Frank Demas' troubles, which I didn't understand either.

While waiting for my sandwich and Si Peterson's security team, I put in a call to Si. He was out, so I left a message for an early callback number even though I was pretty sure our telephone security precautions were a waste of time at this point. The horse wasn't just out of the barn, he was in the next county.

My Reuben and Si's security team arrived at the same time. I offered the team leader, a solidly built First Sergeant named George Biber, half my Reuben, which he gratefully accepted and we munched corned beef while discussing what needed to be done.

When we were through, George made quick work of deploying his dayshift team and got his other two shifts squared away. Clearly, George didn't make Top Kick by lolygaggin'.

It was about then that Annie showed up with copies of the vault installation technician's report I asked her to have typed. I slipped the original handwritten report and two of the copies into a dispatch case I had for carrying such things. The key to the office over the vault was already in the case.

I asked Annie to send the remaining copy of the report to an address at the San Francisco Presidio. She said it would go out in the afternoon mail. Between Annie and George Biber I was actually getting things done.

Around two-thirty Elinor, the receptionist, tracked me down with a message she thought was awfully strange. It simply said, "#7." I thanked her and said it made perfect sense to me.

Things were more or less under control at Optitronics and now I had a good excuse to get out of there for a while. I headed the Army's Dodge south on Sepulveda until I came to a Chevron service station at Grand Avenue with a public phone. It was three o'clock, precisely the time Si Peterson specified in his message for my secure telephone call to him.

"Hi, Johnny. What's new?"

"Good afternoon, Si. Sorry to drag you out to do the telephone routine, but we discovered a couple of things this morning I thought you ought to be in on."

"I hope they're good news. HQ is about ready to start taking scalps."

"I'm not sure if this part is good news or not, but I now know how a secure vault was opened without the combination."

"I'm all ears."

I explained how the wires ended up on top of the vault and accessible through a hole in the floor of the office above, and I told Si how our thief used the sloppy installation to his advantage. When I finished the story Si said, "Well, isn't that something? So maybe this isn't an inside job after all?"

"I still think it is. The vault was installed shortly after Demas finalized the occuscope design. It doesn't seem likely Japan or Germany even knew Optitronics existed at that point, let alone that they were developing the occuscope. I think it's more likely someone at the plant watched the vault installation and saw how the cable could be accessed, and then used the information when the time was right."

"Could be. Anything else?"

"Yes, two things. First, we got a break because Demas used some gizmos he calls black boxes in manufacturing the occuscopes. They're electrical components sealed in plastic—three different boxes in each scope. He personally assembled them at home and says nobody else knows what components are inside the boxes, and Demas claims the occuscope can't be duplicated without knowing what's in the boxes. He also says trying to open the boxes will destroy them without revealing their secrets. I'm hoping the boxes buy us a little time to find the missing occuscope.

"There are however more than five hundred completed black boxes that haven't been used yet and they're . . ."

Si interrupted, "Don't say it, even on a safe line."

"I was going to say they're reasonably well hidden. That's the good news."

"I just knew you had another shoe to drop."

"Hey, if this was easy, you wouldn't need me."

Peterson chuckled. "Okay, Johnny what's the bad news."

Despite the safe connection I slipped into code talk. "There is a treasure map that shows the whole scheme and it's hidden at the end of the rainbow, the first place a smart leprechaun would look for it."

"Oh, hell."

"Si, if we want to keep anything further from getting out, you need to move Optitronics lock, stock and barrel to someplace that's really secure, and soon. Your team arrived and George Biber seems capable, but not if we let Frank Demas tie the sergeant's hands by insisting on keeping his own secrets."

"I see your point, Johnny. Sergeant Biber is scheduled to call me tonight. I'd like his take on how we can accomplish what you're suggesting, then I'll sell the idea to HQ. In the meantime, are you able to devote a hundred percent of your time to looking for the missing occuscope?"

"Yes, now I am. With Sergeant Biber in charge of plant security, I can get on with my investigation, although I still don't have a whole hell of a lot to go on."

"Hey, Spicer, if it was easy, we wouldn't need you."

"Touché."

By three-thirty Annie Bishop and I were making the rounds of the ribbon clerks whose offices were on the first floor near the vault. We weren't having much luck until we talked to a woman in payroll named Elsie Clayton.

I asked if she recalled seeing anything unusual in the past week or so. She said she couldn't think of anything, but as Annie and I thanked her and turned to leave, Elsie said, "There was one thing that struck me as out of the ordinary."

That got my attention. "What was it, Elsie?"

With an expression that meant she was either constipated or trying hard to remember the details accurately, Elsie said, "Well, it was Monday afternoon, maybe between two and two-thirty. I'm not exactly sure, but about then."

With waning patience, I asked, "What did you see?"

"I took the monthly payroll summaries up to Annie's office,

and as I left, I saw one of the custodians coming up the stairs from the first floor."

Annie interrupted, "Yes, I remember you bringing the summaries in, and it was before two-thirty, but are you sure it was a custodian you saw? They don't come in until after six."

"Yes, that's what struck me as odd. He's an oriental fellow I've seen here when I've worked late to get payroll out. I also remember he looked away from me like he didn't want me to recognize him."

Writing as fast as I could in my notebook, I asked, "Where did he go when he got to the top of the stairs?"

"He passed me in the hall outside Annie's office and I went back downstairs. I don't know where he went from there."

I looked at Annie and she sort of shrugged. "I can't imagine what a custodian was doing here at that hour."

I could easily imagine what a custodian might be doing there at that hour. Turning back to Elsie, I said, "Can you tell from time cards or something if the custodian you saw worked Monday night?"

She was surprised at my question. "Well, he was here, so he must have worked."

"Please humor me and check it."

Elsie dug into one of the file folders in her in-basket. After shuffling through some papers, she said, "Well, I'll be. He didn't report for work Monday night, or last night either."

"Do you have his name and address there?"

"I have his name and I can get his address from our personnel files. His name is Takuya Nakagawa." Elsie spelled the name for me, and then handed me a three-by-five card from a file box on her desk. It showed Nakagawa's address as "1141 West 105th Street, Apartment #8, Westmont, Calif." I jotted the address below his name in my notebook and said to Annie, "I don't recall seeing this name on the employee roster you gave me."

"No, it wouldn't have been there because that was our regular payroll roster and the custodians and gardeners are paid out of a different fund."

I thanked Elsie and led Annie out to the lobby. I was pleased to see George Biber's man on his toes and looking in all directions at once. I nodded to him and approached the reception desk.

"Elinor, I need your help for just a minute."

"Sure, Mister Spicer. What do you need?"

"I would like you to think back to day before yesterday. That was Monday. Did anyone come in during the afternoon and open the key cabinet?"

Elinor turned and looked at the key cabinet on the wall behind her desk.   Next she turned and looked around the room, apparently trying to remember as far back as Monday afternoon. Finally, Elinor turned to me, and for a moment I thought she was surprised to see me standing there.   Fortunately, she wasn't quite that oblivious to the world around her.

"Yes, Mister Spicer, I think someone did come in and get a key."

"Who got the key, Elinor?"

"That's the part I don't remember.   I know it was someone different."

Annie took a shot at it.   "Ellie, what do you mean it was someone different?"

Elinor tilted her head to the side a little and said, "It wasn't somebody I see very often, like I see you and a lot of the others every day, but not this person."

I tried to narrow it down a little.   "Do you recall if it was a woman or a man?"

She started to say something, and then stopped and thought about it.   Finally, she said, "It was a man.   I remember because he had a pair of pliers in his back pocket and women don't keep pliers in their back pockets."

Annie tried again.   "Do remember what color his pants were?"

"I think they were gray.   They matched his jacket."

Annie was doing well with Elinor, but she'd come to the end of the line.   The receptionist couldn't remember anything else about what the man looked like or what he did.

Back in Annie's office, I said, "What do you think?"

"I think Elsie was right about the man she saw being a custodian.   What Elinor can remember fits that idea, but what was he up to and why didn't he sign in for work?"

"I think it's a pretty safe bet the key he took was for the office next door and he didn't sign in because he was hiding in that office waiting for the other custodians to leave.   When they left, he used those wires under the floor to open the vault, and then went down and got an occuscope.   After that he relocked the vault door and left."

Eyes wide, Annie said, "You think that's what happened?   He was right next door the whole time?"

"I think so.   That scenario fits the circumstances perfectly. I'm going to see if Mister Nakagawa is still at the address you have for him, assuming he was ever there to begin with.   That part is a long shot, but it's worth a try."

It doesn't happen often, but sometimes cases break like that. About the time I'm desperate for a lead, one pops up out of nowhere. During the past fifteen minutes I not only learned who stole the occuscope prototype, but when they stole it and where to pick up his trail. At least I hoped that's what I learned.

On the way out I hunted down George Biber and asked if he could spare a man for about an hour so I would have someone to watch the backdoor when I called on Takuya Nakagawa. George said he thought he could slip away for an hour.

Fifteen

Hilltop Apartments – 1141 W. 105th Street, Westmont

As long as I've lived in Los Angeles, I was pretty sure there wasn't a community in the county I didn't know about, but I have to admit I never heard of Westmont. Fortunately Annie Bishop had a Thomas Brothers LA map book in her office. Turns out Westmont is a residential community about seven miles east of Los Angeles Airport.

Once we knew where we were going, First Sergeant Biber and I climbed into the Army's Dodge and we were off. I noticed that, even though it was December, Biber was wearing his cotton summer uniform—khaki pants, shirt and tie topped off with a matching overseas cap—rather than his heavy wool winter garb. Considering the temperature was somewhere in the high sixties, his choice of uniform made damned good sense.

The Top Kick was a large man and, with his sidearm holster hanging from his belt, he gave the impression of being all business. Biber was a guy you wanted with you rather than against you.

When we got to the right neighborhood, I turned east off Western onto 105th and continued another three blocks until we got to 1141. The Hilltop Apartments were not on top of any hill I could see. Instead, they were in a long narrow two story building squeezed between a similar building on the right and an alley on the left.

The ground floor front apartment, displaying a faded sign reading, "Manager," faced the street. All of the other units had to be approached from a walkway down the right side of the building beside a driveway belonging to the apartment complex next door.

The Hilltop Apartments had a total of eight rental units, four on the ground floor and four more on the second floor.

The building was painted a pinkish beige with faded brown trim. It looked like the Hilltop Apartments were a pretty nice place to live at one time, but that time was in the past. Now signs of neglect were everywhere and the alleyway along the left side of the building was scattered with trash, all of which made the joint look right at home in a declining neighborhood.

I slowed slightly as we drove past 1141, but kept going. That gave us a chance to reconnoiter the situation without making it obvious we had business there.

Looking the place over as we passed, Sergeant Biber observed, "I think the even numbered apartments are on the second floor. That doesn't leave us many choices about how to handle this."

"No, it doesn't. I'd say the best approach is one of us downstairs while the other goes up and knocks on the door. That puts us in the best positions to corner the guy in case he's actually there and tries to run. You want the downstairs position?"

"Fine with me. Major Spicer, is this a shoot-to-kill situation?"

"Sergeant, I honestly don't think there's going to be anyone to shoot at, but if there is, the guy isn't going to do us a bit of good if he's dead. The people we need are the ones who sent him to steal the occuscope.

"Understood, Major."

I turned around at the end of the block and drove back to 1141, pulling to the curb near the alleyway on the left side of the building. Parking there hid the Dodge from the apartments on the right side of the building, adding to whatever element of surprise we might have in our favor. Then we split up with Biber on the ground and me climbing the stairs to the second floor walkway that led past apartments two, four, and six to number eight at the back of the building.

Apartment eight's front window was just beyond the door, so I positioned myself a little to the left of the door, making it more difficult to take a shot at me through the window if anyone was so inclined. Then I looked over the edge of the porch to make sure Biber was in place. He was, so I turned back and gave the front door three hard raps, shouting, "Military police, open the door!"

When nearly a minute passed with no result, I repeated the routine. That got me nothing but another minute of utter silence.

Leaning over the upstairs porch railing I told Biber I was going around to the manager's office to get a key. He nodded and backed up a pace or two so he could watch apartment number eight's door.

I did a little better getting a response to my knock on the manager's door. A middle-aged woman with her graying hair in curlers and wearing a filthy yellow apron over a faded blue housedress opened the door and stared at me blankly.

Showing her my MID ID, I said, "We're looking for Mister Takuya Nakagawa. We understand he rents apartment number eight from you. Is that right?"

It was fortunate I wasn't smoking because the alcohol fumes on her breath would have sent the whole damned building up in flames. "Yeah, tha bassard was in eight, but he skipped withou' payin' his December rent, the bassard. You gonna 'rest him?"

"Maybe, but for now we just want to take a look inside his apartment, may I please borrow the key?"

"I tol' you he ain't there no more."

"Yes, you did, but we'd like to see what he left behind when he took off. Have you cleaned the apartment yet?"

In the haughtiest tone the woman could muster, she said, "No, I got more 'portant stuff to do. Wait a minnit an I'll get the key."

With the key to apartment eight in my hand I signaled Sergeant Biber to come up the second floor with me. With his Colt forty-five pistol drawn, he took up a position behind me on the left side of the door. Then I leaned over and pushed the key into the lock. I looked over my shoulder at Biber, he nodded, and I turned the key.

The lock clicked and I gave the door a push. It swung in on a Spartan living room furnished with scarred secondhand furniture and a strong stink of rotting fish.

We moved through the small single bedroom apartment quickly, checking all the places a man could hide. There were no men hiding in apartment number eight, so we turned our attention to the trash Nakagawa left behind. There wasn't even much of that.

Biber and I separated to speed up our search. In the living room I found a minor treasure in the drawer of a small writing desk. Mister Nakagawa left behind two of the alligator clip jumper wires he used on the Optitronics vault and a small wiring diagram with notes in Japanese characters.

While I was transferring the jumper cables and diagram to my coat pocket, I heard Sergeant Biber yell from the kitchen, "I found the stinking fish . . ."

A thunderclap enveloped the apartment and shook the building so hard the front window cracked and the writing desk

67

next to me was propelled several feet across the room. A floor lamp toppled and two cheap art prints in cardboard frames flew off the walls.

At first the explosion came from everywhere at once, but as the echoes died away, wisps of smoke led the way to the kitchen. There, I found a galvanized metal garbage pail with its charred opening folded back like a peeled banana. A few feet away Sergeant Biber lay on the floor, his head in a pool of blood and the lid to the garbage pail still in his left hand.

If it weren't for the sergeant's uniform, I wouldn't have recognized him. His face just wasn't there anymore. I swallowed a couple of times to quiet my stomach and spent several minutes looking for a pulse I was pretty certain I wouldn't find. I didn't.

Sirens that started out some distance away suddenly sounded as if they were right outside the door. I went back to the living room and discovered there actually was a firetruck right outside the door. It was parked in the driveway of the next-door apartment.

Moments later a fireman with "Chief" lettered on his bright red helmet and an ax in his hand appeared in the front doorway. I held up my MID ID, saying, "Major Spicer, US Army Military Intelligence Division. We tracked a Japanese espionage agent to this location, but he left a booby trap. My partner, First Sergeant George Biber is in the kitchen. The blast killed him.

The Fire Chief simply nodded and started giving directions to his men who were filing into apartment number eight a couple at a time. While they went about their business, I walked back into the bedroom to look for anything else Nakagawa might have left behind, explosive or otherwise.

I wasn't expecting to find the missing occuscope sitting on the closet shelf and I didn't. Instead, I found what I expected to find, nothing. As I returned to the living room, a pair of ambulance attendants in white jackets were carrying Sergeant Biber out on a canvas stretcher covered with a blanket. I stopped them and removed Biber's sidearm from his holster. Then I offered a casual salute to a soldier who died in the service of his country, although few would ever know that.

Next the Fire Chief came over with a clipboard in his hand and I wondered if I needed a clipboard. These days everyone has a clipboard. The Chief said, "Major Spicer, I have to fill out this arson investigation form. Where it says 'Cause of Fire' I put 'Booby trap left by previous tenant.' Is that right?"

I nodded. "For a brief explanation, that's as accurate as

anything you could write there."

"Good. I also need to put your information in as a witness and the dead fellow's information as a victim. Can you give me that?"

"Yes. I see you've already got my name and rank there. Below that, write US Army Military Intelligence Division, Building 100, Presidio, San Francisco, California. You can use the same address for First Sergeant George Biber. The people at that address will take care of details like claiming the body when the coroner is done. If you need me during the next two or three days I'm staying at Patmar's Motel on Sepulveda near the airport."

The Fire Chief finished writing and said, "Thank you, Major Spicer. You were lucky you weren't in the kitchen when that bomb went off. The guy who built it knew what he was doing."

I nodded, thinking I now had two good reasons to catch up with Mister Takuya Nakagawa. I was also thinking it would be a meeting he wasn't likely to survive.

Sixteen

After leaving the Hilltop Apartments in even worse shape than I found them, I drove west to Sepulveda Boulevard and turned north. My destination was the YMCA in Westchester, a mile or two beyond the airport. Since there were no military accommodations available in the area, Si Peterson's security team was staying there, and they needed to know their leader wasn't coming back. It was my job to tell them.

Specifically, the man I needed to see was Corporal Russ Pierce. He was the teams' second in command. I spotted Pierce about a block from my destination. The Y was in a pleasant residential district—a far cry from Westmont—and Pierce was getting in some running before the sun set. I wonder if those guys ever take a day off from training.

Pierce recognized me as I pulled to the curb and leaned in the passenger side window. He immediately noticed George Biber's sidearm on the seat beside me, and gave me a quizzical look. I said, "Get in, Corporal. We have some talking to do."

I drove somewhat aimlessly through the residential area around the YMCA as I told Pierce George Biber was dead and how he died. I concluded the story saying, "There was no reason for Nakagawa to booby trap that apartment except pure meanness. I'm telling you that so you have a clear picture of the people we're up against. Pass that on to your team, okay?"

"Yes, sir, I'll be sure they get the picture."

"Good. Corporal, George said he had a safe call to Colonel Peterson scheduled for tonight. Do you know the time and number? I'm asking because it's urgent that I speak with Peterson

70

about the Japanese spy we uncovered and how Sergeant Biber died, but if Peterson is waiting for a call at a safe phone, the only way I can reach him quickly is through Sergeant Biber's scheduled call to that safe phone."

A little reluctantly, Pierce said, "Yes, sir, I have the time and number."

"Okay, how 'bout I go with you to place the call and you tell the Colonel I'm there and need to talk with him."

Sounding relieved, Pierce said, "Thank you, sir. I don't want to break any security protocols."

I nodded. "You and me both, Corporal."

Pierce looked at his watch and said, "I'll need to make that call in about fifteen minutes. There's a small neighborhood grocery on Sepulveda at Manchester. They have a public telephone."

"Okay, then that's where we're headed.

I parked near the payphone booth and leaned against the Dodge's fender while Pierce made Biber's safe call to Si Peterson. Corporal Pierce explained why he was calling instead of Sergeant Biber and that I needed to talk to the colonel. A few seconds later Pierce said, "Sir, Colonel Peterson would like to speak with you."

The corporal and I exchanged places in the telephone booth and I spoke into the receiver. "Hi, Si."

"Hello, Spicer. We lost Biber?"

"Yes we did, due entirely to an act of senseless meanness."

"What happened?"

I related the story, starting with how we identified the Japanese occuscope thief and concluding with, "any chance you've got anything on this Nakagawa?"

"I'll check as soon as I get back to the office. He's probably using an alias, though. Do you think you can get any fingerprints from his apartment?"

"We might if I had a field fingerprint kit, but I don't."

Pierce, who was standing close enough to hear my comment, said, "I have one, Major Spicer."

I nodded to Pierce and said, "Si, Pierce says he has a kit. As soon as you're through talking with him, we'll go to the apartment and see what we can find."

"Good, and if you find any prints, try to get them on a plane for San Francisco tonight. I'll have someone pick them up whenever they arrive and get our people working on trying to make a match from the files. That's likely to take a day or two, though."

"Understood. In the meantime I'll go over everything again

here and see if I can pick up some kind of a trail."

In a somber tone, Peterson said, "Johnny, Biber was a good man, one of the best we had. I want you to find that agent and his pals."

"Yes, sir, that is my intention. Here's Pierce again."

Half an hour later I was entering Hillside Apartments, number eight again, this time with Corporal Pierce in tow. I still had the landlady's key, but we didn't need it. The door was only hanging by one hinge. Next we looked around for something that might have Nakagawa's fingerprints, but nobody else's.

Fortunately the furnished apartment came complete with a four-place setting of cheap plastic plates, bowls, and coffee mugs. Being in a cupboard and plastic, they survived the blast more or less intact, and Corporal Pierce was able to lift good prints from one plate and two coffee mugs. When he finished lifting the prints, we carefully wrapped the plate and mugs in a dishtowel and took them with us so we still had the prints available if something happened to the set Pierce made.

Then, after I dropped Pierce off at the YMCA, I drove over to the military hanger at Los Angeles Airport. There wasn't much going on, but the operations officer, an Army second lieutenant, told me an Army DC-3 transport was expected in half an hour, and it would be turning right around to fly a diplomatic pouch to San Francisco.

I asked him for a manila envelope, which I addressed to Colonel Si Peterson's attention at MID headquarters, Building 100, Presidio, San Francisco. After slipping the fingerprint samples into the envelope, I sealed it and wrote across the flap in large letters, "TOP SECRET." Below those words, I signed my rank, name, and service number.

When I handed the envelope to the lieutenant, he took one look at the address and almost came to attention. "Yes, sir. I'll personally make sure this gets on the plane and that Colonel Peterson is called the moment it arrives. In fact, sir, if you'd like, I'll call the Colonel when the plane leaves to let him know the envelope is on its way."

"I would appreciate that, Lieutenant. Thank you for your help."

He snapped off a salute and said, "Yes, sir!"

Since I was feeling a bit peckish when I got back to Patmar's Motel, I stopped at the coffee shop for a roast beef sandwich and some French fried potatoes to eat in my room. There, I kicked off my shoes, sat at the room's small table and picked at the sandwich.

It turned out I wasn't as hungry as I thought.

They say people respond to crises in different ways. In my case, I've always been able to push my emotions aside and deal with whatever the situation required. Then, when I'd done all I could and tried to relax, the emotions I'd shoved aside returned in force. Thinking about Sergeant Biber and how he died left me feeling pretty low.

I randomly selected a telephone in front of the coffee shop and put in a call to Susan. I didn't really have anything important to tell her, I just thought hearing her voice would perk me up. It did.

Seventeen

Optitronics, Inc. – 2001 E. Mariposa Avenue, El Segundo

If all my years as a private detective taught me anything, it's that solving a caper is ninety-nine-percent legwork, and the return on that legwork comes out to about one-percent, if you're lucky. I pulled up at Optitronics around three in the afternoon after spending a day proving the accuracy of that formula.

I hunted down and questioned Optitronics custodians. Nobody knew anything useful about Takuya Nakagawa, so I went to the Hilltop Apartments yet again and interviewed everyone who was home. Nobody knew anything about Takuya Nakagawa, so I drove up to the LAPD's Pacific precinct in Westchester, where they checked their files and found nothing on Takuya Nakagawa. Then I went to the El Segundo cop shop and asked them to check their files. Nothing. Nobody knew a damned thing about Takuya Nakagawa. He was the little man who wasn't there.

Feeling pretty well spent, I walked into the lobby where Corporal Pierce was watching the Optitronics entrance. The corporal said, "Major Spicer, Colonel Peterson called. He asked that you call him at HQ the minute you came in."

Since Si didn't specify a safe telephone number, what he needed to tell me wasn't highly classified. Still, I thought a phone with a little privacy would be nice. I found what I was looking for out on the loading dock and placed my long distance call to San Francisco.

"Hi, Johnny. How are you coming?"

"To be painfully honest, I'm not. I've gone sniffing in every place I could think of where there might be some trace of a trail and it all amounts to a big fat zero."

"That's too bad."

"Yeah, it's been a disappointing day."

"No, I meant I could have saved you some shoe leather if there'd been a way to get in touch with you directly."

"Oh?"

"Yes. When your package got here last night I put a couple of our best people right on it. Just before lunch this morning they surprised me with a match."

"Well hallelujah. Nice going, Si."

"I'm not sure how much good the ID is right now, but I've got other people working on locating the guy. I'm hoping they'll have something by the time you get up here tomorrow evening."

"I take it I'm needed elsewhere?"

"You are. See me at the office when you arrive tomorrow evening and I'll give you the details over dinner. Have a safe trip."

"Thanks, Si, but wait a minute. I'm going to try and kill two birds with one stone. If you need me tonight, I'll be at Santa Barbara number in my file. I've got a piece of unfinished personal business to attend to there."

"Okay, Johnny. See you tomorrow."

Returning to Optitronics' lobby, I told Corporal Pierce our trip to the Hilltop Apartments the night before apparently paid off and I was on my way back to San Francisco to work on tracking the guy who belonged to the fingerprints we found."

Piece said, "Great, Major. Good luck!"

At Patmar's motel I packed my gear and checked out before slipping into a public telephone booth and calling the Casa Sobre El Mar. It was just four o'clock and I caught Susan as she was heading for the door.

"What's cookin', good lookin'?"

"Johnny! Two calls in two days? You're going to spoil me."

"That's the idea. I'm even going to buy your dinner tonight."

One thing about Susan, when she gets excited about something the whole world knows it. "Really, Johnny? That's really swell! When will you get here? Are you here already?"

"No, I'm just leaving LA. It'll take me about two hours and some change with the traffic. That okay?"

"Absolutely. Can you stay overnight?"

"I can if you've got a little extra room in your bed."

"Mister Whiskers is sleeping on the chair tonight!"

"Then it's a deal. I'll see you between six and six-thirty."

"See you then, darling."

Suddenly I wasn't feeling quite as spent as I was earlier. In fact, I found myself humming Helen O'Connell's Green Eyes as I drove over the Sepulveda Pass and connected with US Route 101 North.

Unfortunately, traffic was especially heavy, so the trip took longer than my estimate. I pulled to a stop in front of Susan's four-unit apartment building at 4312 State Street a little after six-thirty. Susan has an upstairs unit with a balcony overlooking the street. She waved and met me at the top of the stairs. Anyone watching us would've thought we hadn't seen each other in years. Love does that sort of thing to you.

She showed me in and I gave Mister Whiskers his pets before heading down the hall to freshen up. When I returned, Susan had some cheddar cheese slices and Ritz Crackers arranged on a plate as an appetizer before we headed out to wherever dinner was to be served. I made sure Mister Whiskers got a little taste of the cheddar cheese and Susan accused me of spoiling him, too. Mister Whiskers didn't seem to mind.

After building up my strength with crackers and cheese, I suggested Joe's Café, a pretty fair restaurant downtown on State Street. Susan said Joe's was fine, but we could go to a hamburger joint for all she cared, just as long as we were together.

Joe had a nice quiet booth for us at the back of the dining room where we took our time over an eclectic meal of crab cakes and thick slices of Norm's Meatloaf. I have no idea who Norm is, but his meatloaf can't be beat.

Artie Shaw's recording of Frenesi was wafting through the dining room when Susan put her hand on mine and said, "I'm sure glad you could get away tonight. It's almost as good as having the weekend."

Tapping the ash off my cigarette, I said, "Yeah, but only almost. Apparently they've got someplace in mind for me to go, and since I'm going there from San Francisco, I'm guessing it's somewhere I can't drive to. I honestly don't know where, though."

"I understand, Johnny. I'm just happy we have tonight. Do you have to leave early in the morning?"

I grinned. "Not before the sun comes up."

"I'm glad to hear that! Just in case, I told them I might be a few minutes late coming in tomorrow morning."

"Unfortunately, Angel, I don't think I'll be making you very late. I've got a dinner date with a Colonel who doesn't like to be kept waiting."

Reaching for her purse, Susan said, "Then we'd better head for home. I want plenty of time for . . . ah . . ."

"Brushing our teeth and combing our hair?"

"Yes," she smiled demurely, "For brushing our hair and combing our teeth.

Eighteen

MID West Coast Command HQ – Building 100, Presidio

By five o'clock I'd checked in at the VOQ and hiked four blocks down to Si's office at the corner of Bliss & Montgomery. Rather than have our conversation in the stuffy soundproof room, Si suggested we go for a walk. Even though the fog was rolling in and it was a little cool outside, I agreed wholeheartedly.

We strolled north along Veterans Boulevard, catching glimpses of the Golden Gate Bridge towers standing tall through the fog, and Si brought me up to date. "The fingerprint match we found identifies your Takuya Nakagawa as Daisuke Kobayashi. Now, that could also be an alias, but the source is an FBI print card and they usually note names and other information that is questionable."

"Was there a mug shot with the prints?"

"There was. I sent a wire photo copy to the LAPD and got them to hand carry it to Pierce at Optitronics this afternoon. He showed it to the employee who noticed Nakagawa, or Kobayashi, at the plant when he shouldn't have been there and she identified the man in the photo as the man she saw. Here's a copy of the FBI photo."

I stared hard at the four-by-five-inch mug shot he handed me, committing the face to memory. "Well, this is a big improvement all by itself. Now I have a face to look for in the crowd."

"We might also have a location in which to look for that face. According to our research people, Daisuke Kobayashi rents an apartment in Pearl City, Hawaii. That's on the outskirts of Honolulu. Here's the address to go with the mug shot."

"What's our confidence level in the address?"

"It's good. The address showed up in encrypted Japanese correspondence about a month ago. It also ties this Daisuke Kobayashi to a known espionage unit operating out of Hawaii, and since the Japanese don't know we're reading their mail, it's likely the address is still current. I have enough confidence in it to send you on an all-expense paid vacation to beautiful Hawaii."

I didn't much care for Si's idea of a vacation. I spent a little time in Hawaii when I was with MID before and I didn't much care for the place then. I didn't figure things had improved much in the past seven or eight years. I said, "Okay, Si. How am I getting there?"

"By the quickest means possible. The Thirty-Eighth Reconnaissance Squadron is moving sixteen of their B-17s to the Philippines. They leave from Hamilton Field tomorrow at 1700 hours. I got you a ride on one of their planes. I'll run you up to Hamilton so you can leave your car here."

"Don't lie to me, Si. You'll run me up to Hamilton to make sure I get on that damned B-17 cattle car for a fourteen hour trip."

Si laughed. "Yeah, that, too. Anyway, the Army Air Force will take you to Hickam Field. I've arranged for a staff car and one of our people to drive you where you need to go. Your driver will be prepared to back up whatever you decide to do about Kobayashi."

"Okay, I've got all that. The only thing you haven't told me is how I'm getting back."

Smiling, he said, "I was saving the best for last. I got you a return ticket on Pan American's *China Clipper*, departing Honolulu at noon on Monday, eight December, or Monday, fifteen December, depending on how quickly you finish your business with Kobayashi. Getting you back by the quickest means is costing the taxpayers a pretty penny."

"As a taxpayer, I whole-heartedly approve."

"I thought you would."

"All right, Si. What do we do if I search Kobayashi's place and don't come up with the occuscope? There's a good possibility the damned thing is already in Tokyo by now. Unless we pick up a lead somewhere, we'll be right back where we started."

Si was quiet for a few moments. "I'm hoping you'll have a chance to . . . let's say . . . talk with Mister Kobayashi and convince him he ought to return the scope or at least tell you where it is. I understand you have not been trained in the most recent methods of . . . interrogation, but your driver has. I'll leave it at that."

"Si, this isn't the inquisition."

"No, Spicer, it isn't. It's war. Hostilities may not have been declared yet, but that's not stopping the Japanese, and I don't intend to let it stop us. There's far too much at stake to play by obsolete rules."

After dinner I wired Susan I would be out of touch for as much as ten days and told her not to worry. Then I organized my gear, laid out a uniform for Saturday, and went to bed.

1500 Hours – Saturday – 6 DEC 41

Flight Line – Hamilton Army Air Force Base, Novato

Sixteen B-17 heavy bombers lined up in a row make a hell of an impression. They took up the entire flight line at Hamilton Army Air Force Base, about 25 miles north San Francisco on Highway 101.

Si dropped me off in front of the operations building and wished me luck. I thanked him and that was the end of our conversation. It was a quiet trip from San Francisco. I had a feeling he lost some faith in me because of my unenthusiastic response to his implication that, if necessary, we should employ torture to make the Japanese espionage agent tell us where the occuscope was.

That was one difference between an experienced field agent and a Colonel who'd been out of the field long enough to have forgotten how things are. Any experienced agent knows he faces the risk of torture if captured, but we tend to believe in doing unto others as we would have them do unto us.

The ops shack was lousy with fliers, all of whom seemed to be intent on harassing a young second lieutenant behind the counter. I took a spot in the line and when I got up to the young man, I showed him my orders.

"Oh, yeah, we were wondering when you were going to show up." He turned and yelled to a pilot standing at the far end of the counter. "Captain Swenson, here's your passenger." Turning back to me, the second lieutenant signed off on my orders and said, "Captain Swenson is flying the ship you drew. He'll tell you what to do from here."

I walked over to Swenson and he pointed to the door next to him. It led outside to the relative quiet of the flight line. Once outside where we could talk, Swenson said, "You're Spicer, huh? Glad to meet you. I'm Ray Swenson."

"Nice to meet you, Ray."

"Let's walk over and stow your gear. You done much flying?"

"Some, but only as a passenger."

Swenson nodded. "I wondered because of that nice leather flying jacket you're wearing. You don't see those on many guys who aren't pilots."

His tone suggested he didn't approve of non-pilots masquerading as fliers. I set him straight on the subject. "But you do see them on guys who have to travel light and may end up God only knows where. Lots of pockets come in handy. The shoulder patch should explain things to anyone who questions the jacket."

Swenson stopped and stepped around to my opposite side to see what the patch was. The yellow, blue and gray Military Intelligence Division emblem obviously impressed him. He let out a low whistle and said, "You're the first spy I ever . . . ah, forgive me. You're the first intelligence officer I ever met, and you're right, you can wear any damned jacket you want and more power to you."

Swenson's B-17 was a C model, USAAF aircraft number 40-2074. It was painted olive drab with no markings except for her number and USA roundels on her wings and fuselage. The ship was a low wing monoplane with four engines, each swinging a giant four-bladed prop. Her top speed was estimated to be in excess of 300 mph, but the exact number was classified.

Captain Swenson explained we were flying with a skeleton crew—pilot, co-pilot, navigator, engineer, and radioman—so we could carry as much fuel as possible. That was also the reason we had guns and a bomb site, but no ammo or bombs.

On hearing that news, I said, "Damn. I'm guess I'm worth about 20 gallons of fuel. I hope we can still make it."

"Don't worry. My flight engineer is the best in the business. He can lean out those engines so the fuel gauges look like they're going up instead of down. We'll make it just fine.

"Major Spicer, I think the most comfortable spot for you is in the bombardier's compartment up front. It's fairly comfortable and the view is spectacular . . . when there's anything to look at.

"So make yourself to home. We'll be warming 'em up in about fifteen minutes. There's coffee and plenty of sandwiches aboard. Oh, and don't worry about the oxygen mask for now. Just wear your throat mike and headphones. If we need to venture above Angels Ten, I'll give the word for oxygen masks. Okay?"

"Thanks, Captain. I appreciate your hospitality."

At precisely 1700 hours the long line of heavy bombers began lumbering toward the active runway. By this time we'd already lost two of our number due to engine problems. It turned out two more turned back shortly after takeoff. That made us a flight of an even dozen.

When 40-2074 was in takeoff position at the end of the runway, Captain Swenson put the coal to her and, as the roar and vibration of four 1200 horsepower engines threatened to shake the ship apart, we started our roll down the runway. Then, as the Army Air Force is so fond of singing when they've had a few beers, off we went into the wild blue yonder.

Nineteen

50 Miles East of Hickam Field – Honolulu, Hawaii

I dozed off for a while and when I rejoined the world it took me a minute to figure out where I was. What woke me up was music playing in my headphones—the kind Harry Owens plays on his Hawaii Calls radio show, but what was Harry Owens doing out in the middle of the ocean?

That was all I could see out my window on the world—ocean and a few puffy white clouds. Then my brain shifted gears and everything made sense. I was in the nose of 40-2074, a B-17C winging its way to Hawaii. Squinting, I could make out a dark line on the horizon. Since there wasn't anything else between California and our destination, I concluded I was looking at Hawaii.

That detail was confirmed a moment later when the music ended and an announcer announced I was listening to radio station KGMB, Honolulu. Then, just as another song began, the music was cut off and I heard Corporal Lucas, our radio operator say, "Captain, I've been trying to get Hickam Field tower on the command set, but all I'm getting is static and strange noises. I can't tell what they are."

Swenson replied, "Pipe it through. Let's hear what you've got."

Lucas was right. What he was getting on Hickam's frequency was a strange racket that sounded more like a shootout on Gangbusters than an airport control tower. Just then, a different voice came through my earphones. It was another pilot in the group reporting he saw a group of escort fighters coming our way from Hawaii. I scanned the sky ahead and spotted the fighters, but they weren't coming to escort us anywhere but into the drink. Bright orange-yellow sparkles—gun muzzle flashes—twinkled continuously around their noses and wings.

I keyed my throat mike and said, "Swenson, that fighter escort is shooting at us."

"Holy shit! They are!"

They were Japanese fighters and they continued to harass our formation the rest of the way in. As we reached the island of O'ahu, another voice on the radio said, "B-17 flight, this is Hickam tower. We are under attack by Japanese aircraft. Use alternate or emergency landing fields. Repeat, Hickam under attack. Use alternate landing fields."

Suddenly it was every B-17 for itself. Swenson held his course, though, probably because the Japanese fighters were after two other ships in the flight and he didn't want to attract their attention. At least I now knew what those Zeke fighters were doing so far from home. The logical conclusion was they arrived from Japan by aircraft carrier. That Jap planes were bombing the hell out of our Pacific fleet wasn't any big surprise either. It was bound to happen.

A few minutes later we cleared a ridge and looked down on Pearl Harbor and Hickam Field. Even from our distant vantage point the scene below was one of complete chaos. Then we were in the thick of it and I had a front row seat. Dozens of silver and pale green dive bombers with big red roundels on their wings were swooping in to drop their bombs on Hickam's runways, hangars, and dozens of US planes conveniently grouped together on the flight line. Northwest of Hickam, dark green torpedo bombers were buzzing low over Pearl Harbor like a hive of angry bees. Explosions erupted from one after another of the warships lined up in neat rows in the harbor like targets in a shooting gallery.

Silver Zeke fighters were everywhere and shooting at anything that moved, which included us. Still, Swenson held his course, which lined us up perfectly with the wide east-west runway at Hickam. I felt and heard the main landing gear come down somewhere behind me. Swenson was taking the most direct route out of the melee, which was right through it.

The radio said, "B-17 on final approach to Hickam, this is Hickam Field tower. We are under attack. Use an alternative field."

Swenson said, "Too late for that, Hickam. We're committed now."

"B-17 on final, watch out for debris and bomb craters on the runway." Then, after a short pause, he added, "Good luck."

The runway was coming up fast. That made sense. Swenson was heading in for a "hot" landing. The sooner we were on the ground, the sooner we could get the hell out of sitting duck number 40-2074.

Just when I thought we might make it through the chaos in one piece, I looked up and saw two Zekes coming directly at us with their wing-mounted .20mm cannons firing steadily. I could hear their large caliber slugs ripping up our sheet metal. That racket was followed by an explosion further back in the ship. Lucas yelled from the radio operator's position, "They hit the flair storage box! We're on fire!"

Low over Hickam's runway, we leap-frogged the tail section of a PBY that was missing an airplane and Swenson chopped the power. The heavy B-17 dropped the last ten feet or so to the runway like a rock, but the gear took the impact and I felt Swenson and Roy Reid, our copilot, applying all the brakes they had.

The ship needed a lot of room to slow down because of Swenson's hot landing, but when our speed permitted, he swung the big B-17 off the runway onto a taxiway and we all started to breathe a little easier. Then the ship broke in two.

I mean the B-17 literally broke into two pieces. The flare fire amidships was so hot it damaged the B-17's structure, and everything aft of the waist gunners' position separated from the front part of the ship and dropped to the ground. Fortunately, our skeleton crew members were all forward of the break, so no one was seriously injured.

Surprisingly, the intercom was still working and I heard Swenson yell, "Everyone out. Spicer, grab the Norden bombsight case and drop it down to the first man on the ground."

"Will do."

The forward hatch was in the floor directly behind me. Roy Reid was already opening it. As the hatch cover swung down, he dropped through the opening. With the bombsight case in hand, I moved to the hatch, "Reid, here's the Norden."

He reached up and I dropped it into his waiting arms like a baby we were rescuing from a house fire. I followed the bombsight to the ground and, as the rest of the crew left the ship, I looked around.

Flames and busted up airplanes were everywhere. The interior of 40-2074 was relatively peaceful compared to the chaos around us. Concussions from bombs shook the ground and the air vibrated with the raucous chatter of the attackers' machine guns overhead and from whatever weapons defenders on the ground found to fight with, including rifles and handguns.

Men, most with grease or blood smeared on their uniforms, ran back and forth to no apparent purpose. Trucks zig-zagged between burning aircraft, trying to move those that could be saved away from the ships already destroyed.

Firefighters tried to put out gasoline fires with water hoses that barely trickled. I watched one fellow with a large fire extinguisher run toward a burning Curtiss P-40. The fighter exploded before he got there and, when the smoke cleared, all that remained was the red fire extinguisher rolling slowly along the flight line.

A few men were manning .30 caliber water-cooled machine guns mounted in sandbag revetments. One fellow firing a machine gun near us was hit by enemy fire and another guy immediately stepped into his place behind the gun. I could also see at least two .40 millimeter Bofors guns blasting away at the invading aircraft. It was hard to say if the gunners were doing any good, but they were certainly giving it their all.

Swenson was the last man through the hatch. He took a look around and said, "Let's make for what's left of that hangar over there. It'll give us some cover."

The six of us took off running with Reid and the bombsight in the lead. We were heading for a ten-foot opening blown in the wall of a hangar by a Japanese bomb. The opening was less than a hundred feet away as the crow flies, but we were running an obstacle course, jogging around airplane pieces and at least one large bomb crater. Our flight engineer was the last man into the hangar. He dove through the opening head first with a strafing Zeke on his heels.

Captain Swenson looked out at Hickam Field's version of Dante's Inferno and said, "What a mess! Why the hell didn't they warn us back at Hamilton there was a war on out here?"

I said, "Because there wasn't a war on then. I'm betting the Japs pulled their usual trick, declaring war only after they've struck the first blow. They've done that before."

Reid mumbled, "Yellow cowards is what they are."

Lucas said, "You sound like the intelligence people knew this was coming. Why the hell didn't you tell someone?"

"Believe me, we did! We told everyone in Washington from FDR on down that the Japs were likely to pull something like this, but nobody wanted to rock the boat."

Lucas shook his head in disgust. "And now the damned boat

is sinking like a rock!"

We were watching the beginning of what was sure to be called the Second World War through a hole in the wall, and as we watched, the scene before us gradually calmed. The firefighters and other emergency crews were still going full speed, but the sky was now clear of Jap aircraft and the sound of gunfire died away.

I said, "I left my travel bag in the ship. I'm going back for it."

Swenson said, "I'll go with you. I want to grab the log book and a couple of other things. Anybody else need anything from the ship?"

Lucas piped up, "If you can get to them, you might bring back the rest of the sandwiches and coffee. It might be a while before we get to a mess hall that isn't blown up."

Swenson laughed. "Always the chow hound, that's our Lucas."

As Swenson and I walked toward what was left of 40-2074 I said, "Nice job of getting us back on the ground in one piece . . . well, two pieces."

Ray Swenson hadn't lost his sense of humor. He laughed again. "Thanks, Spicer, but a lot of it was luck. The Japs had us cold, but I guess it just wasn't our time to die yet. By the way, thanks for identifying that first batch of Zekes we encountered."

"No thanks necessary. I was looking out for my own hide as much as anything."

As we arrived under the nose of 40-2074, Swenson looked at his ship and said, "Well, I'd make you an honorary crew member if we still had a ship to be the crew of."

"Thanks, Ray."

"The fuselage hatch is blocked so we'll have to get in the way we got out, through the nose hatch. Listen, Spicer, there's no sense to both of us climbing around in there. You stay down here and I'll drop the stuff through the hatch. You'll have to give me a boost up, though. With the tail missing, the nose is quite a bit higher than it should be."

Returning to the hangar with the gear we recovered, Swenson said, "Okay, Lucas, here are your sandwiches. Anybody else want one?"

It turned out we were all hungry enough to eat a sandwich and there were plenty to go around, so we chowed down. As I was finishing off a baloney on white, a four-door olive drab Plymouth staff car pulled up just outside the hangar and a burly master sergeant climbed out. He approached our hole in the wall and said, "Would one of you gentlemen in there be Major Spicer?"

"That's me."

"Good. I'm your MID driver, sir. You ready to go?"

"Sure." Turning to Captain Swenson, I said, "Ray, you guys need a lift anywhere?"

Swenson shook his head. "No, thanks. We just need to walk over to what's left of the ops shack and check in or something—at least let 'em know we're here." Offering his hand, he added, "Nice having you aboard, Spicer. Sorry about the turbulence at the end."

We both laughed and I said, "No problem, Ray. Maybe you can glue the pieces together and get her flyin' again."

After saying goodbye to the rest of the crew, I threw my travel bag in the back of the staff car and we were off. As we bobbed and weaved our way through the debris, my driver offered his hand. "I'm Ed Carson, Major. They didn't tell me a whole lot about what we're up to, just that I'm to take you wherever you need to go and help you do whatever you're here to do."

I briefed Carson on the basics of our mission and gave him Daisuke Kobayashi's address. The note Peterson gave me said, "329 Kaluamoi Drive, Pearl City, Hawaii."

Twenty

En Route: Hickam Field to Pearl City – Honolulu, Hawaii

Master Sergeant Ed Carson studied Daisuke Kobayashi's address for a moment. "Pearl City, huh? That's going to take a little time."

"It's a long way?"

"No, actually it's only four or five miles, but the roads in that direction are a mess. Everybody's out to get a look at the damage in the harbor or they're trying to get somewhere they think is safe. The traffic is bumper to bumper from here to Pearl City and beyond. We'll get there, we just have to be patient."

Leaving Hickam, Carson turned left onto a broad street called Kamehameha, which I presume is named for the guy who established the kingdom of Hawaii as an independent country. His highway follows the eastern shoreline of Pearl Harbor and at the moment was jammed with automobiles not going anywhere in a big hurry. Off to our left a pall of thick black smoke still hung over what was left of the American Pacific fleet. The view to our right was mostly pineapple fields.

Our staff car was equipped with a red light and siren, and Carson made use of both, but most drivers just ignored them. Eventually, he resorted to driving on the shoulder of the road, forcing pedestrians to dive out of our path.

Carson asked me to look in the glove compartment for a map. He said he'd seen the street name, but wasn't sure where it was. The Shell Oil Company map of Honolulu included Pearl City and, after getting it folded down to a manageable size, I found our street.

Kaluamoi Drive ran along a thin strip of land between

Kamehameha Road and the harbor. Since one end of Kaluamoi intersected Kamehameha, a left turn there would take us to our destination. The navigation was simple, pronouncing the names of the streets was not.

After a while, the pineapple plantations on our right gradually became clusters of small houses that weren't much more than shacks. Carson nodded toward the houses. "Pearl City."

It was almost eleven-fifteen when we made our left turn onto Kaluamoi Drive, and the minute we did, I got a bad feeling. This part of Pearl City was right on the edge of the harbor and the Jap attackers weren't too particular about their targets. Several of the houses we passed were badly shot up, and when we got to our destination, the situation was even worse. An American gunner on one of the ships in the harbor apparently shot straight and true enough to knock a Zeke out of the sky. It came down on 329 Kaluamoi Drive and plowed on into the house next door.

The houses weren't much to begin with and the fighter had reduced the one we wanted to rubble. The only good luck was the Zeke crashed without burning, but the strong smell of aviation fuel warned that situation could change at any moment.

Carson and I got out of the staff car and took a good look around us at the neighborhood. There was nobody in sight, so we ventured into the rubble for a closer inspection. On the surface it appeared most of what was there consisted of the personal belongings and furnishings you'd expect to find in someone's house.

Before getting too involved in the search, though, I unholstered my revolver and looked into the Zeke's cockpit. Half a dozen bullet holes were strung in a vertical line up the right side of the cockpit, and since the fighter has no armor to protect the pilot in that area, I found what I hoped to find, one very dead Jap pilot.

While I was checking on the pilot, Carson was knee deep in the remains of the house. He hadn't been at it long before he yelled, "Major Spicer, take a look at this."

I climbed over the rubble and studied the sheet of paper in his hand. It was a commercially printed map of Pearl Harbor on which the outlines of ships had been hand-drawn, each identified by Japanese characters.

Carson growled, "Those bastards were planning this for a long time. I bet this map shows every ship in the harbor."

Nodding, I said, "If nothing else, it proves we were too complacent. Let's see what else is here."

After another twenty minutes or so of searching Carson said,

"Found something else, Major."

"Carson, I bet you were a whiz on Easter egg hunts as a kid."

Looking down into the rubble at his feet, Carson said, "Yeah, well this ain't no Easter egg."

I looked where he was looking and saw a leg in blue denim and a foot in a sandal. We cleared away enough garbage from the body for me to recognize Daisuke Kobayashi, the Jap who stole the occuscope and whose booby trap killed Sergeant Biber. Somehow there was justice in the irony of him being killed by the wreck of a Jap aircraft.

"What do you want to do with him, Major?"

"Leave the bastard right where he is. The local officials will get around to him sooner or later and right now I don't much care whether a Jap spy gets a proper burial or not."

"This guy was a spy?"

"And a cold-blooded killer."

Carson took another look at Kobayashi and went back to hunting Easter eggs.

We dug around for another half an hour or so and I was thinking we'd found everything we were going to find without a bulldozer to scrape the rubble aside. That's when a piece of cardboard caught my eye. I could only see about three inches of it, but the cardboard was exactly the right color.

"Hey, Sergeant, come over here and give me a hand."

He trotted over and I pointed to a ceiling truss laying on top of what I wanted. "Help me lift this so I can get ahold of that cardboard under it."

He picked a spot from which to lift and I picked another. "Okay, on three. One . . . two . . . THREE."

With both of us putting our backs into it, the truss came up enough for me to grab the cardboard and jerk it free. What I had in my hand was a three-by-two-and-a-half-foot box that was custom made to fit an occuscope.

Holding my breath, I lifted the box lid. Against all odds, I was looking at the occuscope stolen from Optitronics' vault nearly a week ago. I muttered, "Well, son of a gun. They didn't get it to Tokyo after all."

Sergeant Carson was looking over my shoulder and observed, "Yeah, but that gizmo is all busted up."

"That's okay, Sergeant, as long as it's our busted up gizmo and not theirs. Let's get the hell out of here."

As Carson negotiated our departure, I studied the cardboard box and its contents. I could clearly see a crease in the cardboard where the ceiling truss hit it. The damage to the occuscope matched the crease—a major dent in the vertical column and one lens bent at an angle.

I couldn't help smiling at another bit of irony. The Jap attack had come before anyone monkeyed with scope or sent it to Tokyo. Things were looking up.

"Where to, Major?"

Having accomplished everything I came to do, the number one priority was my departure from paradise. "Where does the Pan Am clipper put in?"

Carson stopped the car and pointed through the smoke toward Ford Island in the middle of the harbor. "Right out there on that point due north of the island."

"Oh swell. Even if we could get over there, I don't imagine we'd find any clippers waiting to fly passengers out of Honolulu."

Sergeant Carson nodded. "I'd say you're probably right about that."

"Where can we find out the status of the *China Clipper* that was supposed to arrive yesterday?"

"Well, this being Sunday, I doubt any of the travel agencies in town would be open even if the Japs hadn't shown up. I think the next best thing would be one of the big hotels. Most of them have travel services to book steamship and airline reservations for guests. Someone like that might know."

"Good idea. Which hotel would you suggest?"

"The biggest is the Moana over in Waikiki. They've got a large staff and they're probably handling the emergency better than the smaller hotels."

"Okay, Sergeant Carson, you convinced me. The Moana it is, and don't spare the horses."

If anything the traffic was worse than when we left Hickam, but Sergeant Carson pushed hard and we pulled into the Moana's Hotel's circular drive about one-thirty. I jammed the occuscope box into my travel bag and told Carson to wait with it while I went in to see what I could find out. A doorman stopped me as I walked toward the hotel entrance and said we couldn't park where we were parked.

I flashed my MID ID. "Mister, in case you haven't noticed, there's a war on. That means I park wherever the hell I need to."

His mouth snapped shut and he stepped back to let me pass. Walking through the entrance doors, I found myself in a very busy and very classy lobby. A bellman hustled past me with one of those little silver trays in his hand they use to deliver messages. I stopped him and asked where their travel service was. He pointed toward a hallway next to the hotel gift shop.

Surprisingly, there were only a couple of customers in the little travel agency and a woman behind the counter was available to answer my questions, although I didn't much care for the answers she came up with."

"Sir, the *China Clipper* had to leave Pearl Harbor because of the attack this morning, but the crew got it safely to Hilo on the Big Island without damage. The information we have is the Clipper will depart tomorrow as scheduled, except from Hilo rather than Pearl."

"Is Pan American providing transportation to Hilo?"

"No, sir, not that I'm aware of. I guess that part is every passenger for himself."

"All right, miss, if you had to catch that Clipper tomorrow, how would you go about getting to Hilo?"

She thought for a moment, and then said, "Under normal conditions, I would take a Hawaiian Airlines flight, but we heard they suspended all service. I have no idea how else to get there short of chartering a boat."

I thanked the woman, made a quick stop in the hotel gift shop, and returned to the car. As Ed drove away from the Moana Hotel I explained the problem. I was surprised when he said, "That's no problem. You want to get to Hilo? I'll have you there before dinner."

We headed out of Honolulu to the east on a road called Kalanianaole—go ahead, say it, I dare you—that skirted the southeastern tip of O'ahu and took us north through a community known as Waimanalo. We drove for about forty-five minutes before coming to a guarded gate in a concrete wall. A white metal sign on the wall with large black letters said:

BELLOWS FIELD
US Military Reservation
No Trespassing

Bellows Army Air Force Field wasn't overlooked by the Jap attackers, but it faired a lot better than Hickam. There were a few bomb craters here and there and some gutted P-40 fighters were bulldozed up against a B-17—probably one of our group—that bellied in for a wheels-up landing.

Otherwise, Bellows appeared to be fully operational. Carson obviously knew who to talk to at Bellows and what to say, because we soon found ourselves aboard an hour-long flight aboard a DC-3 in military garb. We did, indeed, have dinner in Hilo.

Before dinner, however, I checked with a woman in a flight stewardess uniform sitting at a table in the Hilo Airport lobby. A hand-lettered sign in front of the table said "Pan American Clipper Service." I wanted to make sure my reservation was still good. The woman explained some reservations had to be cancelled because of priority military travel, but after looking at my MID ID, she found my name on a list, made a note next to it, and confirmed that my ticket and reservation would be honored.

Spending the night at Hilo Airport because all the local hotels were booked up, Sergeant Carson and I took turns keeping watch over the occuscope. In the morning, I thanked Carson for his help and he got a lift back to Bellows on another Army DC-3 heading in the right direction. Then I boarded a bus carrying Pan American's San Francisco-bound passengers to the *China Clipper* moored in Hilo Harbor.

Twenty-One

Pan American China Clipper – En Route to San Francisco

The *China Clipper's* four big engines were already spinning their propellers when dock hands cast off the mooring lines and the huge flying boat glided smoothly away from the dock at Hilo. It was precisely noon by my watch. Despite the war, Pan American was operating on schedule.

I found myself nervously watching the skies around us for the first half hour of the flight, expecting Jap fighters with blazing guns to pop out of the clouds any minute. After a while, though, I relaxed and began enjoying my luxurious surroundings.

Unlike most airliners with rows of seats down both sides of a central aisle, the *China Clipper's* passenger areas were divided into compartments spanning the width of the airplane, about ten to twelve feet. According to an information brochure on the Martin M-130 flying boat I found beside my seat, there were nine of these interconnected rooms.

Starting at the front of the airplane on the lower deck—the crew occupied an upper deck—was a compartment designed to carry six passengers on overnight flights like Hawaii to San Francisco. Six seats and two couches converted into six bunks for sleeping. This was Compartment One and it happened to be the one I was in.

What surprised me was I had the compartment all to myself. After my conversation with the woman at Hilo airport, I expected every seat on the Clipper to be occupied, but it was only carrying 12 passengers—just one-third of the ship's capacity for an overnight flight. The difficulty of getting to Hilo might have caused some to miss the departure, and a one-way fare of $278 dollars might also help explain the light load. The same amount of money will rent you a nice house in LA for at least a year.

The next compartment aft of mine was devoted to baggage and restrooms. Compartment Two also had a spiral staircase leading to crew areas on the upper deck.

The second passenger compartment came next and it was identical in design to the first. Aft of the second passenger compartment was a large main lounge which was converted into a dining room at mealtimes.

Moving further aft you came to compartments three, four and five, all of which were laid out identically to the first two passenger compartments. More restrooms occupied the next space, and they were followed by the last compartment in the ship, designated the "Deluxe Suite." For that matter, everything on the plane looked pretty deluxe to me.

The compartments alternated color schemes between turquoise carpets with pale green walls and rust carpets with beige walls. The comfortable seats were upholstered in soothing colors, the carpets were thick, the soft lighting was relaxing, and the soundproofing was excellent. On top of all that, delicious meals were served on fine china, food and drinks were always available, and the cabin stewards remained close at hand to accommodate our every wish. Flying in the Clipper is like floating along on your own private cloud.

Lunch was served promptly at one o' clock in the main lounge. The meal, consisting of celery hearts and stuffed green olives, a hearty Pan American Chef's Salad with French dressing, chocolate ice cream, and coffee, was well prepared and tasty. After lunch, I propped my travel bag up against the side of the compartment, leaned against it to make sure nobody bothered its top secret contents, and took myself a nap.

After nearly 20 hours, even the lap of luxury gets tiresome, so I was delighted to see the endless ocean outside my window become beaches, and then the coastal hills west of San Francisco Bay. Our course took us directly over the Golden Gate and east almost to Treasure Island before the captain made a turn to the southeast that lined us up for a landing behind a breakwater on the south side of Alameda Naval Air Station. From there a short taxi took us across a manmade lagoon especially designed for the Pan American Clippers.

Five minutes later we were moored and I heard the forward hatch just ahead of my compartment open. I simply picked up my travel bag and walked off the ship into a bright sunny California day. It was ten-thirty Tuesday morning.

As I walked up a ramp from the floating dock, I was surprised to see Si Peterson waiting for me at the top along with two armed enlisted men. I expected some security because I sent him a cable explaining I was bringing him a pineapple from Hawaii, which he correctly translated to mean I recovered the occuscope, but I didn't expect him to take time out to be part of the welcoming committee.

We shook hands and Si asked, "The pineapple is in the suitcase?"

"Sure enough. It's a little banged up from having a Jap fighter land on it, but the scope is still intact."

Si put a mile-wide smile on his face. "Great job, Johnny. You really earned your keep this trip. Let's get your pineapple back to the Presidio so we can lock it up, and on the way I'll tell you what else is going on."

In the backseat of Si's staff car I unzipped my travel bag and slid the occuscope's cardboard box onto his lap. He opened the box and shook his head. "What a mess."

"And it is now officially your mess."

He chuckled. "You can't imagine how happy I am to have it." After a short pause, he added, "Well, maybe you can."

"I think I've got a pretty good idea."

As our driver negotiated the Oakland approach to the Bay Bridge, Si said, "The latest news here has mostly to do with Optitronics. HQ agreed with your assessment of the situation and decided the scopes are too valuable to leave in the hands of people who have no idea how to run a secure plant. Corporal Russ Pierce—you remember him—is supervising the security aspects of Optitronics' move to Naval Air Station Lakehurst. All of the manufacturing and testing will be done there with the Navy providing security except when an occuscope leaves the base. Then it becomes our problem again."

"I see."

"Now, what I want you to do when you've rested up from your vacation in romantic Hawaii and write me a report on how you recovered this thing, is get down to El Segundo to make sure everything is properly cleaned up there. Then stand by because the Navy tells us they're about to send a blimp west to do some testing out here. That includes putting the occuscope through its paces. I'll want you and a man of your choosing ready to go wherever the damned Navy points that bag of hot air."

"Actually, I wrote up your report on the flight back, so you can have that right now. As for a man to work with, is Pierce available?"

Si nodded. "I thought he might be your choice. He's available as soon as he's done riding shotgun on Optitronics' move to Lakehurst. He'll need to stay back there a few days to get things sorted out, but he can probably ride back on the blimp they send west for testing."

"Good. How soon do you expect them to be done moving Optitronics?"

"The most important parts, the completed scopes, all Fred Demas' damned black boxes, and the parts inventory are being assembled for shipping. Pierce will be moving that stuff aboard two DC-3 transports, so if something happens to one plane, they won't lose the whole shebang. We expect the DC-3s to be loaded and gone in a day or two. We can't do it sooner because Lakehurst won't be ready to receive classified stuff for a few more days."

"Okay, I'll head down there first thing tomorrow morning. Oh, and Si, I'd like Pierce to have a field promotion to sergeant. That would be a more appropriate rank for the responsibility we're piling on him."

Si nodded enthusiastically. "Agreed. I'll put him in for it as soon as we get back to the Presidio."

"Good. I'm certainly no expert, but winning this war will take the best we've got, both on the front lines and in intelligence."

Si's expression turned serious. "That bad, huh?"

"Let's just say our boys in the Pacific have their hands full."

Twenty-Two

1200 Hours – Wednesday – 10 DEC 41

Casa Sobre El Mar – 1051 Fairway Road, Montecito

I left the Presidio before sunup on Wednesday so I could get to Santa Barbara by lunchtime. I hit town about eleven-forty-five and called Susan at work to wrangle a lunch invitation.

"This is Susan Jackson."

"Good, that's just who I wanted to talk to."

"Johnny! Are you okay?"

"I'm fine, Angel. How about I come by for lunch in about fifteen minutes?"

"Yes! I'll get us a couple of sandwiches and salads from the kitchen. That way we won't waste any time going somewhere."

"Sounds good. I'll see you soon."

Susan met me out on the redwood veranda surrounding the clinic. She had a white paper sack in each hand and managed to drop both of them when she threw her arms around me.

"Easy, Angel. Everything is fine."

She had an expression that looked like fear on her pretty face. "No it isn't! We're at war. I heard the whole thing on the radio Sunday."

I'd debated about how much to tell her and decided lying to her would catch up with me sooner or later. Besides that, I had a small present for Susan I'd picked up at the Moana Hotel gift shop on my way through, and it wasn't something I'd be likely to have if I wasn't in Hawaii.

I took a deep breath and said, "Yeah, I know. I saw it firsthand."

"You were there? At Pearl Harbor? Sunday morning?"

"Yes, I flew over there as a passenger on a B-17 bomber and

99

we arrived at Hickam Field just as the Japs were attacking."

Her hands flew up to her face. "Oh, gosh. I got your wire, but I kept expecting you to call when I heard the news on the radio. No wonder you didn't."

"I would have, if I could have. The telephones weren't working too well at that particular time."

"But you're okay? Really?"

"I'm fine, Angel. I flew back yesterday on the *China Clipper*."

"I won't ask what you were doing in Hawaii, but I hope there was a darn good reason for being there."

"A lot of the time what I was doing was thinking of you. In fact, I brought you something. Come on, let's sit and I'll give it to you while we have lunch."

I picked up our lunch sacks and we walked to a bench with a terrific ocean view through the pine trees. We sat and I held up the bags, "Are these the same?"

"No. One is Cheddar cheese and the other is tuna. Pick the one that sounds best to you."

I was about to pick the cheese sandwich when she leaned over and put her arms around me again. "I'm sorry, Johnny, but I was worried sick about you. I'll do better, I promise."

"Angel, I know this isn't easy for you, but . . ."

"I know; we don't have any choice in the matter. Stupid Army! Now show me what you brought me from Hawaii on the *China Clipper*."

I reached into the side pocket of my sport coat and brought out a white gift box. "Here you go, Angel, all the way from O'ahu."

While she opened the box, I opened the Cheddar cheese sandwich and took a bite. I was hungry.

Under a layer of tissue paper she found a kukui nut necklace with a little stylized wooden sea turtle dangling from it. "Oh, Johnny, how pretty! Tell me about it, there has to be a story."

"Well, about all I know is that those brown round things are polished kukui nuts from kukui trees. In the Islands they're used for just about everything from candles to making dyes. The myth is the nuts are symbolic of enlightenment and peace, and kukui nut leis are worn at weddings by the bride and groom for luck. The sea turtle is symbolic of long life and good fortune."

"I love it, Johnny. Thank you so much. Here, help me put it on. I want to show off my kookoo nuts."

She turned around and I put my sandwich down long enough to fasten the necklace around her neck. I said, "And by the way, that's pronounced ku-ku-ee."

"Well, however you say it, they're beautiful, simple and beautiful."

"I'm glad you like them, Angel. I just wanted you to know I was thinking about you."

"I don't need a present to know that. I could feel it the whole time you were away. That much I knew for sure."

After finishing our lunches, we sat holding hands and staring out at the ocean until Susan looked at her wristwatch. "Oh, damn. It's almost time to get back to work."

"And I need to get back on the road. What's your work schedule for the weekend?"

"I have the weekend off. You think you might be able to come back?"

"There's a good possibility I'll have some time to kill while . . . while I wait for some stuff to get done."

Susan grinned. "They say Santa Barbara is a great place to kill time."

"I've always found that to be so. I'll give you a call tomorrow or Friday, just as soon as I know what my schedule will be. And don't worry Angel, nobody will be shooting at me between now and then."

"They'd better not be!"

We said our goodbyes and, after filling up the Dodge's gas tank, I got back on US 101 in the southbound direction. I arrived at Optitronics a few minutes before six and turned into the alleyway alongside the loading dock. There I saw three canvas covered stake-bed trucks and a member of Pierce's team holding a .45 caliber M3 submachine gun at the ready. Pierce had definitely stepped up Optitronics' security.

I showed the guard my MID identification, which he examined very closely, and asked him where I could find Corporal Pierce. The fellow finally lowered his grease gun and told me Corporal Pierce was in the building, but I would have to go in through the front entrance; the loading dock entrances were sealed.

I found Pierce in the lobby giving one of his team members instructions for the night shift. He looked up and saluted me, as did the private he was talking to, and said, "Good evening, Major. I'll be right with you. I just need to finish going over some last-minute details."

"Take your time, Corporal."

When Pierce dismissed his team member, he hurried over, saying, "It's good to see you here, Major."

"Considering that I just got back from a weekend trip to Pearl Harbor, it feels damned good to be here."

"You were there Sunday morning, sir?"

"Yes, I was and there are some things about that trip you need to know. When are you through here tonight?"

"I'm done now, Major."

"Then let's go get some dinner and have us a talk. Do you have wheels here?"

"Yes, sir."

"Then meet me up at the Patmar Motel's coffee shop. It's on the west side of Sepulveda just this side of Imperial. Go ahead and get us a table. I need to rent a room before they're all gone."

"Yes, sir. See you there."

Twenty-Three

Patmar Motel Coffee Shop – 949 N. Sepulveda Blvd., El Segundo

By the time I got myself registered at the motel, Pierce was already through one Coke and starting on his second in the coffee shop. He found us a quiet table off by itself and, as I joined him there, Pierce said, "Major Spicer, before we discuss what you've got on your mind, I want to thank you for recommending my field promotion. Colonel Peterson called this morning and told me a promotion of two full grades was approved and he submitted it on your recommendation."

"Well, then, Staff Sergeant Pierce, congratulations. You deserve a rank commensurate with the responsibility you've accepted."

"Thank you, sir."

Our waitress showed up then to take our dinner orders. Pierce opted for healthy grilled Alaskan Salmon with rice and I picked pot roast with mashed potatoes and gravy.

As I watched her clip our order to the stainless steel order wheel in the kitchen pass-through, I said, "Now I've got some news for you, Sergeant Pierce. I already told you I was in Hawaii Sunday. Now I'll tell you why. Do you remember those fingerprints you pulled off of the dish and cups in Nakagawa's apartment?"

"Yes, sir."

"It turned out we got quite lucky with those prints. In less than 24 hours Colonel Peterson's people matched them to a known Japanese espionage agent working under the name Daisuke Kobayashi, and better yet, they found an address for him in Hawaii."

Pierce looked as impressed as he sounded. "Wow!"

"Yeah. We work for a pretty good outfit. Anyway, Colonel Peterson decided the address was recent enough that it might still be good, so he put me on a B-17 being ferried to Manila via Hawaii from Hamilton Field. We left as a flight of 12 unarmed ships Saturday and arrived at Hickam Field Sunday morning just in time to meet the Japs."

"Oh, geez!"

"Fortunately, our pilot, an AAF captain named Swenson, knew his stuff and did a hell of a job getting us on the ground at Hickam. The ship was wrecked, but nobody in the crew was seriously injured. That was a miracle in itself."

Slowly shaking his head, Pierce said, "On the radio news reports they said most of the fleet in the harbor was badly damaged or sunk and hundreds of planes were destroyed on the ground at Hickam and some other airfields."

"That's fairly accurate. It's a hell of a mess over there. Anyway, Colonel Peterson arranged for a driver to pick me up at Hickam and we went to Kobayashi's address in Pearl City. When we got there we found the house was destroyed by a crashed Jap fighter, but we went through the debris anyway and found the missing occuscope still in its cardboard carton."

"No kiddin'?"

"No kidding. The scope is pretty beat up, but all the pieces are there and no one had opened it up yet to see what makes an occuscope tick. Colonel Peterson has it now and I imagine it will eventually be sent to Lakehurst for repair or whatever they do with those things."

"That's great! I've been thinking all of our security efforts were too little too late. I feel better now."

"You should feel better, especially since it was your fingerprint kit and the prints you lifted that got the scope back."

Pierce looked thoughtful. "Speaking of Kobayashi, were you able to find him, too?"

I nodded. "Yes. He was in the house when the Jap fighter hit it. Kobayashi met with a fitting end."

"Good. That guy was mean as a snake."

"He was, but that's history. You and I have a new assignment which is likely to have us meeting up with more snakes."

"Colonel Peterson said something about working with you, but he said you'd explain the details."

"Actually, it's simple to explain. As long as the occuscopes are on the base at Lakehurst, they are the Navy's problem. When one or more leave the base for testing or something like that, they're MID's problem."

"I see."

"As soon as you finish your current project—moving the scopes and other stuff to Lakehurst—the Navy is going to send a blimp west for testing in the Pacific. One of the things they plan to test is the occuscope. So, when that blimp leaves Lakehurst with an occuscope aboard, you'll be on it, too, and we'll get together wherever the thing ends up out here. At the moment the only completed airship facility on the west coast is Moffett Field, up by San Francisco, but I suppose they could tie one of the damned gas bags down just about anywhere."

"Got it. I only have one question."

"Shoot."

"Who will be in charge of the Optitronics stuff in Lakehurst? Nobody's told me who I'm supposed to contact there."

"Nobody's told me, either, but unless you hear different, I would hunt down Lieutenant Commander Edward Nugent. Nugent is a big stick back there at Lakehurst. He came out here when they first handed me the Optitronics assignment and I couldn't get rid of him fast enough. I imagine you'll feel the same."

Our dinners arrived and we both chowed down with enthusiasm. Afterwards, Staff Sergeant Pierce headed for the YMCA in Westchester and I retired to my room at the Patmar Motel.

Since I was wearing civvies on this assignment, I unpacked a clean shirt and slacks for tomorrow. While I was rummaging around in one of the zippered side pockets of my travel bag for a pair of socks, I came across the occuscope prototype photo Si gave me. I was putting it aside when the light caught it just right and I noticed some words on the back written with a very light pencil. I hadn't seen the printing before and I took a closer look. The patterns of characters made no sense, so I figured they were a code of some sort.

Making myself a mental note to return the photo to Si, I decided it might be fun to take a shot at cracking the code myself. As unlikely as that was, it was something interesting to do until bedtime.

I began the puzzle by copying the encrypted message on a piece of motel stationary. After studying it for a few minutes, I decided it was a simple substitution, or monoalphabetic, code. That means the person who encrypted the message just substituted an alphabet with randomly mixed up letters for the

English alphabet.

XEESZX KRQBWESR WZJ OWBDU AP ARRCKRAD/
ODRE FSEQSZ EQSGEV JWVK/
EGWZKBSE JUSLGV SZKEGCRESAZK/ KD

Monoalphabetic encryptions are relatively easy to decode using the frequency of occurrence method. Frequency of occurrence simply refers to the letters of the alphabet occurring most frequently in English text. For example, the letter you see most often in English words is *E*. It is followed in frequency by *T A O I N S* and so on.

You use this decoding method by counting the number of times each letter occurs in the encryption and replacing the most frequently used letter with an *E*, and the letter that occurs next most often is replaced by *T*, and so on. Typically you have to play with the sequence a little, but the method usually solves the puzzle.

The encrypted letter occurring most often, 11 times, in the message I had was *E*. When I saw that, I knew I had a problem. It's highly unlikely a real letter *E* would be replaced with an encrypted letter *E*. Replacing *I*, the next most frequently occurring letter, with *T* worked a little better, but I was still missing something critical.

I picked up what little encryption knowledge I have when I was with MID before. There was an encryption expert we called "Professor" and he liked nothing better than showing those of us outside the encryption department how encryption worked. Unfortunately, I'd already used up most of what I learned from him, except for some warning rules.

Warning number one was be sure you know what language the message was in originally. The frequency of occurrence sequence he gave us only applied to English. I had no way of knowing for sure, but I was reasonably certain the original language was not Japanese, so there was a good chance it was English.

Warning number two: beware of short messages. This also has to do with the frequency of occurrence. The sequence used is based on average occurrences in long pieces of text—at least a few thousand words. In shorter texts the frequency of occurrence can easily change. For example, my message was less than a hundred characters, and that alone could account for discrepancies in the frequency of occurrence.

The Professor's third warning was sort of a catchall, but I thought it was the most important caveat of all: beware of messages encrypted by people whose encryptions you have not seen before. A cryptologist can easily slip in an anomaly that is known to the recipient of the message, but not to you. In the Professor's words, "If you are certain you are working on a monoalphabetic encryption, and you've tried everything you can think of to break it, look for the anomaly—the little personal touch a cryptologist uses to throw you off the track."

Even with those warnings, I got nowhere. After an hour of staring at the jumble of letters in front of me, my eyelids began drooping and I figured it was time to hit the sack. I was a little disappointed I hadn't cracked a relatively simple code, but cracking codes, even simple ones, isn't my job. I decided to leave it to the experts and went to bed.

Twenty-Four

Optitronics, Inc. – 2001 E. Mariposa Ave., El Segundo

Optitronics was a beehive of activity when I got there Thursday morning. The canvas covers on the stake bed trucks at the loading dock were pulled back and lines of employees were carrying boxes onto the trucks. A member of Sergeant Pierce's security team was stationed on each truck with a clipboard, apparently making sure the arriving boxes were on the right truck and were accounted for on some sort of master inventory. It looked complicated, but I wasn't carrying a clipboard, so it wasn't my problem.

Staff Sergeant Pierce was overseeing the activity and he did have a clipboard. When I approached, he was deep in calculation. To himself, he was saying, "DC-3 range is 1,600 miles. Los Angeles to Lakehurst is 2,800 miles. Dividing 2,800 by 1,600, I get ..."

I said, "One-point-seven-five, which means you have to make at least one fuel stop along the way."

"Thanks, Major Spicer. Arithmetic was never my best subject in school."

"Sergeant, you have an experienced flight crew to figure this stuff out. Why are you fooling with it?"

"Check and double check, sir. We've got a lot riding on those transports. I want to know for sure the crews are giving me the straight dope."

"Admirable, Sergeant. I imagine that's why Colonel Peterson thinks you're the man for this job. When are you scheduled for takeoff?"

"Ten-hundred-hours. They say we'll be staying overnight at

Offutt Army Air Force Base near Omaha and we'll get there around twenty-two-hundred-hours tonight. That's a long time in the air."

"Don't forget the time zones. Omaha is in the central time zone so that adds two hours to your local arrival time."

Frustrated, Pierce said, "Damn. I forgot about that. So we're only in the air about ten hours."

"That sounds about right and you should have a flight of roughly eight hours to Lakehurst on Friday."

"Thank you, sir. I'm not sure I'm cut out for all this detail stuff. There are just too many things to think about."

"You're doing fine, Sergeant, and this isn't something you'll be doing all the time."

"I sure hope not, Major."

"What all are you taking on the DC-3s?"

Sergeant Pierce counted the categories off on his fingers. "The completed occuscopes, all of Mister Demas' black boxes, the current inventory of parts, and the portable equipment from the assembly rooms."

"What's being done about Demas' schematics?"

"Well, sir, that's a matter of some contention. Mister Demas' absolutely refuses to turn them over. He claims they're his property. Colonel Peterson is letting him have his way, but the Colonel isn't happy about it."

"I bet he isn't. Leaving those schematics in private hands is very unusual." I made myself a mental note to look into the matter of the schematics. If Pierce had his story straight, something was out of whack.

Pierce looked at the last page on his clipboard. "The office furniture, files and that kind of stuff will have to be moved, but Optitronics and Lyon Van Lines are handling that part of things, so our last responsibility will be handing all this stuff over to the Navy in Lakehurst on Friday. After that I'll get my team on their way home to San Francisco and wait for orders to accompany the blimp that's coming out here."

"You aren't leaving any of your team here until the building is completely empty?"

"No, sir. I asked Colonel Peterson about that, and he said there was no need to guard a bunch of desks and unclassified paperwork. That gives me a full team to divide up between the two DC-3s."

"Okay, sounds like you've got everything under control." I handed him a three-by-five card and said, "Here are all the telephone numbers where I might be between now and the time you head west again. At least, all the numbers I know about at this point. Tonight I'll be at Patmar's Motel. Okay?"

Pierce carefully slid the three-by-five card into his wallet. "I think I've got it, sir."

"I'm sure you have, Sergeant. It also looks as if the loading is winding down."

He studied the three trucks at the dock, and then said, "I guess I'd better check the loads and get ready to roll."

Shaking Pierce's hand, I said, "Are you scheduled to check in with Colonel Peterson anywhere along the way?"

"Yes, sir. He said to call him when we arrive at Lakehurst, so I'll be talking to him tomorrow night."

"Good. I'm sure he'll breathe easier knowing those damned scopes are out of our hands."

Pierce gave me a sharp salute. "Yes, sir, I will, too. Thank you for your help with the arithmetic, Major Spicer."

The Sergeant and his crew double checked the load on each truck, after which they tied the canvas covers down and rolled away from the loading dock. With the trucks gone, I walked into the Optitronics building and headed upstairs to look for Annie Bishop.

I found Annie in her office busily packing cardboard boxes with file folders full of papers. I knocked lightly on the door frame and said, "Hello, Annie."

She jerked her head up as if I'd startled her, even though I was careful to make my presence known before speaking. Maybe she was a little on edge about packing for the move.

Annie said, "Oh, hello, Major Spicer. It's good to see you again."

"Getting all packed up and ready for your move to Lakehurst?"

Her expression changed to anger. "Packing, yes. Moving, no. I wouldn't live in New Jersey for twice the money they pay me."

"Well, I haven't spent much time in the Garden State, but I guess I can understand that."

"It's a darn shame, too. This was a good job and I enjoyed working with the people here. If the Army would just butt out . . ." Annie suddenly realized she was talking to the enemy and quickly said, "I'm sorry Major. I meant no offence to you personally."

I smiled. "None taken, Annie, and I'm sorry this move isn't working out for you. It's necessary because, despite the vault, security here was almost nonexistent. That's not your fault, but you can see why changes had to be made."

"I guess."

"Incidentally, I was able to recover the missing occuscope. It was in Hawaii on its way to Tokyo. We caught up with it just in time."

That news cheered her up a little and I left to see Frank Demas. He, too, was packing, but in his case the boxes were filling up with scientific-looking books. His door was only partially closed, so I peeked in and knocked.

"Oh, it's you again."

"You sure don't make a guy feel welcome around here, Demas."

"There's no reason you should feel welcome. All of our problems started when you showed up."

That was the last straw. "Demas, your problems started when one of your employees walked past your lousy security and stole a device that should have been so well protected nobody could get within a hundred feet of it. Don't blame me for problems you brought on yourself. And another thing, where the hell are those schematics?"

With anger in his tone, he said, "They're somewhere safe. That's all you need to know."

It was a trick that sometimes worked if you caught a person off guard. On hearing the word "schematics" he automatically looked toward the calendar hiding the wall safe in his office. So, even though Demas was no longer willing to tell me where the schematics were, it was a pretty sure bet the schematics were right where they'd been all along.

"You know, Demas, if those plans turn up missing you can be arrested on a charge of treason for not turning them over to a federal organization that could protect them properly."

"Those schematics are my property and nobody is getting their hands on them, not you and not the Japs. Now get out of here. I've got work to do."

I got out of there and thought about what to do next. My job was guaranteeing the security of the occuscopes. That included its schematics, but short of pulling a gun on him, nothing was going to make Demas hand them over.

Sticking my head into Annie's office again, I said, "Do you know if anyone has arranged to have the private security guards back tonight now that the Army security team has left?"

"I don't think so. Mister Demas says there's no reason to have security if there's nothing left to steal. He also laid off the custodians."

Wishing she was right about there being nothing left to steal, I went downstairs and asked Elinor for a set of front door keys from the key cabinet. The good thing about Elinor is, once she knew who was in charge, she did what she was told without question.

She handed me two keys. One was a normal brass Schlage door key and the other was a small, oddly shaped silver key that was used to activate and deactivate the building's primitive alarm system. I thanked Elinor, dropped the keys into my jacket pocket, and left the lobby via the front door.

It seemed unlikely I was the only one who knew Demas still had the occuscope schematics. The fuss over them was sure to have made it around the company, and even without the hint Demas involuntarily gave me about where the schematics were, the first place anyone would look for them was where they were last, in the wall safe.

I decided to call Si Peterson and bring him up to date on the situation at Optitronics. I called from a pay telephone at the burger joint and made it a short conversation. In our casual "code," I told him I made an attempt to convince Demas he should hand over the schematics, but was unsuccessful. I also told Si I was pretty sure the schematics were still where they'd been all along.

I mentioned the schematics in the hope he would give me some specific orders concerning them. He didn't, so I was on my own in that department. That still struck me as odd.

After ending the call, I sat in the car a few moments thinking about how to handle the schematics problem. Since no security was scheduled, if I wanted to be certain nobody walked off with the papers in Demas' safe tonight, I had two options. One was to crack Demas' safe after everybody went home and stash the schematics somewhere safer.

Ultimately that was the most effective solution, but it was also risky. I had no authorization to confiscate the schematics, and doing so could get me into hot water.

My second option was to spend the night at Optitronics and personally make sure nobody else confiscated the schematics. Thinking about the pros and cons of that idea, I realized what I had was another potential baited trap situation like we had at Moffett Field. It was one way to turn a lousy situation to our advantage and possibly nail a Jap espionage agent, assuming they were still interested in occuscopes. Besides that, it was the only legitimate option I had.

According to my wristwatch it was ten-forty-five. If I ate an early lunch, I could be in bed by noon. That would give me about five hours sleep before I came back to play night watchman at Optitronics.

Twenty-Five

Optitronics, Inc. – 2001 E. Mariposa Ave., El Segundo

After stopping at Rod's burger joint again to pick up a take-out sandwich for my dinner later, I parked across Mariposa Avenue from Optitronics and watched the neighborhood for a while. By seven o'clock, all the employees were out of the building and it was time for me to go in. I pulled up the block a hundred feet or so and walked back to Optitronics so my car wouldn't be so obvious. Making sure not to look if anyone was watching, which is always a sure giveaway you're doing something you're not supposed to be doing, I used the silver key to turn off the alarm system and the brass key to open the front door. I locked it behind me and took a quiet tour of both floors. If there was anyone else in the building they ate cheese and squeaked.

I'd already thought about where I was going to position myself to see a burglar before he saw me. The first and second floor loading dock interior doors were locked and the roll-up doors were closed and secured. The first floor back door was locked and barred, so the only way into the building was the front door. What I wanted to see, though, was Demas' office where the schematics were hidden.

The best observation spot for that view was through the door at the top of the loading dock stairs. The door to the loading dock stairs had a wire safety glass window, and because the two rows of manufacturing rooms had waist-high to ceiling windows on the interior sides, I had a clear view of the entire second floor, right up to the doors of the three offices across the front of the building.

All I needed was a little more light than was coming through the outside windows. I walked down the side hall and turned on the overhead lights in the hall outside the offices. If anybody wondered why they were on, I hoped they'd think someone just forgot to turn them off. Back on my perch outside the door to the loading dock stairs, I positioned a stool on the landing. After that all I had to do was wait.

Around eight o'clock I heard a soft noise that sounded like it came from the ground floor. Thinking the noise could be someone coming in through the front door, I waited more than long enough for them to get up to the second floor. When nobody showed, I decided to take a look downstairs.

Down on the loading dock I peeked through the window in the first floor door. There was nobody in sight. Thinking it was possible the sound I heard was just the building settling or something like that, I climbed back up the loading dock stairs.

Just as I got high enough to see through the window a movement caught my eye. Someone was on the second floor and moving quickly along the hall past the three offices at the front of the building. He turned the corner next to Annie Bishop's office and started down the front stairs. Whoever it was must have come up the stairs from the lobby while I was coming down the loading dock stairs to check the ground floor, and if I was going to catch him, I had to get to the lobby before he got out the front door.

I tore down the loading dock stairs and ran toward the ground floor door. I was almost there when a bolt of lightning struck somewhere over my head. The whole second floor lit up in a flash of brilliant white light. A percussive clap of thunder knocked me off my feet and sent me sliding headfirst across the concrete floor. At the same time a hailstorm of broken glass and other debris rained down on me. A stack of cardboard boxes finally stopped my slide, but it took me a minute to figure out what the hell happened.

As best I could figure, someone just blew up the Optitronics plant with me in it. I looked up toward the second floor and saw another kind of light blazing away. This time it was a fire set off by the detonation. I could smell the smoke and hear crackling sounds that meant it wasn't just a fire, but a damned hot fire. Time for Johnny Spicer to get his butt out of there.

I flew through the ground floor loading dock door toward the lobby and, as I passed the front stairway, I looked up and saw a raging inferno burning its way across the second floor. Whoever blew the place up didn't bother to shut the front door on their way out. I ran through it and looked up and down the street. The only movement I saw was a car turning the corner two blocks east on

Mariposa Avenue.

There was, however, a lot of sound going on. Behind me the fire was busy blowing out second floor windows and roaring like a hungry lion. From somewhere in front of me there were sirens— lots of them. Sirens seemed like a good thing, so I walked across Mariposa to put a little more distance between me and the lion while I waited for the sirens.

Standing on the curb across the street from raging inferno I was reminded of the explosion at the Hilltop Apartments. Apparently the Japs had a surplus of explosives on hand because they seemed intent on blowing things up everywhere they went.

Not more than three or four minutes passed before the first siren arrived. It was attached to a big red fire engine. By this time the fire was lighting up the whole block, so the firemen had plenty of light by which to string their hoses from fire hydrants to the burning building. They quickly got busy pouring water on the second floor.

The next sirens arrived in quick succession and belonged to a fire chief's car, two police cars, and a second fire engine. More sirens were wailing in the distance, but the fellows who'd already arrived seemed to have the situation in hand, which amounted to keeping the fire from spreading to the nearby businesses. The Optitronics building was already a lost cause.

A sergeant I recalled seeing at the El Segundo PD recognized me, and walked over. "You're the Military Intelligence guy, right?"

"Well, Sergeant, I'm not feeling terribly intelligent at the moment, but you remember correctly."

"What the hell started this? Did something go wrong in the plant?"

"No. In fact, the plant was being disassembled before this started. They're moving to another location and all of the classified stuff left this morning."

He looked puzzled. "Then what . . ."

"I was inside because we expected someone might break in tonight, so I can give you my best guess about what happened. First, there was someone else in the plant. I saw him just before the explosion."

The sergeant was taking notes now. "An explosion started this?"

"Absolutely, and if I had to guess, I'd say it was some well-placed Composition B."

"What on earth is Composition B?"

"It's a military grade explosive—a composition of TNT,

another explosive called RDX, and plasticizing wax to make the finished product flexible. The flexibility allows the charge to be molded into the shape that will do the most damage. The TNT and RDX make a hell of a bang on their own, and an expert can wreck a lot of havoc with the stuff by shaping the charge just right. Of course, I don't know for sure the explosive was Comp B until we can get in there, but that's my guess."

The sergeant stopped writing for a moment to ask, "Where would a burglar get military grade explosives?"

"A common burglar probably wouldn't, but a Jap espionage agent would have no problem getting his hands on it. Just about every country on the planet makes some form of Composition B."

Now the sergeant looked worried. "If a Jap spy did this, I'm afraid the El Segundo Police Department is a little out of our league."

"That's where I come in Sergeant. While I'll admit I haven't done such a great job with this one so far, catching espionage agents is my business. I suggest you write the incident up as potential espionage case based on your interview with me and send the report and a letter to the Military Intelligence Division requesting that the MID handle the investigation. Above all, I would not let the press know it might have been sabotage. If that gets out, we're liable to have the local folks seeing Japs behind every lamppost and shooting each other."

The sergeant jotted a few more notes and said, "Okay, Major Spicer. I'll have to run all this by my Captain, but he's not going to be any more interested in chasing spies to Japan and back than I am. Can you give me the exact address where we should send that request to MID?'

"Sure. Send it to the attention of Colonel Simon Peterson, US Army Military Intelligence Division, Building 100, Presidio, San Francisco, California."

"Thank you Major. Will you be around in case I need to ask any further questions?"

"I'm not sure yet, Sergeant. I will definitely be around until this building cools down to the point where I can get up to the second floor and see exactly what caused the explosion." I didn't mention I was also anxious to see a certain wall safe in one of the offices. "After that, where I'll be depends on my boss. In fact, I'm going to take a few minutes right now to go up the street and use a pay telephone to tell him what happened here."

I picked the public telephone at Rod's Hamburger stand again because they also had coffee, and I was feeling the need for a jolt of wake up juice. First, though, I entered the booth and placed a person to person call to Peterson's home telephone. When there was no answer, I called the office. There I got a Major Downey on the line.

I've never met Major Downey, but I know his name. He's Si Peterson's second in command. Downey told me Si was in Denver for a meeting with some other MID brass and didn't expect to be back until Saturday. Downey promised, however, to pass the information about the Optitronics fire on to Si as soon as he called in. I said I would check back with more details when I had them. Finally, I told him to keep an eye out for a letter to Si from the El Segundo Police Department.

When I got back to what was left of Optitronics, the fire appeared to be out and I asked the fire chief when I could get into the building. He gave the still smoking ruins a long thoughtful look and said, "I wouldn't suggest it for several more hours. Flair ups are a strong possibility, plus the building is structurally damaged and parts of it are subject to collapse."

I said I'd see him around dawn, diplomatically not mentioning that the three front offices were damned unlikely to collapse sitting as they were atop a steel vault. Instead, I drove back to the motel and spent an unproductive few hours trying to make some sense out of the evening's events.

Twenty-Six

Optitronics, Inc. – 2001 E. Mariposa Ave., El Segundo

Arson investigation is a science unto itself. An experienced arson investigator can map out exactly how and where a fire started, and where it went from there. Unfortunately, I'm not an experienced arson investigator or even an inexperienced one.

All I could do when I finally had access to the Optitronics building was observe the obvious clues and make what sense of them I could. The El Segundo Fire Chief said an arson investigator from the county would conduct his own investigation and MID might get a copy of it. I'd only been there a few minutes and the Chief's snooty attitude was already ticking me off.

Walking along the hallway past the three front offices on the second floor was a little tricky because there wasn't much of it left. The rest of the second floor beyond the hallway collapsed and was now mixed in with the rubble on the first floor. The only reason part of the hall and the three front offices were still on the second floor was the sturdy fireproof steel vault below them.

Most of the door to Frank Demas' office was missing, and what was left fell off its hinges when I pushed on it. The Fire Chief started to give me hell for disturbing evidence, but I gave him a glare that shut him up in midsentence. I don't like sharing crime scenes, especially with arrogant bastards like this guy.

I went straight to the wall that held the office safe. The safe door was open. I expected that, but there was no sign that explosives were used to open it. Hell, as much explosive as the culprit used would have blown the safe and the entire wall clear into the next county.

No, the safe was picked by hand and the explosive charge was

119

laid against the opposite wall near the door, where it opened a huge gaping hole out into the hall. It was a good location from a damage point of view. The force of the blast blew right through the thin wall and kept going straight back into the glass enclosed manufacturing areas.

The Fire Chief got down on his knees to look at what remained of the floor below where the explosive was set. The linoleum on the floor was peeled back from the wall and even from where I was standing I could see the residue I was taught to expect when Comp B was used. The Fire Chief picked up some of the residue on his finger and sniffed it. I thought he was going to taste it next. I said, "Chief, do you know what you've got there?"

"Some kind of residue left by the explosive. I'll take a sample back to our lab. They'll know what it is."

"I think you'll find it's something your lab people haven't seen before unless they have a military background. What you have there is residue from Composition B."

The chief glared up at me. "Is that so? I didn't know you were an expert on arson."

Already regretting offering the guy information, I said, "I'm not an arson expert, but I know a little something about explosives. The explosion that started this fire had all the earmarks of Comp B. Ah, you do know what Composition B is, don't you?'

The blank look on his face told me he didn't. With a small smile, I said, "Well, you will."

I had one more thing to check, so I left the Chief on his hands and knees and went down what remained of the stairs. In the lobby I stopped at the front door. The door was open when the explosion went off, so aside from being a little charred by the fire, it was mostly undamaged. A close look told me neither the lock nor the doorframe showed any signs of a forced entry.

When I'd seen all I thought there was to see in the remains of the building, I went back to the Army's Dodge and jotted the conclusions I drew from my inspection into my notebook. First, I'd been right about the explosive used. It was Composition B or something very similar. That spelled "professional."

Second, I'd seen the culprit, but only briefly and from a distance. I knew he was a male of average size. He wore a hat and a suit coat. That was all I had time to see.

Third, the front door lock had either been picked or opened with a key and the alarm was disabled. That meant I was dealing with an insider or a pro.

Fourth, it was likely whoever walked through that front door knew there was no human security and that he wouldn't encounter any custodians because they'd been given their walking papers. That made it, to at least some extent, an inside job.

The fifth conclusion I could draw was the most significant. Whoever pulled off the heist knew Demas still had the schematics and where he kept them. That they were in the safe was pretty easy to guess, but that information was worthless unless you knew Demas hadn't turned the schematics over to us. He was making a fuss about it, though, so it wouldn't be stretching things too far to conclude someone in his company knew or guessed he still had them.

The difficult part about those conclusions was that one person wasn't likely to be both an insider and a professional, especially since all Optitronics employees, except the damned custodians, underwent security checks. It was more likely somebody inside the company told someone else about the schematics. Maybe.

There was another part of the whole deal that puzzled me: why the big boom? Since the explosion had nothing to do with opening Demas' wall safe, it must have been intended as some sort of diversion. On the other hand, if he hadn't set off the explosive, the culprit would have had more time before it was discovered the schematics were missing. At the rate I was moving, though, I wasn't exactly hot on his heels.

Then a big question mark popped up over my head like in a Bugs Bunny cartoon. There was a flaw in my facts. My conclusions were all valid assuming the schematics were in Demas' safe, but were they? My only evidence that they were there was Demas glancing at his safe when I had him on the spot and asked about the schematics. That was hardly irrefutable proof.

It was enough to justify me standing guard at Optitronics last night, but it wasn't enough to prove the schematics were now missing. Before going off on a wild goose chase, I needed confirmation that there was actually a goose to chase.

That one was still bouncing around in my brain when I looked up and saw Annie Bishop standing across the street staring at her former place of employment. She didn't look any happier than I felt.

I got out of the Dodge and walked over to her. When she saw me, Annie said, "My God, Major Spicer, what happened?"

"The short answer is somebody blew up Optitronics last night."

"For heaven's sake, why? Was it vandals?"

Deciding not to mention the schematics, I said, "We know it was arson, but there are very few clues as to who did it. The El Segundo Fire Chief is inside investigating now. He might tell you more when he comes out."

"Well, I guess this pretty much finishes the packing job."

"On that score, most of the stuff already out on the loading dock seems to be intact. A lot of debris fell in there, and some boxes have water damage, but a lot of what's in them should be salvageable."

"Do you know if anyone has told Mister Demas?"

"The police tried to call him at home last night, but they couldn't find a telephone number for him. I don't know if he's been here or not since the fire. If he has, I didn't see him."

"Do you think we should comb through the mess to see what can be recovered?"

"That's a question you need to ask the Fire Chief and Demas. The building has some serious structural damage, so it would be dangerous for you to be working in there until some precautions are taken. I'd suggest you gather your employees out here as they show up, and then wait for the Fire Chief to come out. Then you'll know what you can and can't do. After that you'll have to ask Demas what he wants done."

"I guess that makes the most sense."

"You could do me one favor, though."

"Certainly. What do you need?"

"Would you mind giving me your home telephone number? I may need more information as I investigate this thing and I sure won't be able to reach you here."

Annie Bishop smiled and said she didn't mind at all giving me her number and I wrote it in my book. Then I said, "While we're at it, do you have a home number for Mister Demas?"

"No, Major Spicer, I do not. He is a very secretive man, but I do have a home address. It was on a piece of correspondence he wanted copied. He very carefully crossed out the address, but all I had to do was hold it up to the light and I could see it clear as day."

"That's great, Annie. What is the address?"

She paused a moment with her head tilted to one side and looked me straight in the eye. "Major Spicer, you are an officer of the law are you not?"

"I am, Annie. What's more, the United States has been at war with Germany and Japan for four days now. That makes providing information important to the war effort even more imperative."

"Thank you, Major Spicer. I am loyal to my employer, but my country has priority in the loyalty department. I didn't recognize the address I copied, so I looked it up in my Thomas Brothers map book. It's clear up in Malibu. From a small address book she read, "Two-two-five-one-five Carbon Mesa Drive."

Twenty-Seven

En Route to Demas Residence – 22515 Carbon Mesa Rd., Malibu

Malibu, with sparkling white beaches against a background of sheer cliffs and oak studded mountains, is a great place to live if you have loads of money and nothing else to do with it. Living there is not, however, worth spending the better part of two hours a day getting to and from work.

It figured to be about 25 miles from Malibu to El Segundo, and in the daily commuter traffic up and down the coast highway, the drive would take close to an hour each way. I'll pass on that, thank you very much.

Demas' house was perched on a hillside with a spectacular view of the ocean. The house itself was nothing fancy, barely more than a shack with lots of windows. Besides the view, however, it also had the advantage of being the only house on the hillside—no noisy neighbors up all night playing their radios too loud.

The gate in a rough wooden fence along the front of the property stood open, so I drove in and parked near a carport attached to the house. There was a shiny new gunmetal blue Cadillac two-door convertible coupe in the carport. It made me think there was more to Frank Demas than met the eye. He certainly didn't strike me as the Cadillac convertible type.

An unpainted and sagging plywood porch provided wobbly access to the front door. Not finding a doorbell button, I knocked. When at least half a minute passed with no response, I knocked again a little louder. Still no response.

Well, maybe Demas was out back looking at the view to forget his troubles. I walked around the house through a yard landscaped by Mother Nature and stepped up on another rudimentary wooden porch, this one supporting a couple of rusty lawn chairs. There was nobody back there and I was about to perform my knocking routine on the backdoor when a spot of color caught my eye.

There was something red in the underbrush about ten feet down the hillside behind the porch. I walked over for a better look. Frank Demas picked a bright, cheerful Hawaiian style shirt to die in. I didn't bother checking for a pulse. The two large caliber bullet holes in his head matched his red shirt.

I kicked a small rock down the hill and said, "Damn!"

It didn't matter much to me one way or another that a brilliant engineer was no longer with us. What made me mad was I'd lost the one man who could tell me if the occuscope schematics were stolen or secure.

I sighed and turned toward the house. I had to get some back-up out here to pick up the body, do an autopsy, go over the house for fingerprints, and all that sort of detective stuff. First, though, I decided to break into Demas' house and see what I could find on my own.

As it turned out, I didn't need to break in. The backdoor was unlocked. Being careful not to leave fingerprints on the doorknob, I walked into Frank Demas' kitchen. From there a reasonably thorough search of the house didn't take very long. For one thing, somebody had already opened every drawer, cabinet and closet in the place looking for something, maybe something they didn't find in Demas' office safe.

For another thing, the place was small, having only a living room, a bathroom, the kitchen, and two bedrooms, the larger of which had been converted into a workshop. Amid the clutter on his workbench I even found the molds Demas used for his black boxes. It was all right there. The only thing I didn't see was a set of schematics.

I walked back into the kitchen and picked up the telephone handset. Demas did have a telephone, he just didn't want anyone to know he had it. I got the long distance operator on the line and called San Francisco. Once again I found myself talking to Major Downey. I had nothing against Downey, but Si Peterson was my boss and I damn well needed him to make some decisions.

"Downey, Spicer. This case is unraveling like a cheap sweater. I just found Frank Demas in his backyard with two bullet holes in his head."

Major Downey groaned. "Oh, no."

"And I've got more cheerful news. There are no longer any

schematics in Demas' wall safe, assuming they were there in the first place. I can also tell you the fire at Optitronics was a pro job. The explosive they used was Comp B."

Downey didn't say anything. Figuring he was too overwhelmed to know what we had to do, I gave him a hint. "We need to get a team down here to clean up the mess at Demas' house and deal with the local cops who will want answers when they find a prominent citizen of Malibu shot down in his own backyard. That sort of thing is considered gauche in the nicer neighborhoods."

Major Downey sounded like the water was at least a foot over his head and rising. "I don't know, Spicer. I'll have to try and get Colonel Peterson on the telephone and . . ."

"Hogwash, Downey! Si left you in charge. Do your damned job and get some people down here by the fastest means possible, and I mean competent people. If you don't, we're gonna have headlines 'til hell won't have it. This thing isn't going away by itself."

The major was quiet for a long moment before saying, "You're right. Hang on the line a minute while I see who I can send down there."

At least five minutes of long distance time passed before Downey came back on the line. "All right, I've got two good people available. I'm sending them over to Crissy Field. There's a plane coming in to fly them down to LA. Can you meet them at the Los Angeles Airport military hanger?"

"I can and will. Who are they?"

"Captain Neil Rogers, he's an experienced forensic investigator, and a civilian crime technician by the name of Mattie Thomas. They should be at the airport by 1430 hours."

"I'll be there. Also, pull some strings and arrange a car for them. I'll lead them to Demas, but after that I have to get back to the other business I'm supposed to be handling down here."

"All right. Look, Spicer, I'm doing the best I can here, but I suddenly found myself running things with no idea what those things are. Thanks for being patient."

"I take it Si's trip to Denver was spur of the moment."

Downey sighed. "It sure was. One minute he was here, and the next he was on his way."

"You're doing fine, Major. Just keep your wits about you and you'll be okay, and thanks for getting things moving. You'll be hearing from me or the people you're sending down here or all of us."

It was quarter past eleven. I had a little over three hours to kill before reinforcements arrived. That gave me plenty of time for the drive down to the airport with a stop for . . ."

From the spot where I happened to be standing at that moment, light coming through a window showed what looked like deep scuff marks in front of the refrigerator on the kitchen floor. I looked closer. That's what they were all right. The marks might have been made when the appliance was installed, but a light push on the front of the fridge showed it was on casters. In order for the scratches to be made, the refrigerator had to have been tipped—something that might happen if one person tried to move it.

I stepped back and took another look at the refrigerator. It was a yellow Crosley Shelvador, whatever the heck that meant. It was squeezed into a narrow space between the end of a kitchen counter and a sort of matching O'Keefe & Merritt four-burner stove. I opened the refrigerator door, got a firm grip, and pulled. The Crosley was a lightweight and moved so easily it rolled out too far and unplugged itself. Since the appliance was out that far anyway, I kept pulling until I could turn the thing and look behind it. The fridge tipped slightly when I rotated it because the casters didn't swivel. Looking down, I saw that's exactly what someone else had done because the front corner of the fridge was sitting squarely on top of the scratches in the floor.

The back of the refrigerator had a bunch of half-inch tubing for the refrigerant. The tubes were mounted so they stood off a few inches from the back of the appliance. That narrow space was where Demas chose to hide a thick roll of papers. I got a grip on the papers and pulled them free. They were bent in half—probably to fit in Demas' office wall safe—and it took some smoothing to straighten the pages so I could unroll them.

Yup. There it was right in the information panel at the lower right corner of each page: "Occuscope Schematic Series – 1 of 14 – June 1, 1941."

I re-rolled the pages and took a look outside the house to make sure I wasn't being watched. Seeing no one around, I trotted out to the Dodge and opened the trunk. I unlocked the fake trunk floor and stashed the schematics under it. Ten minutes later I was heading back down the coast highway toward Los Angeles Airport. I had the goods and a brand new set of puzzles to solve, but first I was going to make damned sure we kept the goods this time.

Twenty-Eight

Military Hangar, Los Angeles Airport – Inglewood

Feeling a whole lot safer surrounded by Army and Navy personnel at the Los Angeles Airport military hangar, I talked the Army Air Force Operations Chief into loaning me two armed Military Policemen to help protect the occuscope schematics, which I now carried in a dispatch case. I was taking no chances. With the MPs in tow, I found a telephone and made Major Downey's day.

"Major, the missing items have been found."

"That's great news, Major Spicer. Good work!"

"And some luck. Listen, Downey, we need to get these items somewhere that's secure. What do you suggest?"

Sounding more confident than the last time we talked, Major Downey said, "Let me check something. Be right back."

Downey used up enough long distance time to make me wonder how much American Telephone and Telegraph stock he owned. "Spicer, the pilot who is bringing your friends in is qualified to handle the items in question. Give them to him and he'll bring them to a safe place where they can be secured. Will that work?"

"That's fine with me."

"I just spoke with the pilot by radio. He's very capable. Also, he knows your Uncle Ed. They're good friends."

Since I have no Uncle Ed, or any other uncles for that matter, I knew Downey just gave me a recognition code. The pilot will tell me my Uncle Ed says hello or something along those lines and I'll know he's the guy who gets the schematics. I was pleased Downey thought of using a code. It meant he was back on the ball.

"Okay, Major. I've got it. I'm at the airport now waiting for the flight to arrive. I'll talk with you later."

"Again, Spicer, my congratulations on a job well done."

I checked my watch for the hundredth time and it said ten minutes past two. Shortly after that the Army Air Force Operations Chief came over and said, "The flight you've been waiting for is in the pattern. They'll be on the ground in ten minutes or so."

"Thanks, Lieutenant. We'll meet 'em out front."

I stood just outside the military hangar side door and waited for the little twin-engine Beechcraft to taxi up. It was an AT-7, a military version of the Beechcraft Model 18 Expeditor. The ship was in its bare aluminum skin, had twin tailfins, and seats for eight passengers. The Army used this model for short passenger flights and other versions for training bombardiers, gunners and radio operators. For a little tyke, it had a very business-like look about it.

So did the two people who climbed out of it. The first was a woman who appeared to be in her early thirties. She carried what looked something like a large doctor's bag. The second passenger out the door was Captain Neil Rogers. He carried two travel bags and a smaller bag under one arm.

We introduced ourselves, and then I sent them to find the Operations Chief and pick up their car. We agreed I would lead them out to Demas' house in Malibu and show them around. After that the show there was all theirs.

Next I introduced myself to a round-faced captain in a leather jacket with an MID shoulder patch and pilots' wings pinned over his left breast. He was lounging against the AT-7's fuselage with all the swagger of a fighter ace. Around the stub of an unlit cigar, he said, "Hello, Major Spicer. Pleased to meet you. Stu Irvin's the name."

"Hi, Stu. Did you have a smooth flight down?"

"Sure did. Not a bump in the sky today." Then he paused, took the cigar out of his mouth and said, "By the way, your Uncle Ed said to say hello if I saw you."

"Thanks, Stu. How is old Uncle Ed?"

With a twinkle in his eye, Stu lowered his voice and said, "He's still a drunken bum."

Smiling, I said, "That's Uncle Ed. Oh, and this is for you to take wherever you're headed next."

He took the dispatch case and looked at the two MPs standing behind me. "I take it these fellows know what's in the case?"

"They do and they are witnesses to the fact that the case and its contents are now officially your problem. Is that right gentlemen?"

Almost in unison the two MPs said, "Yes, sir, that is correct."

Stu tossed a salute in my direction and said, "Okay, Spicer. I'll get aboard and get movin'. We need to pick up some fuel here and I want to get where we're going before dinner."

"Have a safe flight."

As Stu and his copilot taxied off, I cut the MPs loose and hunted down my crime scene team. They were out behind the hangar stowing their gear in an olive drab Plymouth sedan with white stars on the back doors. I asked, "All set and ready to go?"

Captain Rogers said, "All set."

"I'll try to keep you in sight behind me, but if the traffic gets heavy, here's a simple map that shows our route."

Rogers studied the map for a moment, saying, "I'm originally from down here, so I think I know where we're headed. Looks like we just take PCH up to Carbon Canyon Road in Malibu, and then turn right on Carbon Mesa Road."

"That's it in a nutshell. We should get up there about sixteen-hundred. That will give you a little time before it gets dark. I imagine you'll want to get Demas' body inside or off the property completely. You should have time to do that."

Mattie Thomas said, "We made arrangements with the Los Angeles County Coroner to handle that part of it. We're to give them a call as soon as we get to the man's home."

Looking skeptical, I asked, "And no questions asked?"

She smiled. "I understand the sensitivity involved, Major Spicer. I have the Coroner's assurance the findings will be handled in the strictest confidence and they'll hold the body as a John Doe until we tell them what to do with it."

Rogers chimed in, "Finding ourselves suddenly in the middle of a war guarantees a lot of cooperation that would be hard to come by otherwise. On top of that, we have orders to handle this one very carefully."

I grinned. "Then I'll keep my big trap shut and take you guys up to Malibu."

By the time we were parked in Demas' yard, it was a little after four o'clock. The traffic was heavier than I expected. I took Rogers on a quick tour of the property as Mattie Thomas called the county coroner.

When I completed the tour, including the body and the repositioned refrigerator, Captain Rogers began making photos of the body. Demas was on the west side of the property, so there was still a little light for photos, but I noticed Rogers was also using flash bulbs.

When Mattie Thomas came out to the yard, she said, "The wagon is on its way."

She walked down the hill to where Captain Roger was inspecting the body and I said, "Okay, I'm going to leave you to your work and do some guard duty. Somebody is very anxious to get their hands on what I found behind that refrigerator earlier. We think they blew up a building last night and killed Demas looking for what I found. Worse, they probably don't know I found it yet.

"Odds are the people we're dealing with are Japanese espionage agents and they play dirty. So stay alert and keep your weapons handy. Most of all, if you run into trouble, don't stand around trying to talk your way out of it. Shoot to kill and ask questions later. Okay?"

I thought Mattie Thomas looked a little pale, but Rogers took my speech the way I intended it, as a warning that might keep them alive. I had the feeling he'd been in similar situations before.

Rogers said, "Thanks, Spicer. We'll keep our guard up. And I think we'll limit our work time up here to daylight hours. We're quite a ways into desolate back country and at night that is a disadvantage."

I nodded and said, "That sounds like a good plan. I'll be walking around keeping my eyes open if you need me. Oh, and before we leave here tonight, I'd like you to bag up the stuff on Demas' workbench. I can't make heads or tails out of it, but somebody else might find it useful."

The county coroner's panel delivery showed up as expected and hauled Frank Demas off to the morgue. After that Rogers and Thomas began their work in the house and I alternated my position between the carport, where I could see the road in both directions, and other spots that gave me a view of the country around Demas' shack.

Half an hour later Rogers came out carrying two large brown paper evidence bags. "This is the workbench stuff. You want us to take it back up to the Presidio when we go?"

"Yeah, along with anything else you think might be of use to the bad guys."

The Captain put the sacks in the trunk of the Plymouth sedan. Then we locked up as well as we could and left Demas' shack to his ghost.

Twenty-Nine

Patmar's Motel – 949 N. Sepulveda Boulevard, El Segundo

When I left Patmar's Motel early that morning I didn't figure on trekking all the way to up Malibu. I found reasonable lodging for Rogers and Thomas on the outskirts of Santa Monica, but all of my own gear was back in El Segundo. It was almost seven o'clock when I got there.

Before going to my room, I stopped at a telephone booth and called Annie Bishop. When she answered, I said, "Hello, Annie, Johnny Spicer here."

"Hello, Major Spicer. I was just thinking about you. Mister Demas never showed up at the plant today and I was wondering if you talked to him."

"Annie, I'm afraid I have more bad news for you. Frank Demas is dead."

A gasp on the other end of the line preceded, "Oh, no! What happened?"

"I don't have all the facts yet, but my best guess is whoever blew up the plant last night was looking for something and when they didn't find it, they went to Frank's house to see if it was there. He refused to hand over what they wanted, so they shot him."

"That's awful! What on earth were they looking for?"

I saw no reason not to answer Annie's question, so I did. She said, "I knew it, I just knew it! Mister Demas really should have turned those darned schematics over to you. He didn't and they got him killed."

"I'm afraid that's about the size of it."

"What are we supposed to do now?"

"When your people arrive in Lakehurst the Navy will be

directing things. The guy in charge back there is Lieutenant Commander Edward Nugent."

"Okay, Major Spicer. Thank you for calling and letting me know what's going on. I'll pass what you've said onto the employees going to Lakehurst."

"You're welcome, Annie. I'm sorry to be bringing bad news, but I thought you ought to know."

Annie Bishop was a trooper, no doubt about that. Optitronics' move to New Jersey was costing them a valuable employee.

When I got to my room a message form slipped under the door informed me I received an urgent telephone call while I was out. The call back number was in Lakehurst, New Jersey and the caller was one Russell Pierce. I hiked back out to a telephone booth and talked to a cute sounding AT&T long distance operator. She might have been uglier than sin, but she sounded cute and I always try to keep an optimistic outlook in such matters.

After the usual clicks and buzzes the telephone company provides free of charge with every long distance call, a voice nearly three thousand miles to the east said, "Lakehurst Airship Operations."

"This is Major Johnathon Spicer calling for Staff Sergeant Russell Pierce. He left this number."

"Oh, yes, Major Spicer, the fellow with MID. He's in the next room. Please hang on the line."

A moment later Pierce said, "Hello, Major Spicer. Thanks for calling back. I'm sure glad to hear from you."

"What's going on, Pierce?"

"Probably nothing, but I've been having trouble getting a hold of anyone. I called Colonel Peterson, but he wasn't there. They said I'd have to talk to a Major Downey, but he was out of the building, too. That's when I decided I'd better call you and find out why nobody's talking to me."

"Well, it's my understanding Colonel Peterson was suddenly called out of town yesterday. Major Downey is his second in command, and he's an okay guy, but he's got his hands full right now. I'm sure he'll talk with you when he's got a minute. How did your delivery go?"

"Like clockwork, sir. We finished unloading the DC-3s earlier this evening and the cargo has been handed over to the Navy. Tomorrow morning they'll move everything to Optitronics' new on-base facility."

"Good work, Pierce."

In addition to sounding relieved, there was a note of pride in

Pierce's voice. "Thank you, sir. The Army's transports are heading back to Los Angeles in the morning and my team will be aboard them. From there they can hitch rides to San Francisco."

"That worked out well."

"Yes, sir, it did. I also learned that the airship carrying the . . . ah . . . device will be leaving here tomorrow. They say it will be going to Reeves Field at San Pedro Naval Air Station near Los Angeles and should arrive Tuesday afternoon. I guess blimps don't go as fast as DC-3s."

I laughed. "They sure don't. Seems to me the K-series blimps they have back there cruise at less than sixty miles per hour."

"That's what they tell me, sir. I guess I'll have plenty of time to see the country between here and there."

"I guess you will, and when you get to Reeves Field, look for me. I'll be there to pick you up."

"Thank you, sir. I'll be glad to be back."

"I'll be happy to have you back. A lot's been happening. I'll give you a full rundown when I see you Tuesday."

"Yes, sir. If there's a change should I leave a message at the Presidio?"

"Yes. That's the best way to make sure I get it. I seem to be talking to Major Downey at least once a day, anyway."

"Understood, sir."

"Okay, Sergeant Pierce. Have a safe, if slow, trip back and I'll see you on Tuesday.

As I walked into the coffee shop for some dinner, I went back over my conversation with Pierce. Something about it was nagging at me, but I couldn't put my finger on it.

Pierce was upset because he couldn't get Si or Downey on the telephone. I knew why he couldn't get to Si and I could guess why he couldn't reach Downey. Depending on when Pierce called, Downey might have already been at Crissy Field to meet Stu Irvin and take delivery of the schematics. I could not recall Downey and I discussing Pierce's delivery to Lakehurst, and with everything else going on, he might not have even been aware the Optitronics materials were in New Jersey already. I could also understand why not finding anyone besides me who gave a damn he'd just pulled off a perfect assignment dealing with some very important cargo might disappoint Pierce.

I was a little disappointed, too. Peterson was suddenly treating a critical part of my assignment—securing the occuscope materials—as if it were nothing. I'm certain he has other irons in the fire, probably a lot of them, but this one was damned important, if for no other reason than two men had died trying to protect the Navy's super-secret gizmo.

Looking at the coffee shop menu, I realized I was more than a little hungry. I didn't stop for lunch on my way to the airport because, once I had the occuscope schematics, I wasn't about to risk leaving them in a burger joint parking lot. The best I could manage when I got to the military hanger was a ten-cent Zag Nut candy bar and a two-cent handful of peanuts from vending machines.

The most appealing item on Patmar's Coffee Shop menu was a pair of Texas tamales with chili and beans. To avoid giving us gringos heartburn, the tamales and chili were a little tamer than what you get south of the border. Otherwise, it was a good dinner. I even treated myself to a slice of Dutch apple pie a la mode. I was living high on Uncle Sam's hog tonight.

I finished dinner a little before nine and, since it was a pleasantly balmy evening, I took a stroll around the motel grounds to work off my tamale dinner. I would not have been so leisurely about getting back if I'd known another telephone message slip was waiting for me under my room door. This time I was to call San Francisco as soon as possible.

Thirty

Patmar's Motel – 949 N. Sepulveda Boulevard, El Segundo

It was about nine o'clock when I stepped into a payphone booth and called the number specified in the second telephone message. When I got Major Fred Downey on the line he sounded a whole lot different than he did seven hours earlier when I called him from Los Angeles Airport. Then he was pleased I recovered the occuscope schematics. Now his voice was edged with panic. Something big was happening and he wasted no time telling me what it was.

"Spicer, MID has a serious problem. There is substantial evidence that Colonel Peterson has turned traitor and gone to ground."

That piece of news threw me for a loop. I said the only thing I could think of. "Are you sure?"

Downey sounded almost broken hearted. "I wish I wasn't. The situation came to a head a little while ago when MID Director Davis called looking for Peterson. He was put through to me and I explained Peterson was at a MID conference in Denver. What it comes down to is there is no MID conference in Denver, or anywhere else for that matter."

"Are we sure that's where Peterson said he was going?"

"Absolutely. He wrote it in his desk calendar and had his secretary make a reservation for him at a downtown Denver hotel—a reservation he never showed up for."

Figuring this was all leading up to something involving me, I asked, "Okay, what are my orders?"

"You are to drop everything else and find Peterson. That comes from the top. General Davis specifically said you were to head the investigation."

When I knew Davis eight years ago he was a Lieutenant Colonel and my immediate superior. It was Davis who put me in for my field promotion to Major. We got along because he liked agents who used initiative and unorthodox methods that weren't necessarily by the book.

He was fond of using me as an example of this approach to counter-espionage. More than once Davis said, "We need more agents like Spicer who pay attention to their hunches and act on them."

"All right, who am I reporting to?"

"General Davis wants you to report to him through me because I'm easier to reach that he is. I'll pass your reports on to him immediately. Also, the general has given me orders to get you anything you need . . . top priority."

"Okay, Downey. I want Staff Sergeant Pierce on my team for this."

"You can have anyone you want. I'll give someone else the assignment of guarding occuscopes when they leave Lakehurst."

"Then have them meet me at San Pedro Naval Air Station Tuesday afternoon. That's when a blimp from Lakehurst will show up with an occuscope and Sergeant Pierce aboard. Just tell 'em to look for the blimp. It shouldn't be too hard to spot."

"Okay, I'll get on that right away. What else do you need?"

I was trying to formulate a plan of attack in my mind as we talked. "A hell of a lot of information I don't have. Look, can you get Stu Irvin and his AT-7 back down here at 0800 hours tomorrow morning?"

"I can. Where do you want to go?"

"Crissy Field. I want everybody and anybody who was close to Si in Building 100 when I get there—I mean his secretary, his driver, his assistants, his house steward . . . anyone who worked with him or around him."

"Got it. What else?"

"Get an all-points bulletin with Peterson's description out to every police agency in the state. You can do that through Sacramento."

"We're already working on that. It should be done by the tomorrow morning."

"Good. We may have to expand it nationally, and that won't be so easy to do. Do we know how Peterson left San Francisco?"

"His driver dropped him off at San Francisco Municipal Airport Thursday morning."

"That would seem to indicate he took a commercial flight to wherever he was headed."

"That's the assumption. Peterson's secretary was surprised he made his own airline reservation. Travel reservations were usually her job."

"It's a safe bet Peterson never intended on flying to Denver, and insisting on making his own reservation likely means he knew there was no flight leaving for Denver that fit whatever schedule he was following. Have someone call the airport and check all the departing flights he could have caught from the time he arrived at the airport up to and including the last flight out Thursday night.

"On second thought, have someone do that in person with a picture of Si in their pocket to see if anyone at the airline ticket counters remembers him. Tell whoever you send to the airport they should pay particular attention to Los Angeles flights. Also have them show Peterson's picture at the car rental agencies."

After a momentary pause during which I pictured Downey feverishly writing my instructions, he said, "Got it. Anything else?"

"Yes, a couple of things. First, check the safe and make sure the damaged occuscope I brought back from Hawaii is still there. Second, if one doesn't already exist, have somebody assemble a dossier on Peterson, right from the day he was born to where he's served, his command performance reviews . . . everything in his file.

"I will complete my interviews with the people he worked with before the end of the day tomorrow, after which I'll need Stu Irvin to fly me back here. I'll take the dossier with me so I can study it as time permits.

"And one more thing. Have the best investigator you've got available go through Si's quarters thoroughly. Tell him to look for anything out of the ordinary—anything that could be a clue as to who he was dealing with on the other side or where he might have gone. Try to get the investigator's findings to me before I leave there tomorrow.

"Finally, get a hold of those investigators you sent down to Frank Demas' house. Tell 'em I won't be back and they're on their own."

"Okay, Spicer, I'll get this stuff in the works." Downey paused for a moment, and then added, "I'm glad General Davis insisted you handle this. Otherwise, I wouldn't know which way to turn."

"Davis has thrown us a tough one. Peterson is a pro. If Si really did switch sides, he did it carefully and covered his tracks well. He's that kind of a guy, and he's got a twenty-four hour head start on us. Finding him now won't be so easy."

While Downey went to work on my shopping list of information, I stretched out on my bed and thought about what I just learned. That was when I realized what had been nagging at me all along about the Optitronics case. It was Si's behavior. Now, everything Si Peterson did suddenly made sense.

He left San Francisco just in time to take advantage of a situation he carefully created. There was to be no security or custodial service at Optitronics Thursday night. He indirectly encouraged that because it left the door wide open for him to break in that night and crack Demas' safe for the schematics I told him were there. I had no doubt that, as an agent, Si long ago learned to crack a simple safe like the one in Demas' office. I also had no doubt he knew how to handle Comp B and exactly how to make the break-in and explosion look like sabotage. Even that made some sort of sense now.

Si's problem was Demas got a step ahead of him. Demas took the schematics home, probably Thursday night, and stashed them behind his refrigerator. When Peterson didn't find what he was looking for in Demas' safe, he went to Demas' home. Obviously Demas refused to tell Si where the schematics were or the plans wouldn't have been there for me to find. The only reason I could think of for Peterson killing Demas was Demas knew who he was and Si had to cover his tracks.

One loose end in my scenario was Peterson telling Russ Pierce to contact him when the occuscope materials were safely in Lakehurst if he knew he was leaving San Francisco before Pierce got to New Jersey. I don't know when that conversation took place, but it must have been before Si heard about the delays in moving due to the Navy's not having the new facility ready. It was a minor flaw in his plan Peterson didn't anticipate. Otherwise everything Si did now made sense, assuming the version of the story I'd just cobbled together was more or less what actually happened.

I wasn't particularly proud of myself for finally putting the pieces of the puzzle together. Si used me like his own private agent, providing him with everything he needed to make his defection work, including having me risk my neck in Hawaii to get the occuscope prototype back from the Japs so he could have it. Did he actually have it now? There was no question in my mind that he did. I fully expected another telephone call from Downey confirming that fact. It came no more than five minutes after our last conversation.

Fred Downey said, "You know the thing you asked me to check in the safe?"

I simply said, "It's missing."

"Yes. The shipping box is still there, but it's empty."

"I was pretty sure that's what you'd find."

"I don't understand. Why the hell did Peterson send you three thousand miles to recover the damned thing from the Japs if he was going to hand it right back to them?"

"Maybe because the Nazis made him a better offer."

"Oh, geez! You think so?"

"I don't think anything yet. That's just one answer that makes sense of Si's behavior. Besides, with the Nazi's using their submarine wolf packs to sink relief convoys to England, they have the greatest motivation to get their hands on an occuscope. "

Being a natural born worrier, I doubted Downey was going to get much sleep. I, on the other hand, was more than a little ready for some shuteye. I was about to do just that when it dawned on me it was past ten o'clock and I hadn't called Susan to tell her I wouldn't be seeing her over the weekend. She answered on the first ring.

"Hi, Angel."

"Hi, Johnny. You sound tired."

"I am. It's been a long damned day and tomorrow is going to be more of the same."

"I'm sorry, honey. Anything I can do?"

The sympathy in Susan's voice made me feel a little better. She cared, and that meant a lot.

"Not that I can think of, except be patient with me. We got hit with a major snafu today and I've been given new orders to resolve it. That means I'm flying to San Francisco for the day tomorrow and I'm going to be putting in more long hours when I get back down here on Sunday"

"Don't worry, Johnny. We knew there would be times like this. I'm just glad you're not some place where they're shooting at each other, and I can be very patient when it comes to you."

"Thanks, Angel. I'm not sure I deserve you, but I'm glad you're in my corner."

"Just be careful and remember I love you."

"I will, Susan, and I promise to be very careful. I'll call again when I light somewhere long enough to dial a telephone."

"Good night, darling."

With those words ringing in my ear, I set my little wind-up

alarm clock and hit the sack. The sack would have been a lot nicer with Susan in it.

Thirty-One

Sylvia Eckert put me in mind of those little Mexican Chihuahua dogs. She was thin with pointed features and so tightly strung she'd have gone straight through the roof if I said "boo."

Miss Eckert became Si Peterson's secretary six months ago and clearly wasn't cut out for the kind of work she was doing at MID. That, I figured, was exactly why Si Peterson picked her for his secretary. Sylvia sat there fidgeting with a small lace hanky while trying her best to answer questions she didn't understand.

All I got out of Sylvia Eckert was confirmation that she made a reservation three days ago at the Oxford Hotel on Seventeenth Street in Denver for the nights of Thursday, December 11 and Friday, December 12. Sylvia said she was surprised when Colonel Peterson made his own flight reservations, and she knew something was terribly wrong when Major Downey asked her to leave a message at the hotel for Colonel Peterson to call him and the hotel said Peterson had not shown up Thursday night.

No, Colonel Peterson did not give her any details about the conference except it was hush-hush and to be held in Denver. That was it. I sent Sylvia home to enjoy the rest of her weekend, which seemed unlikely.

Staff Sergeant Ralph Fisher, a driver at the base motor pool, came across as a different breed entirely. He was a bulldog of a man—short, barrel-chested, and scrappy. I also got the definite impression his feelings about officers were the same as a bulldog has for fireplugs.

Describing Si Peterson, he said, "No disrespect intended, sir, but Colonel Peterson struck me as a phony from the day I met him. He was too hoity-toity, if you get my meaning . . . like he was better than everyone else."

"I appreciate your opinion, Sergeant, but you'll want to be careful describing an officer as a 'phony,' even if it turns out he was. Now, I understand you drove him to San Francisco Municipal Airport last Thursday morning. Is that correct?"

My admonition about calling Peterson a phony no doubt put me in company with every other officer Fisher ever knew, but it prompted cooperation that was a little more respectful. "Yes, sir. We arrived at the airport about ten-thirty."

"Did you go into the airport with him?"

"No, sir. He said he could handle his bag, so I waited at the curb for fifteen minutes or so, just in case there was a problem with his flight or something, and then I drove back here."

"Did he say anything about the flight he was taking, like the name of the airline or the departure time?"

"No, sir. Colonel Peterson was never very talkative."

"How much luggage did Colonel Peterson have with him?"

"Just one Army Air Force pilot's suitcase. You know, sir, the kind that folds open in the middle and has big zipper side pouches."

"I don't suppose you happened to see inside it, did you?"

"No, sir. Colonel Peterson carried the suitcase out to the car and it was on the back seat beside him the whole time."

Even though he had more to say than Sylvia Eckert, I really wasn't learning much more from Sergeant Fisher than I already knew, and I was running out of questions. I asked the last one I could think of.

"What kind of car did you take to the airport, Sergeant?"

"The nice staff car, sir. It's a year-old Buick sedan."

I thanked Sergeant Fisher for his cooperation and, as he left, I wondered how long it would be before he called an officer a phony in front of the wrong person. It was the kind of remark that would cost him a stripe and earn him time in the stockade.

Private First Class Paolo Ocampo was the next interview Major Downey scheduled for me. Ocampo was what in civilian life is called a houseboy. In the US Army, however, he wears the title, "house steward." Ocampo is Filipino and grew up in a little town across the bay from San Francisco called Vallejo. For reasons that escaped me, the private was very proud of this fact.

Ocampo was the Golden Retriever in the MID kennel—intelligent, well trained, and eager to please. He was also the only person I interviewed who contributed anything useful to my investigation—actually, something very useful. What's more, what Ocampo knew was not learned in the performance of his duties, but something he observed on his night off.

It seems Paolo has Friday nights off and is in the habit of meeting his girlfriend, who lives in the Castro District south of the Presidio, to take in a show at one of the movie houses in the area. On the particular Friday night in question, which was three weeks ago, Paolo and his girlfriend were leaving the Castro Theater where they saw a new Disney feature-length animated film about a flying elephant. They were walking half a block north to a bus stop on Market Street when he spotted Colonel Peterson leaving the Twin Peaks Tavern at the corner of Market and Castro with a pretty blonde woman.

Paolo passed directly behind them and got a good look at the woman. He also heard a few words of their conversation. They were speaking a foreign language he did not understand, but his girlfriend seemed sure was German.

Feeling I was on the verge of finally learning something important, I asked Ocampo to sit tight for a minute while I went out and found Downey. I knew MID maintained something like police mug books with pictures of known alien espionage agents. I asked Downey for the book that would have female Nazi agents in it. He got it for me and I walked back into the interview room with my fingers crossed.

Setting the book down in front of Ocampo, I asked him to look through it and see if he recognized the woman he saw with Si Peterson. The book was thick, but most of the photos were of men, so it only took about five minutes to single out a picture.

Pointing to a black and white photo taken on a city street somewhere, Paolo said, "That's her."

According to the information under the photo, the woman's name was Hilda Albrecht. She was known to have strong Nazi ties in Germany, but was thought to be a sleeper—an agent in place awaiting an assignment. Her last known address was an apartment in Anaheim, southeast of Los Angeles.

I gave Paolo Ocampo a hearty handshake and thanked him for his cooperation. After Private Ocampo left, I handed the Nazi mug book back to Downey and asked him to get me a copy of Hilda Albrecht's photo and information. I also asked him to obtain Federal Arrest Warrants for Hilda Albrecht, Simon Peterson, and one John Doe warrant. Downey said he'd get to work on it, but the warrants would take a few days because of the weekend. I suggested he send them down with the two guys who would be taking Pierce's and my places guarding the occuscope aboard the blimp.

My last three interviewees were civilians who came into regular contact with Colonel Peterson during the course of MID business. They were information analysts from various departments and impressed me as the Dachshunds in the MID doghouse—smart, observant, and eager to be part of whatever was going on. Unfortunately they were also as puzzled about the colonel being absent without leave as I was. Si covered his tracks very well.

Over a late lunch at the Presidio O-Club, Major Downey briefed me on what his man learned at the San Francisco Airport. It wasn't much. The first flights leaving after Peterson's ten-thirty arrival at the airport went to Salt Lake City, Portland, and Los Angeles. After that there wasn't much going out until around dinner time when there was another flight to LA and flights to Omaha, Chicago, and New York City. Nobody at any of the three ticket counters or the car rental outfits recognized Peterson's picture. The morning LA departure did, however, fit nicely into my hunch about Peterson's activities on Thursday.

Nothing useful came of searching Peterson's residence on Officer's Row. Si was much too professional to leave evidence laying around his house.

Doing a thorough investigation is a process of elimination. My job is to eliminate all of the impossibilities until I get down to one possibility I can't eliminate. It's the right way to do the job, but it can be an aggravatingly slow process.

Around two o'clock I climbed aboard Stu Irwin's AT-7 with Peterson's dossier, my notes from the dog pound, and the photo of Hilda Albrecht in my dispatch case. It wasn't a lot to go on, but it was a start. What's that Chinese saying? A journey of a thousand miles begins with a single step? Hopefully, I just took that step.

Thirty-Two

Hilda Albrecht Residence – 500 W. Illinois St., #2, Anaheim

A week has passed since the Japs attacked Pearl Harbor, and now we are at war with Japan and Germany. We are also at war with Italy, but Congress didn't get around to including the Italians on the list of countries we don't like until a couple of days ago.

The American public is still getting used to the idea that we are entering a fight with a pretty good-sized chunk of the world, but aside from my untimely arrival at Hickam Field a week ago, my part of the war is fought in small corners of the home front. There are no tanks on the roads, no bombers overhead, and no battleships lobbing sixteen-inch projectiles from twenty miles out at sea, but fighting an espionage war can get you just as dead as any other war and, worse, the enemies aren't wearing swastikas or waving rising sun flags. No, my enemies looked just like anyone else on the street in any American city.

These thoughts were running through my mind because at the moment I was surrounded by thousands of Germans as I drove along Santa Ana Street in Anaheim. The town of Anaheim was settled by immigrants from Germany, and even though most of the Germans here have lived in the US for generations and think of themselves as Americans, people with names like Schneider, Wagner, and Schultz were immediately suspect in the minds of "real" Americans, whoever they might be.

The situation for people of Japanese heritage living in this country is even worse. For one thing, they look different—Japs stand out in a crowd. For another thing, Japan attacked us without warning. That makes the Japanese the worst kind of bad guys. They don't play fair.

Another difference about my part of the war is the number of enemies I fight at any one time. At the moment, for example, I was up against only two enemies—one a Nazi, and the other a traitor to the United States.

I began my hunt yesterday in San Francisco, and when Stu Irvin dropped me at Los Angeles Airport late yesterday afternoon, I pointed the Army's Dodge east by southeast and made the 40 mile, hour-long trip to Anaheim, where I parked myself in a decent looking tourist trap on West Lincoln Avenue called the Chaparral Auto Court. These days anywhere I hang my hat is home.

Now, refreshed by a good night's rest and a quick call to Susan, I was back on the trail of the enemy. The information with the photo in MID's mug book gave Hilda Albrecht's address as 500 West Illinois Street, Number Two, and I was on my way to take a look at Miss Albrecht's digs. I needed to get the lay of the land, and I was hoping I wouldn't find Si sitting on the porch sipping lemonade. He would certainly recognize the automobile he gave me to drive.

It turns out 500 S. Illinois is a duplex at the corner of Santa Ana and Illinois Streets in the middle of a housing tract dating back to the 1920s. The building is a hacienda style place surrounded on all sides by heavy foliage and a separate garage out back.

Driving more or less south on Santa Ana, I kept going past Illinois and turned left at the next street, which happened to be West Street. I followed West around a curve to the left and found myself at the other end of Illinois' 500 block. I made another left turn, in effect going around the block, and when I got back to Santa Ana Street I pulled to a stop at the curb in front of Hilda Albrecht's duplex.

That's when I saw the small sign tacked to a low picket fence in front of the porch. It informed me an apartment was available. I supposed it could be apartment number one, but that isn't the kind of break I usually get in situations like this.

The walkway led from the curb across a grass road verge strip and, beyond the sidewalk, through the foliage up to a semi-enclosed porch with a door at each end. As I got closer, I could read the fine print on the sign. It simply said, "Inquire at apartment number one." Yup, that figured.

Hoping whoever lived in apartment number one wasn't at church or a late sleeper, I rapped my knuckles below a small metal numeral "1" nailed to the doorframe at the left end of the porch. I heard movement inside almost immediately, so I got my MID ID card ready and hoped to hell the duplex wasn't a nest full of Nazi spies. If it was, I was about to give myself away. There were other approaches I could use, but I wasn't feeling tricky.

A moment after I saw the curtain in the front window to my right move, a blonde woman opened the door. She was short, less than five feet, but what she lacked in height, she made up for in girth. She had at least twenty pounds on me. The woman was a caricature of an old world housfrau, except she had no accent. Despite her excellent English, however, I knew German or something like it was her first language. The thing that gave her away was the way she phrased sentences. For example, in English we say "Many people are standing in line." The German phrasing would be "Many people are in line standing."

"Yes, what is it you are wanting?"

I held my ID up and said, "My name is Spicer. I'm with the US Army Military Intelligence Division. I'm here to ask you some questions about the woman who rented your other apartment."

The hausfrau studied my ID carefully before blurting, "I am not surprised that woman is in trouble. She is a horrible person."

I pulled my notebook from my inside jacket pocket and asked, "May I have your name for my notes?"

"Yes, I am Bertha Becker and I am for the past ten years an American citizen."

I made note of those facts and held up my copy of Hilda Albrecht's picture from the MID Nazi mug book. "Is this the woman who rented your apartment?"

"Yes, she is the woman."

"What name did give you when she rented the apartment?"

"She called herself Miss Mary Smith. I did not believe that was her true name, but she paid her rent on time. What she chose to call herself is of no difference to me."

"How long was she here?"

Frau Becker gave that a moment's thought before saying, "I will check the rental agreement if you must have the exact date, but it was the middle of last June when she rented the apartment."

"And when did she leave?"

"Yesterday. She paid her rent in advance by the month and she is leaving without giving me notice, so Miss Smith is forfeiting two week's rent."

I added that detail to my notes on Hilda Albrecht and asked the jackpot question. "You described Miss Smith as a horrible person. What makes you think that?"

"A man she had staying in her apartment! I will not allow

unmarried women tenants to do such a thing."

I got that tingling sensation I always felt when I sense I'm closing in on a piece of the puzzle. "Can you describe the man?"

"I hardly saw him, but I could hear them night and day talking over there. They were talking in both English and Deutsch . . . German. The one time I really saw him he was wearing a dark green uniform, so he is a soldier I am thinking."

"I don't imagine you got his name."

"No, but Miss Smith was calling him 'colonel' on several occasions."

"When did he arrive here?"

She thought about her answer, but only briefly. "On Thursday night they arrived together. It was almost midnight and they woke me up when they got here."

"Did this man leave yesterday with Miss Smith?"

"Yes he did. I saw them loading into a taxicab their luggage."

"Did you notice the name of the taxicab company?"

"No, but red and yellow were the colors it was painted."

I was jotting notes as fast as I could scribble. Si Peterson was way ahead of me, but the trail was still warm. "Miss Becker, what time did you see them leave in the cab yesterday?"

"It was just before the lunch time."

"And did Miss Smith take all of her belongings from the apartment?"

"Yes. I went over to see the condition of the apartment when I saw them leave, but it was neat as a pin. I could not find so much as a scrap of paper she left behind. That is how I am able to so soon be showing the apartment for renting."

Sensing she was growing weary of my questions, I said, "Miss Becker, you have been most helpful. I just have one or two more questions for now. Did Miss Smith have a telephone?"

"Yes. The apartment comes with a telephone connection, but the tenant must pay for the service."

"Did Miss Smith have telephone service?"

"Yes. PRospect-four-one-eight-nine was her number."

"Thank you very much for your cooperation, Miss Becker. Uncle Sam appreciates your help."

With a proud smile, Bertha Becker said, "You will please tell Mister Sam I am a good American and happy to help him."

Thirty-Three

Village Taxicab Company – 559 S. Anaheim Blvd., Anaheim

I drove around Anaheim for a while in search of a red and yellow taxicab. I found one parked out in front of an Episcopal Church, where the cabbie was no doubt waiting for services to end and praying for a fare. I told the driver I needed to talk to his dispatcher and he directed me to the Village Taxicab Company's office at the corner of Water Street and Anaheim Boulevard.

The dispatch office was also where they parked out of service taxis and the big garage was full to overflowing with Dodge sedans. Apparently the demand for cabs on Sunday mornings isn't high in Anaheim. In the middle of the red and yellow sheet metal sea inside sat a swarthy fellow at an elevated desk with a buzzing shortwave radio. At the moment of my arrival he was intently studying the Sunday paper's funny pages. Since he was the only guy in the building, I deduced he might be the dispatcher.

I weaved my way through the Dodges and, as I approached his desk, the fellow looked up. Glaring, he took the stub of a well-chewed cigar out of this mouth and snarled, "If ya wanna cab, call on the phone. We don't take no walk -in fares."

"I don't want a cab. I want . . ."

"Then get the hell out of here. We don't allow no salesmen, either."

I thought about just shooting him, but that involved more paperwork than it was worth. Instead, I held up my MID ID and said, "Do you allow federal law officers who can throw your butt into Leavenworth for the rest of your natural life?"

"Huh?"

"One of your cabs picked two passengers up at 500 South

Illinois Street around noon yesterday. You've got one minute to tell me where he took those fares before I slap the cuffs on you and drag your butt to the Federal Building in LA, where they will ask you the same question, only not as politely."

Still squinting at my ID, he said, "Yeah, sure. Ya don't gotta get all hot under the collar about it. I'll look it up for ya right away. Ya got the cab number?"

"No, the witness didn't get it."

From a filing cabinet behind his desk he removed a manila folder into which were stuffed at least fifty forms with a lot of sloppy handwriting on them. I leaned against the nearest Dodge while he thumbed through the forms looking for the one that had my information on it.

His system must have been more efficient than it looked because he found the answer for me in less than five minutes. "Here it is. It was cab number 4178 and he dropped two fares at the Greyhound bus depot at twelve-forty-five yesterday. That what you want to know?"

"Where's the Greyhound bus depot?"

He jerked a thumb over his shoulder. "Just go straight up Anaheim Boulevard out in front about a mile. It's on your left when you get to Winston Road."

I jotted that into my notebook and asked, "What is the name and the address of the driver who took the fares to the bus depot?"

He removed a black cardboard address book from his desk, turned a few pages, and read off, "Mario Russo, thirty-one-thirty-one West Catalina Avenue, number four."

"Anaheim?"

"Yeah, Anaheim."

"And for the record, what's your name?"

He hesitated a moment, as if telling me his name would get him into more trouble, but finally said, "Enzo Moretti. Is that all ya need?"

"That's all for now. Don't lose that form with the cab ride on it, though. We may need it and Mister Russo in court later on."

Turning back to his funny pages, Moretti mumbled, "Yeah, yeah."

I thought about using a tire iron to smash holes in the windshields of a few red and yellow cabs on my way out to express my gratitude for Mister Moretti's cooperation, but he looked like the sort of guy who wouldn't appreciate the sentiment behind such a gesture. Instead, I drove a mile up Anaheim Boulevard to the Greyhound bus depot.

The bus depot wasn't any busier than the Village Cab Company. In fact, the middle-aged woman behind the counter looked as if she might have been snoozing before I came in. I woke her up with my MID ID and started my interview by showing her the mug shot photo of Hilda Albrecht. The bus lady didn't recall ever seeing Hilda.

Next, I asked about any Army officers she might have seen on Saturday. None. Then I thought to ask if she worked on Saturday. No. Turns out the person who worked Saturday only works Wednesdays, Fridays, and Saturdays. No, she didn't know how to get in touch with him or her, she wasn't sure which. I took a Greyhound schedule from a rack on her counter and thanked the woman for her invaluable cooperation to her country's security.

Sick and tired of Anaheim, I made a left on Ball Road, and worked my way north and west on the major arteries that connect the distant points within Orange and Los Angeles Counties. Finally, about one-thirty I came to Sepulveda Boulevard and turned north toward what was left of Optitronics. I have no idea why I went there, except it seemed like a good idea to keep an eye on the remains as long as I was in the area. The remains looked just about as they did when I saw them last on Friday, except the cardboard boxes stacked out on the loading dock then were gone.

It seemed like a lot longer than two days since I was last there. I'd been running the whole time and Si Peterson was still ahead of me. By now he could be halfway to Berlin, or wherever turncoat US Army colonels hang out in the fatherland these days. There was no remaining doubt in my mind that the term "turncoat" fit Si Peterson like a glove.

With those dismal thoughts churning around in my head, I stopped at Rod's hamburger joint for a cup of coffee and a telephone. It was time to call Major Downey and face the music. I got the coffee first and, drinking it out of a cardboard cup, I placed a call to San Francisco.

"Major Downey."

"It's Spicer, Major."

"Spicer, please tell me you have some good news."

I swallowed another sip of coffee. "The good news is I can now provide a fairly accurate accounting of Peterson's time since he was last seen. You want me to give it to you now, or do you want to set up a safe call?"

Downey seemed to be thinking about my question for a moment, and then he said, "Go ahead now. I doubt we'll be discussing anything the enemy doesn't already know."

"All right. Keep in mind some of this is conjecture, but I have confidence in the overall scenario. It goes like this: Peterson caught the United Air Lines flight to Los Angeles that left San Francisco late Thursday morning. Si had the occuscope and was ready to defect, but he knew from what I told him that Demas' black boxes made the scope worthless for the Nazi's purposes. They wanted to know how the thing works and for that they needed the schematics.

"Hilda Albrecht, the Nazi sleeper in your mug book met him in Los Angeles and they ended up at Optitronics Thursday evening to break in and get the schematics from Demas' safe. Peterson was most likely the man I saw in the building leaving Frank Demas' office just before the big bang.

"Since the schematics weren't in the office safe, though, they went to Frank Demas' house up in Malibu, hoping to find what they were after there. Peterson probably tried to talk Demas out of the schematics using his MID authority, and when that approach failed, I'm guessing he and the Albrecht woman threatened Demas at gunpoint. When that also failed, one or the other of them shot Demas and they searched his house.

"After failing to find the schematics, Albrecht drove Peterson to her duplex apartment in Anaheim. According to the landlady, they got there around midnight. Peterson stayed with the woman until yesterday around noon when a taxicab picked them up with their luggage. I traced the cab to the Anaheim Greyhound bus depot and that's where I hit a brick wall."

Major Downey didn't sound as disappointed as I anticipated. "That's not bad, especially since you've only been on the case for a day and a half. Do you think they'll give up on the schematics or keep looking?

"By now Si has to be getting antsy. He'll know were on his trail, so I think he'll go with what he has."

"Do you have anything else to go on?"

"Yes, one lead, but it's a weak one. The Albrecht woman had a telephone. Can you have someone check with the telephone company down there and find out what calls she made and received during the past ten days or so?"

"Sure. What's the number?"

I read Hilda Albrecht's telephone number from my notebook. "It's PRospect four-one-eight-nine in Anaheim."

Downey repeated the number. "PRospect four-one-eight-nine. That right?"

"That's it. I'll check in with you before noon tomorrow. See if you can get the information back from the telephone company by then."

"Will do. Anything else?"

"Nothing I can think of. The telephone records might come to nothing, but it's the only thing I've got for the moment. By the way, I just drove by the Optitronics plant to see what was going on there. It looks like they cleaned out everything salvageable.

"Anyway, since I've got nowhere else to look at the moment, I'm going to focus on Peterson's Dossier and a couple of other bits and pieces until I call you late tomorrow morning. If you need me before then I'll be at the Santa Barbara number in my file. Do you have anything for me at that end?"

"Not right now. I'll pass your report on to General Davis as soon as we hang up. Good work, Spicer."

I hung up wondering whether he meant the "good work" part or he was just trying to keep me motivated. If it was the latter, he was wasting his time. I'm a realist about my job. I also had a much better source of motivation in mind. I got the long distance operator again and placed a collect call to MOntecito four-nine-five-six in Santa Barbara.

Thirty-Four

Susan Jackson Residence – 3412 State St., #3, Santa Barbara

The sun was drooping low in the western sky by the time I got to Susan's, but her exuberance on the telephone when I said I was coming up for the night reminded me of all the reasons seeing her was worth the drive. She said her brother Jack was coming over for dinner and wanted to know if I'd rather she asked him to come another time. Hell, I like Jack. I told her it would be good to see him again.

Jack met me at the door because Susan was busy being a chef. By the time we shook hands and made it to the kitchen, a casserole was in the oven and she was studying a cookbook to make sure she hadn't forgotten anything. Susan greeted me enthusiastically and Mister Whiskers even looked up from the large tuna can he was busy cleaning to say, "Meow."

Susan said, "I hope you don't mind potluck tonight. I filled in a shift today for one of my nurses who wasn't feeling well, and I'm not up to fancy cooking tonight. We're having tuna-noodle casserole and a salad for dinner. That okay with you two?"

Jack said, "Hey, a home-cooked meal beats the heck out of the mess hall any day."

I added, "My sentiments exactly, even though I seem to end up eating in greasy spoons more often than mess halls."

Jack said, "They're keepin' you hoppin', huh?"

Susan, who was leaning against me with her arm around my waist, said, "They sure are. Do you know where he was last Sunday?" Then a thought dawned on her and, looking sheepish, she said, "Oops. Maybe I can't tell you where he was last Sunday."

I gave her a nudge with my hip. "You can tell him, Angel. My

155

being there was no big secret."

Looking curious, Jack asked, "All right, where the hell was he last Sunday?"

Susan looked up at me and said, "He was at Pearl Harbor, that's where. Right when the Japanese were dropping bombs all over it!"

Jack looked surprised. "You were? Wow, you didn't waste any time getting into the thick of things!"

I chuckled. "Well, more accurately, I was at Hickam Field, but there were just as many bombs and bullets there as there were in the harbor. I was damned lucky."

"Yeah," Jack said, "The reports I saw made things look pretty bad. Thank God our carriers were out to sea, otherwise there wouldn't be anything left of the Pacific Fleet."

Susan piped up again, saying, "I told Johnny he can't do that sort of thing anymore."

Laughing, I said, "I passed that on to the general, and he said, since it was you making the request, he'd see what he could do." Then, to Jack, I said, "How's your end of the war? I keep hearing rumors about Japs invading Lompoc."

Jack laughed. "I wouldn't hold my breath waiting for that to happen. We've got coastal guns, patrol boats, flying boats . . . all kinds of stuff to keep the Japs away. They're even sending us blimps to watch the coast. Hell, next the fish will have to start showing ID cards."

"I understand the blimps will be a while getting here."

"Yeah, but that's okay. At the moment the Navy only has one airship base out here where they can park the dang things. They're planning more bases, but that's going to take a while, too. I haven't even seen a blimp yet."

Phrasing my comment carefully, I said, "After Tuesday you might get a chance to see one if you're anywhere near San Pedro."

"Oh? That's interesting. I've got a TDI assignment at San Pedro Naval Air Station beginning Wednesday. That's quite a coincidence, isn't it?"

I grinned. "Now you see why I have a job. The Japs are even better at putting two and two together than you and I are."

Susan asked, "What does TDI mean?"

Jack replied, "It's military talk that means a temporary duty assignment for training or instruction. This one is only overnight, but they can last for weeks depending on the type of training."

Nodding her understanding, Susan said, "Oh." At the same time a cheerful little "ding" came from the kitchen and she announced dinner was ready.

A few minutes later we were all seated around the kitchen table chowing down on some pretty decent tuna-noodle casserole. Mister Whiskers was there, too. He went from chair to chair looking up hopefully. So far as I could tell, the only success he had was at Jack's chair, but the glare Susan gave her brother ended the chances of any further such success.

Over dinner a thought occurred to me. I said, "Jack, can I get your help with something for a minute?"

"Sure, Johnny. Whatcha got?"

"Well, I'm looking for a guy who was in southern California up until around noon yesterday. He'll be trying to leave the country and I need to figure out how he's going to do it. There's a statewide APB out on him, but I never expect much from "be on the lookout" bulletins. Thinking about it from seafarer's point of view, how would you get out of the country undetected?"

He frowned in thought for a few moments, and then shook his head. "That's a tough one. Despite our stepped-up international security, there are still a lot of holes in our borders a smart guy can slip through, but they're rapidly closing up.

"Now, if it were me, I'd head for Canada. Mexico might work, but his options from there would be more limited depending on his final destination, and he might run into language problems unless he's fluent in Spanish.

"Canada has better border security, but once he got into Canada, getting to . . . where do you think he wants to end up?"

"Let's say Berlin."

Jack raised his eyebrows. "I see. Well, if he made it across Canada, he could probably find transportation to Germany from the eastern seaboard, but you want to get him before he leaves the US, right?"

"If he hasn't gotten out already."

"If the guy's sharp and planned ahead, that's a possibility. On the other hand, if he was still around yesterday, I'd bet his departure plans are just going into effect, so you might still have a shot at catching him. Can you tell me where was he seen last?"

"At the Greyhound bus depot in Anaheim."

Jack frowned again. "That doesn't help much. To answer your original question, I'd bet on Canada." After a pause, he added, "By boat, if possible. A small freighter or large fishing boat could make the trip and stands a good chance of putting in somewhere along the Canadian coast unnoticed by authorities. They have a lot of maritime activity up there and a vessel like I described could easily get lost in the shuffle."

"Thanks, Jack. I appreciate your thoughts. I hadn't considered the ship idea, but it makes sense."

"You're welcome, Johnny. I don't envy you the job of finding this guy with nothing more to go on."

After dinner Jack left, saying he needed to get back to the base. I'm pretty sure his hasty departure had more to do with giving his sister and me some time together than it did with any Coast Guard business.

I helped Susan with the dishes—I washed and she dried—after which I asked if she minded me taking about an hour of our time for some Army business. Our conversation about Si Peterson's escape route was making me feel guilty about neglecting my duty.

Thirty-Five

Susan Jackson Residence – 3412 State St., #3, Santa Barbara

Besides Peterson's dossier, which I read from cover to cover during yesterday's flight back to LA, the only thing I had to work on until I got Hilda Albrecht's telephone records from Downey was the encoded message on the back of the occuscope prototype photo I got from Si. The fact that Si was now among the missing and that he gave me the photo apparently unaware of what was on the back gave the message new importance. I decided to have one more go at decoding it before shipping the message up to Major Downey and letting the experts figure it out.

I removed the occuscope photo and the notes I'd made on Patmar Motel stationary from my bag and laid them out on Susan's kitchen table. She sat down next to me and went to work on the crossword puzzle in the Sunday *Santa Barbara News Press.*

Staring at the message, I once again looked for the reason I wasn't able to decrypt it using the normal substitution method based on letter frequency. I kept ending up with gibberish and nothing I did to the mish-mash of letters gave me anything but more gibberish. The damned thing shouldn't be that difficult to solve, so what was I missing?

Intent on her crossword, Susan seemed to be having letter problems of her own. She was busy erasing a word she just added to the puzzle. In frustration, she muttered, "Damn. I wish I was better at this. I keep leaving letters out. That's why I don't do these puzzles in ink!" Then Susan realized I was trying to concentrate and quickly said, "Oh, I'm sorry, Johnny. I'll keep my dumb mistakes to myself."

Suddenly the Professor's third rule of encryption popped into my mind: "If you are certain you are working on a monoalphabetic encryption, and you've tried everything you can think of to break it, look for the anomaly—the little personal touch a cryptologist might use to throw you off the track." That's when I put two and two together and realized how I'd been tricked.

I said, "Angel, I could kiss you. You just gave me the solution to a problem that's had me stumped for a week."

She looked at my notes. "Are all those letters supposed to make sense?"

XEESZX KRQBWESR WZJ OWBDU AP ARRCKRAD/
ODRE FSEQSZ EQSGEV JWVK/
EGWZKBSE JUSLGV SZKEGCRESAZK/ KD

"They will if they're decrypted correctly. This is a message encrypted with what's called a simple substitution code. That just means one letter of the alphabet is substituted for each letter used in the original message. The decoding method is based on the frequency with which letters typically occur in the English language, only whoever encrypted the message threw in something extra to make the code harder to break, and you just told me what he did."

"I did? What did I say?"

"You said you kept leaving letters out. I think that is exactly what whoever encrypted this message did to make it harder to decrypt. I think he left out the most commonly used letter in the English language. That's why my substitution decoding method hasn't worked so far."

"Okay, I'll bite. What's the most commonly used letter in the English language?"

"On average, it's the letter E, but I think he wrote the original message leaving all of the Es out. That would throw the letter frequency system out of whack, but the message would still be readable as long as whoever received it knew the Es were missing. Let's see if I'm right. The second most commonly used letter in English is T and the most common letter in the encrypted message is E, so let's replace all of the Es with Ts."

```
_TT___ _____T__ ___ _____ __ _____/

     __T __T___ T___T_ ____/

 T_____T _____ ___T___T____/ __
```

The *T*s seemed to be in logical places and it dawned on me the guy who did the encryption substituted the letter *E* for the most common letter in the message as a way to tell the recipient what he did. It was all starting to make sense, so I tried replacing the next most common letter in the message, *S*, with the next most common letter in English, *A*. That didn't look right, so I tried the fourth most common English letter, *O*. That didn't look right, either, so I moved on to the fifth most common English letter, *I*.

```
 _ T T I _ _  _ _ _ _ _ T I _  _ _ _  _ _ _ _ _ _  _ _  _ _ _ _ _ _ _ _/
         _ _ _ T  _ I T _ I _....T _ I _ T _  _ _ _ _/
     T _ _ _ _ _ I T  _ _ I _ _ _  I _ _ T _ _ _ T I _ _ _/  _ _
```

The *I* insertions looked good. I could even see at least one word that might end in "ion" or "ing," common word end combinations. Now I was getting somewhere. The letter frequencies were off some, probably due to the short length of the message, but they were close enough that playing around with them ultimately gave me:

GTTING SCHMATIC AND XAMPLE OF OCCUSCOP/
XPCT WITHIN THIRTY DAYS/
TRANSMIT DLIVRY INSTRUCTIONS/ SP

I turned my worksheet to face Susan and said, "It worked! Go ahead, Angel. Read the message. Just remember all the *E*s are missing and the slash symbols indicate the ends of sentences."

She looked at the words for a moment, and then began reading the message. "Getting . . . ah . . . schematic and example of . . . occuscop?"

"That word has an *E* on the end."

"Oh. Okay. Occuscope. Expect within thirty days. Transmit . . . delivery instructions. And it seems to be signed SP."

"Perfect, and the "SP" stands for Simon Peterson, which makes this message proof positive I'm after the right man. I had no doubt of that, but if we can match his handwriting to the original message encryption, we've got evidence that will stand up in court."

"That's wonderful, darling. Now, I believe something was said about a kiss."

Thirty-Six

Susan Jackson Residence – 3412 State St., #3, Santa Barbara

Susan left for work about seven-thirty and I killed time reading Peterson's squeaky clean dossier for the third time and playing chase-the-string with Mister Whiskers. Playing with Mister Whiskers was more productive.

I wanted to get going, but I had no idea where I should get going to. I was hoping the records from Hilda Albrecht's telephone would solve that problem for me, but Downey wasn't going to have those until at least mid-morning, so I waited.

Impatience finally got the better of me around ten, so I called San Francisco. Even if Downey didn't have anything for me, I had something for him. I had the decryption of Si Peterson's message from the back of the occuscope photo.

When Downey came on the line, he said, "Your timing is perfect, Spicer. I just got the information you asked for from the telephone company in Orange County."

"Great. Before you give it to me, though, I have something for you that may come in handy."

"What's that?"

"Back when Peterson handed me the Optitronics detail, he gave me a photo of the occuscope prototype so I'd know it if I saw it. What he didn't realize is he used the back of that particular photo to jot down an encrypted message."

"Oh? Send it up here and I'll have the cypher people decrypt it."

"I'll send it to you, but I've already decrypted it. The encryption he used was just a simple substitution code with an anomaly and I stumbled onto the solution. You're gonna love this.

"The message reads as follows: 'Getting schematic and example of occuscope. Expect within thirty days. Transmit delivery instructions.' It's signed with the initials SP. He wrote the message he encrypted in longhand so you might be able to match it to his handwriting."

"You're kidding!"

"Nope, we've got him dead to rights in black and white. The only thing we don't know his who he sent it to and how he sent it. You might be able to come up with those details from that end."

Downey was quiet for a moment and I thought he might be making himself some notes on what I'd just given him. Then he said, "I can't believe Colonel Peterson was that careless. When can you send us the original?"

"Unless you want to entrust it to the US Post Office, when I can send it by a more secure method depends on what you've got for me."

"Okay, what I've got for you is short, but sweet. During the past 30-some days, Hilda Albrecht made only two telephone calls from her apartment. Interestingly, one was to our number here. I assume she was probably calling Peterson. The other call was Saturday to the Village Taxicab Company."

"Damn! I was hoping there'd be a lead in there somewhere."

"Oh, but there is. Remember, Spicer, telephones also receive calls, and she got a very interesting call on Friday, 12 December. It was long-distance from a number in Seattle belonging to DDG Kosmos, which happens to be a German steamship line."

"Well, I'll be damned."

"I've got our research people checking on the company, but I don't have anything back from them yet."

"Have them get recent or upcoming sailings from the west coast. That could be the lead we need."

"I've already told them we need that information."

"Good. In the meantime, I've got a local contact here who might fill in some of the blanks for us. I'll check with him and then head for Los Angeles Airport so I can get the encrypted message to you if there's a courier flight going north this afternoon. I'll check in with you then."

"All right, Spicer, and good work on the decryption of Peterson's message."

My next call was to Susan at work. I told her I was headed south and asked her for Jack's telephone number at the Coast Guard facility.

"Lieutenant Jackson speaking."

"Hi, Jack, Johnny Spicer. Do you remember that hypothetical question I asked you last night?"

"Sure."

"Well, I just got a little more information and I'm hoping you can help me make use of it. Do you know anything about a German steamship line called DDG Kosmos?"

Jack was quiet for several seconds and I heard some papers shuffling at his end. "As a matter of fact, I do. Something came in about the Kosmos line toward the end of last week. I'm looking for the dispatch. Here it is.

"'The passenger steamship *Ammon* of German registry and owned by the DDG Kosmos line, put into Los Angeles Harbor on 11 December, 1941 at oh-seven-hundred-hours. The ship's intended destination was Seattle, Washington, but because a state of war now exists between Germany and the United States, the DDG Kosmos line canceled the rest of the voyage. Due to the fact that the passenger manifest includes citizens of several nationalities, permission was requested from, and granted by, the State Department for the *Ammon* to remain in Los Angeles harbor up to seven days for the purposes of refueling and re-provisioning for their return to Hamburg. The deadline for the ship's departure is 18 December, 1941.' That would be this coming Thursday. Does that help any, Johnny?"

"It sure does. Do you know if the State Department is allowing the *Ammon* to take on new passengers while she's in Los Angeles?"

"It most certainly is not. Why? You think somebody is going to board her as a passenger?"

"I'm pretty sure two somebodies have already boarded her, but that's hush-hush until we are in a position to take them into custody, assuming the ship hasn't left yet. Can you find out?"

"Sure, you still at Sis' place?"

"Yes, but I'm about to head south. How long will it take you to find out if the ship has sailed?"

"All I have to do is call the Coast Guard detachment on Terminal Island. They have the responsibility for keeping an eye on the German ship. I should be able to call you back in five minutes."

"Then I'll stand by until I hear from you."

While I waited for Jack's call back, I took a look at the Greyhound bus schedule I picked up in Anaheim. Sure enough, a bus for Santa Monica with stops in Wilmington and San Pedro left at one-thirty Saturday afternoon, right after Peterson and the

Albrecht woman got to the depot. Wilmington and San Pedro were likely destinations for someone planning on boarding a ship in Los Angeles Harbor. Now, if the German ship will just stay put long enough for us to act on the information I'd put together, we might just have Si Peterson in the bag.

Jack was as good as his word. The telephone rang less than five minutes after we ended our first conversation. His news was also good.

"You lead a charmed life, Johnny. I was afraid the *Ammon* would be long gone by now, but there was a problem paying for their fuel. Under the circumstances, Standard Oil wants cash on the barrelhead and the Captain doesn't have it. Funds are being sent from Hamburg by international wire, but Standard Oil won't get the money until Tuesday. Unless something changes, that means the *Ammon* can't put to sea before Wednesday or possibly Thursday."

"Good for Standard Oil and thank you for digging up the information. I owe you a lot."

With a smile in his voice, Jack said, "And I'll collect, too!"

On that happy note I pointed the Army's Dodge south on Route 101 and made the best time I possible to Los Angeles Airport so I could unload the occuscope photo and get to Los Angeles Harbor.

On the way I thought about how I was going to take Peterson and Albrecht into custody. Sergeant Pierce would be here by then to back my play, but I also needed someone with a knowledge of Los Angeles Harbor and maritime law. I knew someone who would be perfect for the job, but I'd have to get Major Downey to pull some strings for me.

Thirty-Seven

Military Hanger, Los Angeles Airport – Inglewood

With Si Peterson's encrypted message locked securely in another dispatch case borrowed from the Army Air Force Operations Chief at Los Angeles Airport, I caught up with the First Looie who flew the DC-3 parked out front. I handed over the dispatch case, got a receipt for it, and arranged to have the case delivered to Major Downey at Crissy Field.

Next, I found an empty telephone booth and called Building 100 at the Presidio. When I got Downey on the line, I said, "The package you're expecting will arrive at Crissy aboard an Army DC-3 at roughly 1645 hours."

"Good. I'll be there to meet it. That's one dispatch case I don't want to go astray. I have some details about the DDG Kosmos steamship line. You ready to copy?"

"Shoot."

Apparently Downey received the same dispatch Jack had on the *Ammon* because he told me almost word for word what Jack Jackson read to me in Santa Barbara. When he was done, I said, "That confirms what I have."

Sounding surprised and a little annoyed, Downey said, "You already had all that?"

"Yeah, but it's good to have it from an official source."

"Damn it, Spicer, you don't need the rest of us for anything, do you? You do your own decryption, research, everything. Hell, I might as well take a vacation in Sun Valley and just wait for you to send Peterson back in a dispatch case."

I couldn't tell by the tone of his voice if Downey was really upset with me or not, so I played it safe. "Begging the Major's pardon, but you're incorrect about that. I do need you. In fact, I need you for something very important."

"What? You out of dispatch cases?"

That was said with a laugh, so I laughed with him and said, "No, I just bum those from the Ops Chief here at the airport. What I need are some strings pulled."

"Who's on the other end of the strings?"

"The US Coast Guard."

"Thank God. I was afraid you wanted me to ask General Davis to get you a battleship from the damned Navy."

"That might be nice, but I don't think the Navy has any of those left in the Pacific."

"True. What do you want from the Coast Guard?"

"Lieutenant Orville Jackson. He's acting commandant at the Coast Guard station in Santa Barbara, and I want him TDY'd to our mission for a couple of weeks. I need him at San Pedro Naval Air Station on Terminal Island early tomorrow afternoon. I'll also need the Coast Guard detachment at Los Angeles Harbor available for an unknown operation."

I could tell Downey was writing my request down. When the major was done, he said, "All right, that's kind of short notice on your Lieutenant, but I'll try to get hold of General Davis and see what he can do."

"Thanks, Downey. Tell Davis I'd have given him more notice, but Peterson didn't let me in on his plans to defect with one of our top secret gizmos."

"Sure, Spicer, I'll give him your message word for word. Where can I get a hold of you later today or tonight?"

"I don't know yet. I'm heading for the harbor to take a look at that German ship, but I don't have a place to stay yet. I'll have to call you."

"All right, call me here, before twenty-hundred-hours if you can."

"Will do."

With my business at the airport completed, I headed south on Sepulveda Boulevard—California Route One—and followed it all the way to Wilmington. The trip is twenty-some miles and took about forty-five minutes with traffic and signals.

Wilmington is a small community just north of Los Angeles Harbor. Aside from providing housing for workers at Los Angeles Harbor and the fishing fleet crews, the town sits on top of the third largest oil field in the country. The refineries, pipelines, and such they built to process the oil make Wilmington a little messy, but money trumps cleanliness every time. I went to Wilmington instead of neighboring San Pedro or Long Beach because past experience told me it offers the shortest and quickest access to the maze of channels and docks comprising the harbor.

Driving into the harbor complex, I was confronted with a dozen or so signs pointing in all directions. Among them were arrows for the Naval Air Station (Reeves Field), the Long Beach Naval Shipyard, and the Terminal Island Coast Guard Base. Since, according to Jack, the Coast Guard has the job of watching the *Ammon*, they ought to know where it was moored, so I followed the arrow on their sign. That eventually brought me to a guarded gate with another sign.

US COAST GUARD
US Government Property
Do Not Enter

I pulled up to the guard shack at the gate and presented my MID ID. The Coast Guard Shore Patrolman at the gate looked at my credentials, had the sense to know they were important, but had no idea what to do with me.

I said, "Call the Officer of the Day and tell him I'm here. He'll take it from there."

That sounded like a good idea to the guard because it got him off the hook. He directed me to a parking spot just outside the gate and went back into his shack to make the call. About five minutes later a gray Chevrolet sedan with "US Coast Guard" lettered on its front doors and large white stars on its back doors pulled up to the gate from the other side. The guy in it had a short conversation with the guard, and then got out and walked to where I was parked.

According to the twin silver bars on the shoulders of his crisp, white uniform, he was a lieutenant. Stepping up to my driver-side window he said, "Good afternoon, sir, I'm Lieutenant Hutchins, Harbor Operations. May I please see your credentials?"

I handed my ID over and he studied it for a few seconds. Then he gave me the typical strange look I get when regular military folks encounter MID agents.

Sounding a trifle hesitant, Hutchins said, "How can I help you, Major Spicer?"

"I'm sorry to show up unannounced, Lieutenant, but I need to know where the German ship that put in to the harbor a few days ago is moored and I figured this was the place to find out. You guys should be getting some orders regarding my business here, but that may take a few more hours and I'm trying to get ahead of the game."

"I understand, sir. I don't see any security problem with giving you the information you want. If you'll please leave your car here, I'll take you around for a look at the German ship."

Fifteen minutes later I was a board a 36-foot Coast Guard motor lifeboat cruising up what Lieutenant Hutchins told me was the harbor's main channel. Another ten minutes had us angling to starboard into a short channel bordered on our port side by several large round fuel storage tanks. A large steamship was moored about fifty yards ahead on our starboard side.

As we entered the channel, Lieutenant Hutchins told the chief petty officer at the helm to cut the engine and let the boat drift. Pointing toward the moored ship, Hutchins said, "This is the harbor's quarantine dock and there is your German ship, Major Spicer. At the moment the *Ammon* is the only vessel here.

The steamship looked to be at least 400 feet in length. The hull was black and the upper parts were white. The ship had a single stack painted black with one red stripe and one white stripe. Across the ship's broad stern in large white letters were the words "AMMON" and "Hamburg."

The lieutenant offered me a pair of binoculars for a closer look. I took a look, but didn't really expect to see Si Peterson lounging in a deck chair on the fantail. However, I did see two armed Coast Guard Shore Patrolmen doing sentry duty on the dock alongside the *Ammon*.

I said, "The last word we had was that there was a problem getting the ship fueled and the earliest sailing date is expected to be Wednesday or Thursday. Is that still the status?"

My host replied, "I haven't heard anything different. I just hope they get that ship out of here by Thursday night. Otherwise we're going to have a mess on our hands taking the passengers into custody."

"Is that the plan?"

"It's not down in writing, but we have orders to impound the vessel if it isn't out of the harbor by midnight Thursday, and doing that would require removing the passengers."

"I see your point."

"Would you like us to pull alongside for a closer look?"

I handed him the binoculars and said, "No, thanks. I've seen everything I need to see, and I'd just as soon keep my distance for now."

The Lieutenant nodded knowingly. "That's kind of what I figured."

On our way back to the base I thought about asking Hutchins how he'd go about extricating a couple of illegal passengers, but decided not to let all the cats out of the bag quite yet. The lieutenant drove me back to my car at the gate and I thanked him for his cooperation. Next stop, finding a place to stay for the night.

Thirty-Eight

1700 Hours – Monday – 15 DEC 41

Hotel Cabrillo – 615 S. Centre St., San Pedro

I went about the task of finding a place to stay in an organized manner—well, organized for me. Long Beach, to the east of the harbor is a resort town with several nice hotels right on the beach. I've stayed in a few of them and, as inviting as they are, it didn't seem right to stick the taxpayers with a tab for first class accommodations, especially since I needed three rooms for a couple of nights.

San Pedro, to the west of the harbor, will never be mistaken for a resort town, but it's a big step up from the oily marshes of Wilmington. For that matter, I can't remember ever seeing a hotel in Wilmington. So San Pedro it is.

I figured the most likely place to find a decent hotel would be in the downtown area, so I picked a main north-south street through the center of town—Centre Street, to be specific—and went in search of reasonable accommodations. Just south of Seventh Street I found what I was looking for, the Cabrillo Hotel.

The Cabrillo is a brick building, half a block long and three stories tall. It was built in three sections with partial light wells between them and a sturdy fire escape zigzagging right down the front. Guest parking was provided on Eighth Street behind the hotel. A two-story vertical sign at the corner of Centre and Eighth spelled out "Cabrillo Hotel," and below that "San Pedro's Finest." Who could resist a recommendation like that?

Inside, the 1920s hotel was beginning to look a little threadbare around the edges of its high-ceilinged, narrow lobby, but the registration desk and its silver bell for summoning bell boys were shined to a sparkling sheen. Best of all, single rooms with baths could be had for two bucks a night, payable in advance. I took one on the third floor and reserved two more for Tuesday and Wednesday nights.

By the time I got my bags up and I was settled into my room, my stomach was grumbling. It's always something when you're on the road. I knew, however, exactly where I wanted to go for dinner.

San Pedro is world famous for a dive called the Shanghai Red Café, and I've never been there. They specialize in Chow Mein and booze with a dance floor on the side. The fellow at the hotel's front desk informed me Shanghai Red's could be found at Fifth and Beacon, so off I went.

If there is a worse part of town, I can't imagine where it would be. Beacon street is right on the waterfront and the businesses— the ones that aren't boarded up—are either pawn shops, bars, or unidentified, and there in the midst of all that iniquity sits the famous Shanghai Red Café. I parked on the street hoping the Army's Dodge would still be there when I came out and walked into what turned out to be a great little joint.

The décor was . . . well, a little of everything, mostly treasures collected by the proprietor in the Orient. The most prominent thing in the room was a bar as long as the building was deep. Sticky plastic tablecloths were tacked to the tables and the menu was simple. A hand-lettered cardboard sign on the wall said:

<u>BILL O' FARE</u>
Chow Mein or Ask

I asked and was rewarded with a huge and delicious shrimp dish with spicy Chinese vegetables over rice. The vegetables were so spicy it took three bottles of Tsingtao beer to cool the heat, but I've never eaten more flavorful Chinese food. What's more, the tab added up to only two bucks, including the imported beer.

Back at the Cabrillo Hotel, I made my eight o'clock call to Major Downey. He answered on the second ring and I said, "Did you get my battleship, Downey?"

He snorted something that might have been a chuckle and said, "Sure, only you'll have to row it yourself."

"Well, hell."

"What I did get you is your Lieutenant Jackson and orders from the Admiral of the Coast Guard, or whatever they call him, for the detachment at Terminal Island to give you whatever you need whenever you need it, no questions asked. Jackson will meet you on the flight line at NAS San Pedro around noon tomorrow. You've got him as long as you need him. Will that get you by?"

"I think so. Thanks, Downey."

"Don't thank me. General Davis made it all happen. Oh, speaking of thanks, thank you for the occuscope photo with Peterson's message on the back. I put the original in our safe, and sent a photographic copy of the message to our decryption people with instructions to see if they can find out anything about the code or the message beyond your translation. I don't imagine they will, but I'm trying to cover all the bases here."

"Sounds like you're doing a good job of it, too."

"Thanks. What have you been up to?"

"I visited the Coast Guard on Terminal Island this afternoon and talked them into taking me to see the German ship. It's there all right, and the situation remains the same—the earliest possible departure date is Wednesday, but Thursday is more likely."

Downey was quiet for a moment, and then he said, "I sure hope Peterson is really on that ship. We've got an awful lot riding on a very slim lead."

"I'm betting he's there. In fact, I'd bet Peterson and his Nazi girlfriend are the real reason the Germans canceled the rest of the ship's itinerary."

"Yes, but what if that ship was sent to throw us off the trail?"

"The *Ammon* just doesn't add up to a red herring. For one thing, what the Germans are going through to have the ship there is too complicated and risky for it to be a fake. For another, there is no other logical reason for the ship to put into Los Angeles. They could just as easily have stayed outside US territorial waters and gone up to Seattle or Vancouver as originally scheduled. I'd also bet fuel wouldn't present a problem in a port they regularly visit."

"I know all that, Spicer. It's just that we jumped to this ship conclusion without looking for other possibilities. That might have been a mistake."

I saw what Downey was doing and I didn't like it one bit. He was covering his tail by questioning the only lead we had. Then he could say "I told you so" if Peterson wasn't aboard the *Ammon*.

That got me a little hot under the collar. "Major, I considered every conceivable route out of the US that would get those two to Germany, and all of them involved sneaking across an international border and a risky flight, train ride, or bus trip across three thousand miles of the US or Canada. That ship sitting in Los Angeles Harbor eliminates most of those risks. Furthermore, the minute the ship clears US waters, Peterson and Albrecht are standing on the equivalent of German soil. Nobody can touch them then without creating an international incident."

"Yes, but they could have gone to Mexico."

"And done what? Ridden a burro to Tampico and rented a rowboat to cross the Atlantic? Look, Downey, if I'm wrong, I'll gladly admit to General Davis I risked all the marbles going with the best lead I had. That'll get you off the hook and protect your precious gold oak leaves."

When he didn't say anything to that, I concluded the telephone call, saying, "If you need me tonight or tomorrow night, I'll be at the Hotel Cabrillo in San Pedro. The number is TErminal 4398 . . . TErminal 4398. Goodnight, Major."

Thirty-Nine

Naval Air Station San Pedro – Terminal Island

NAS San Pedro is located between some railroad tracks and a part of the harbor called San Pedro Bay along the southern shore of Terminal Island. As Navy airfields go, it's kind of puny with just two narrow paved runways and a protected lagoon for landing seaplanes. In keeping with the military tradition of making everything as confusing as possible, the base has one name and the airfield another, so I was standing on the Reeves Field flight line at Naval Air Station San Pedro, if that makes any sense.

Up until we found ourselves at war, NAS San Pedro served as a Naval Reserve flight training facility, but now plans were underway to use the base for other more urgently needed activities. Judging by the number of factory fresh aircraft from the nearby Lockheed and Douglas plants parked around the field I have a pretty good idea what those activities might be, but the plans are still classified, so I'll keep it to myself for now.

In addition to the runways and the seaplane lagoon, the base has two medium-sized hangers, an engine shop, an aircraft repair shop, and accommodations for a few dozen men. Again, there are indications the facility will be undergoing expansion in the near future.

I was a little surprised to see a few Army P-39s and P-40s parked in revetments around the field's perimeter. Unless the Navy brought them in just so I'd feel more at home, I have no idea what Army fighter planes were doing at a naval air station.

I arrived at NAS San Pedro under a high, thick coastal overcast early Tuesday morning. Wearing my spit and polish Army suit, I checked in with the base commandant and was given the run of the field because the commandant already had the word about who I was and that I was there to make the base safer for one of their blimps on its way from New Jersey. Well, that wasn't entirely true, but it wasn't entirely wrong, either.

Even though there was little activity because of the fog, I spent the next few hours observing the field. I wasn't observing anything in particular, just keeping my eyes open for anyone who seemed suspicious or anything that didn't look like it ought to be there. Of course, the Navy has its own security, but we were looking for different things.

Around eleven two armed MID enlisted men found me on the flight line and explained they were the new security detail to replace Sergeant Pierce when he arrived on the blimp from Lakehurst. They also handed me the Federal Arrest Warrants I asked Downey to obtain for me, along with a search warrant for the German steamship.

Shortly after the MID fellows arrived, a Navy staff car pulled up with Jack Jackson aboard. "Hi, Jack, or I guess I should say 'welcome aboard.'"

Jack smiled. "Yes, 'welcome aboard' would be more 'Navy,' but then I'd feel compelled to salute the ensign flag and ask permission to come aboard. How 'bout we just shake hands?"

"That does seem a lot less complicated."

Jack and I shook hands and I said, "I'm sorry to have your duty assignment switched on such short notice, but I need your kind of help, so I got some strings pulled."

"I guess you did! My orders came by teletype late yesterday afternoon directly from Washington, D.C. Your outfit carries some weight, even with the Coast Guard. Exactly what did you get me into?"

Checking to make sure I wasn't standing next to a drum of aviation gas, I lit a Lucky Strike. "Do you remember me asking you about a German ship belonging to the DDG Kosmos line yesterday?"

"Sure. I told you it was here in LA Harbor."

"You did, and your information was right on the money. I saw the ship yesterday afternoon, courtesy of the Terminal Island Coast Guard detachment."

"Oh, yeah? How come all the interest in this Kraut steamer? Or can you tell me?"

Flicking an ash from my cigarette, I said, "You have the necessary security clearance, and since you are now officially on assignment to MID, you have a need to know, so I can let you in on all the classified dope. Our in interest in the *Ammon* is due to my belief there's an American traitor on that ship carrying the prototype of a top secret Navy gizmo. He's accompanied by a Nazi spy, a woman named Hilda Albrecht."

With an infectious grin on his face that reminded me of Susan, Jack said, "And I'll bet that's what's behind the question you asked me at dinner the other night—the one about how to get from here to Berlin."

"Correct, and you nailed that one on the head when you said you would use a ship to leave the US. The only difference is this ship isn't going to Canada, it's headed straight for Hamburg with two passengers who aren't likely to be on the purser's list."

"Well, how about that? I got one right."

"That's why you're here."

Looking thoughtful, Jack said, "So how are we going to get these two nefarious stowaways off the *Ammon*?"

"That's another reason you're here. We need a plan for capturing them, and since you have a knowledge of maritime law and procedures, I figured you'd come in handy. We'll get to work on that as soon as the third member of our team arrives."

"Who's that?"

Field stripping the Lucky, I said, "Staff Sergeant Russ Pierce. He's MID and we've worked together before. I picked him because he's savvy, tough, and as conscientious as the day is long. He'll be arriving on one of the Navy's blimps very soon now."

"I figured there was a blimp in this story somewhere because of what you said the other night about coincidences."

Smiling, I said, "I figured you figured that."

"And we're gonna try to pull this operation off with just three guys?"

"Not exactly. I got a few more strings pulled with the Coast Guard. The entire detachment at the Terminal Island Coast Guard station is at our disposal."

Jack smiled again. "Geez, Johnny, you're one hell of a string puller!"

"It's not that I'm particularly important, Jack. It's because the guy we're after is so damned important. As much as it pains me to admit it, he was the MID's head man on the west coast—my former boss."

"Holy cow!"

"I'd put it a little more colorfully, but yeah, holy cow."

I was still explaining our assignment to Jack when a flatbed truck with a portable airship mooring mast mounted on the back rumbled past us heading for the northern perimeter of the field. That, in turn, got everybody looking up toward the eastern sky. There, gradually materializing out of the overcast like some enormous mythical flying beast, was the unmistakable shape of a blimp heading in our direction.

As it drew closer we could make out the control car gondola with an engine on each side. Soon we could hear the rasp of those engines and see the word "NAVY" in large black letters on the huge silver-gray gas bag.

At that moment a Navy Chevrolet pulled up behind us and the driver yelled, "You guys need a lift out to the blimp?"

Jack and I piled into the big sedan along with the two MID enlisted men and off we went around the perimeter of Reeves Field to its northern edge where the mooring mast truck was parked.

The blimp, now down to less than a hundred feet above the ground, slowly crossed over the railroad tracks. We could hear the airship's twin engines maneuvering her into position for mooring and we could make out the designation "ZNP-K-3" on the side of the gondola. From what Lieutenant Commander Nugent told us at my initial briefing on the airship assignment, I knew I was looking at the third K-type airship built by the Goodyear Company for the Navy.

While the blimp was jockeying into position, a sailor climbed the twelve-foot portable mooring mast and hooked a rope dangling from the blimp's underside. He made the line fast to the mast and the airship shut down its engines.

It was quite a spectacle for those who never saw a blimp dock before. Each step of the mooring process was carried out with deliberate care and by-the-book precision. The Navy clearly had blimp landing down to a science. Then it crossed my mind to wonder if Si Peterson watched the airship's arrival from aboard the *Ammon* moored only a mile or so away.

When the blimp's gondola was nearly touching the ground, a rope ladder dropped from the hatch on the starboard side. Then, one by one, the blimp's passengers scrambled down the ladder. They were all wearing Navy blue except for the last man out. He wore Army green.

Pierce gave me a snappy salute, demonstrating to the Navy that the Army knew how to do things right. He said, "Reporting for duty, Major Spicer."

Returning his salute, I said, "Welcome back to California, Sergeant. I want you to meet Lieutenant Jack Jackson. He's on temporary assignment to our operation. I'll tell you what's going on in a minute, but you should probably brief your replacement team over there first."

To Jack, I said, "You might want to tag along with Sergeant Pierce and get an introduction to the Navy's wonderful new gizmo, the occuscope."

Pierce set about showing Jack and the two-man MID replacement team around the blimp. They paid particular attention to an inverted dome on the underside of the control car. When Pierce finished his tour and instructions, he wished his MID replacements good luck, picked up his bag, and we climbed into the Navy's Chevrolet for a ride back to the Army's Dodge, which I left next to one of the hangers on the flight line.

In route to our next stop, I told Russ the whole sorry story about Si Peterson and the occuscope prototype. He was careful not to show it in front of Jack, but I could tell Russ shared my feelings about Peterson's defection. It put MID in a bad light when we were most needed.

Now that our little team was complete, however, we were going to erase that black mark from our record. Next step: figure out how to extricate one Army Colonel, one female Nazi spy, and one top secret Navy gizmo from a German passenger ship.

Forty

When I arrived at the Coast Guard's gate this time I was welcomed with open arms. After I told the security guard why I was there, he made a telephone call and we were sent directly to Dock Easy-Six, the same dock from which Lieutenant Elmer Hutchins and I headed out on my first visit to the *Ammon*. Hutchins was waiting for us aboard what looked like the same motor lifeboat.

Hutchins, looking surprised to see a fellow Coast Guard officer in our group, welcomed us aboard and we putted over to see the *Ammon*. Nothing had changed since I saw the ship yesterday, but I wanted Jack and Pierce to get the lay of the land— or water—from the channel.

On the way, I briefed Hutchins on the specifics of our mission, recovering the occuscope and two Nazi spies. After we stared at the German steamship for a few minutes, Hutchins said, "Have you fellows figured out how we're gonna do this?"

He seemed to be directing his question to Jack, which was natural, but Jack deferred to me. "Not yet. I wanted the rest of the team to see the layout before we figured out our strategy. I do have Federal Arrest Warrants for the two people we're after and a third John Doe warrant just in case. We also have a search warrant for the ship, although I don't know how much good all that paperwork is going to do when push comes to shove."

Hutchins said, "Maybe none, but it's best to do things by the book in situations like this."

"And does your book suggest the best way to serve those warrants without losing our suspects or setting off an international fracas?"

Shaking his head, he said, "I'm afraid it doesn't. I have no idea how I'd go about it if I were in your shoes. All I can tell you is we have orders to back your play, whatever it is. Assuming, that is, the operation is at least somewhat legal."

"It will be that, Lieutenant. I have no intention of losing our suspects on a technicality. I figure we've got one shot at this and we have to make it work."

Jack, who was listening to our conversation while he studied the ship through Hutchins' binoculars, said, "If I may make a suggestion, I think a straight forward approach with a strong show of force is our best bet."

I nodded and said, "What do you have in mind, Jack?"

"I'd position three armed motor patrol boats around the ship—one off the bow, one at the stern, and one mid-channel off her port side. Their job would be to make a show of force and prevent anyone from going over the side and escaping that way.

"Then I would position, say, twenty armed men on the dock along her starboard side to prevent anyone from making an escape in that direction. Finally, I would instruct the vessel's captain to come down on the dock for a powwow so we could tell him what we want and what we intend to do if he doesn't comply."

I said, "Sounds good so far, but exactly what is it we intend to do if the captain tells us to go pound sand?"

Hutchins added, "Yeah, I was wondering that, myself."

"We do the only thing we can do. We quarantine the ship and prevent her from refueling. That will keep the *Ammon* here after the Department of State deadline, which means we take everyone aboard into custody and impound the ship."

Hutchins groaned. "Do you have any idea what that entails, Lieutenant Jackson?"

"I do, but I don't think the Germans will let it come to that."

I asked, "And if they call our bluff?"

"In that case we have no choice. The thing we have to remember is there are at least a hundred places on a ship that size where two people can hide. It could take twenty men a couple of days or longer to do a thorough search. There isn't much difference between doing that and what would have to be done if the *Ammon* stayed past the State Department's deadline without our interference."

Jack paused a moment, and then threw the sixty-four-dollar question on the table. "Gentlemen, it all comes down to just how important this gizmo really is."

Everyone stared at me while I thought about that. Finally, I gave them the only answer I had. "According to the Navy, their gadget could save hundreds of lives and dozens of ships in the Atlantic alone, but if the Nazis get their hands on it and figure out how to defeat the thing, it's worthless. That makes it pretty damned important."

Then everyone stared at Hutchins. Looking resigned to a fate worse than death, he nodded and said, "Then I guess we pull out all the stops and go for broke, but I wish we could get an 'okay' for this scheme from the Department of State or somebody else with a whole lot more authority than we have because, if something goes wrong, our necks are on the chopping block."

Now everybody was staring at me again. Hutchins wanted to cover his butt and I couldn't really blame him. I sighed and said, "Get me to a telephone and I'll see what I can do."

It was a little before two o'clock, or almost five o'clock east coast time, when I picked up the telephone in Hutchins' office and asked the base operator for a number in Washington, D.C. When the call was answered a woman said, "United States Army, Military Intelligence Division. Please state your business."

I said exactly what I was taught to say in such situations. "This is Major Jonathon Spicer, MID ID three-three-eight-seven-two-one. I'm requesting a priority Able call to General Davis."

It took her a minute to match my name to her master list of ID numbers and then to verify I have the authority to make a priority Able request. I do and she said, "It will take a few minutes to make your connection, Major Spicer. Please hold on the line."

That response told me Davis was someplace other than his office. They, of course, knew exactly where he was and would connect me to that location through their switchboard. The wires hummed and I waited.

I recognized Davis' voice the minute I heard it. "This better really be priority Able, Major, because you're making me late for a dinner engagement." He laughed, and then added, "What's going on, Johnny, and how can I help?"

It took a couple of minutes for me to explain the situation and what I needed. He listened without interruption until I finished. One thing I always admired about Davis is he never leaves his people hanging. He makes decisions quickly and stands by them.

The general said, "Ask your Coast Guard Lieutenant if a verbal authorization from Cordell Hull would satisfy him."

I glanced at Hutchins and said into the telephone, "I'm sure it would, General."

"Go ahead and ask him, Johnny. I don't want to waste Hull's time if it's going to take FDR to make the Coast Guard happy."

"Yes, sir."

Holding the phone aside, I turned to Lieutenant Hutchins and said, "My boss, Major General Chester Davis, wants to know if authorization for this operation from Secretary of State Cordell Hull will satisfy you, or if you need it directly from the President."

Hutchins suddenly looked like he just stepped knee-deep in cow manure. He quickly said, "No, no. A directive from Secretary Hull would be more than satisfactory."

Putting the phone back to my ear, I said, "General, he thinks Hull will do."

Davis laughed again. "He damned well better think so. Okay, I think I know where Hull is at the moment. Give me your number there and about 30 minutes. I'll ask him to call you directly. That fast enough for you?"

It was my turn to laugh. "Well, sir, yesterday would be better, but I think we can make thirty minutes work. Thank you, General Davis."

"You're welcome, and listen, Johnny, I know we owe you a lot for taking the crappy end of the stick on this one. When it's all over I'm going to fly out there and buy you a thick steak at that place on Hollywood Boulevard where we used to go back in the good old days, if it's still there."

"Musso and Frank is still there, and I'll hold you to that steak, sir." I gave him Lieutenant Hutchins' number and hung up.

Turning to Hutchins again, I said, "Expect a call on that line in thirty minutes from Cordell Hull."

Hutchins now looked almost stupefied. We were obviously playing in a league well beyond his rank. Jack had a whimsical grin on his kisser. He already knew how we played the string-pulling game. Pierce just stood a little taller, like he was proud of his outfit.

Frowning, Hutchins said, "Okay, but there's one thing still bothering me about all this."

Allowing a hint of impatience into my tone, I said, "What's that, Lieutenant?"

"What if the people you want aren't aboard the *Ammon*? What if they're somewhere else entirely, or waiting to board her at the last minute before she sails?"

I nodded. "That's a fair question. The answer is we have reliable intelligence that says they plan to leave the country via the Ammon, and the safest place for them to wait for the ship's departure is aboard her. Since the *Ammon* is relatively protected by international law, hiding anywhere else puts them at greater risk of being discovered.

"If they aren't there, well, the Germans should be more than willing to prove it to us and we'll end up with a little egg on our faces. Under the circumstances, that's a chance we have to take."

Looking like he was stuck between the same rock and hard place as the rest of us, Hutchins said, "All right, Major Spicer, I see your point." After a pause, he added, "Anybody want a sandwich or coffee while we wait?"

Pierce, Jack and I all agreed we could use a cup of Joe. Hutchins buzzed his secretary and she showed up a few minutes later carrying a tray of white ceramic mugs with blue anchor designs on them and a pot of coffee.

At precisely two-forty-five, the telephone on Hutchins' desk jangled making us all jump a little. He picked it up. "Lieutenant Hutchins speaking."

After a moment, he said, "Yes, I'll hold the line."

A few more seconds passed and he said, "Yes, sir, this is Lieutenant Hutchins."

The male voice on the other end of the line was loud enough for the rest of us in the room to hear, but not quite clear enough to make out the words. It was obvious from the range of expressions on his face as he listened, Hutchins could make the words out just fine.

He listened for quite a while, and then said, "Yes, sir. I understand, sir, and we will proceed accordingly. Thank you, Secretary Hull."

We all heard the click that came over the line before Hutchins replaced the receiver on its cradle and said, "That was Secretary of State Cordell Hull. He has specifically instructed us to do whatever is necessary up to and including sinking the Ammon in order to capture the spies and recover the Navy's device. In his words, 'We're already at war with the damned Germans, how much worse can it get?' He also said we would receive approval in writing by telegram later tonight."

Glad the waiting was over, I stood up and said, "All right, gentlemen, let's get moving. Jack, this is your plan, so work with Lieutenant Hutchins and Sergeant Pierce arranging for the necessary men and equipment. We'll launch the operation at ten-hundred-hours tomorrow."

When preparations were complete, Jack, Pierce and I moved our gear from the Hotel Cabrillo to a large wooden dormitory sort of place within the Coast Guard facility called the Temporary Personnel Quarters or TPQ. Because space on the base was limited, the Coast Guard simply combined a Visiting Officers Quarters and the visiting enlisted men's barracks into one building. Officers got the second floor and enlisted men got the first.

Forty-One

Terminal Island Coast Guard Base – Los Angeles Harbor

Wednesday morning dawned under another heavy marine layer, or fog, as we natives call it. Tiny droplets of mist swirled in the beams of our headlights and ran down the Dodge's windshield in thin rivulets as we drove through the Terminal Island Coast Guard facility.

At dock Easy-Six the vail of fog added an ethereal quality to a scene that looked for all the world like the staging area for a major amphibious assault. A convoy of vehicles parked along the road next to the dock was headed up by a gray staff sedan followed by a little General Purpose vehicle, also gray. The Jeep was followed by three tarpaulin-covered deuce-and-a-half trucks designed for carrying personnel and equipment.

The personnel those trucks were here to carry, a ghostly army of about two dozen Coast Guardsmen in full combat regalia, milled around the convoy in the fog. Each man carried either an M1 Garand rifle or a Thompson submachine gun. If nothing else, our mission was providing the Coast Guard with a swell training exercise.

In the water, three gray eighty-foot patrol boats bobbed up and down, nudging their bows gently against the dock like giant dolphins. Each boat mounted a fifty-caliber water-cooled machine gun on its foredeck—more than enough firepower against an unarmed passenger ship. Besides, the patrol boats were there as much for effect as any other purpose.

I stood on the dock with Jack, Sergeant Pierce, and Lieutenant Hutchins while a guy with a heavy field radio strapped to his back discussed radio call signs with Hutchins. The command team, meaning Jack, Hutchins and I, would be Charlie-George-One, the patrol boats were Charlie-George-Two through Charlie-George-Four. Sergeant Pierce, whose job was leading the troops on the dock got the designation Charlie-George-Five.

To be honest, I felt a little silly going through all the military combat rigmarole. I wasn't here to play soldier, I was here to catch a jerk who betrayed his country and stole a valuable piece of equipment on my watch. Si Peterson was going to pay dearly for that.

Finally, around nine-forty-five, we were ready to get under way. I climbed onto the front seat alongside the driver of the staff sedan, while Jack and Hutchins got in the back. The radioman rode in the Jeep with a medic, although I have no idea why he was there—maybe to apply a bandage in case someone tripped and skinned a knee. Russ Pierce rode up front in the first truck.

We halted our convoy behind a warehouse just before we got to the dock where the *Ammon* was moored and sat silently in the fog waiting for the patrol boats to arrive. When Charlie-George-Two reported all boats into position, we led our little convoy out onto the dock and Sergeant Pierce dispersed his men along the length of the *Ammon*. I stood with Jack and Hutchings at the foot of the gangplank. While all that was happening, I saw passengers and members of the ship's crew lining the rails to see what was going on.

When all was ready, Jack picked up a megaphone and glanced at a piece of paper on which Hutchins had written the name of the *Ammon's* captain. Then in a loud clear voice Jack said, "Ahoy aboard the *Ammon*. This is the United States Coast Guard. We request a meeting with Captain Brandt on the dock. Captain Brandt, please come ashore."

Jack's purpose for requesting a meeting with the captain on the dock was to give us an opportunity for stating our business and serving our warrants before boarding the ship. A technicality, but we were going by the book.

When two minutes passed by my wristwatch with no response or any indication a response was forthcoming, I said, "Try it again, Jack, a little more forcefully."

Jack nodded and raised the megaphone to his mouth again. "Ahoy aboard the *Ammon*. This is the United States Coast Guard. We are here to meet with Captain Brandt. Captain Brandt, you are ordered to come ashore immediately."

A minute later a young ship's officer appeared at the top of the gangplank. He shouted, "I am First Mate Walter Hoffmann. What is the subject you are wishing to discuss with Captain Brandt?"

Jack looked at me and said, "This has all the earmarks of a stall."

"I'd say so, but what are they hoping to gain by putting off the inevitable? Tell him we'll only talk with the Captain."

"*Ammon*, the subject is confidential. We will discuss it only with your captain. Send him down here now."

The first officer shouted back, "One minute, bitte," and disappeared inside the ship.

When I looked at my watch again, nearly fifteen minutes had elapsed since we initially arrived on the dock. The Germans' stall techniques were working quite well, but I still couldn't figure out what they hoped to gain . . . That was when I noticed wisps of smoke rising into the overcast from the ship's stack. Turning to the bridge, I saw an older officer I suspected might be the captain moving out into the mist on the starboard bridge wing. He was looking aft. Now I knew what the Germans hoped to gain by stalling us.

I opened my mouth to give warning, but Hutchins' radioman beat me to the punch. "Sir, Charlie-George-Four reports the ship's port screw has begun turning."

I said to Jack, "Tell them if they attempt to leave the dock we will be forced to fire on them."

Sounding near panic, Hutchins said, "We can't do that with innocent passengers on board!"

I said, "I know that, but maybe the Germans don't."

Jack spoke through the megaphone yet again, "*Ammon*, do not attempt to leave your mooring or we will be forced to fire on you."

Even at a distance of fifty or so feet I could hear a collective "ohh" from the passengers closest to us along the railing. The first mate appeared again and promptly called our bluff. "Herr Coast Guard, I doubt very much that you have the authorization to fire on an unarmed passenger vessel, but if that is what you must do, by all means, proceed."

The *Ammon* was moored with two lines forward and two lines aft. I glanced toward the bow just in time to see first one, and then the second mooring line fall away from the ship.

Jack said, "They're cutting the hawsers!"

The radioman announced, "Charlie-George-Four reports the starboard screw is now turning and requests their orders if the *Ammon* begins moving."

To Hutchins, I said, "If they intend to leave, how will they do it?"

Hutchins pointed aft of the ship and said, "They'll back out to the main channel where they have room to swing the bow around and proceed seaward."

"Any chance we can block them in and keep them here?"

Hutchins shook his head. "Not with the boats we have available. The *Ammon* might be damaged slightly, but it would plow right over our patrol boats."

To the radioman I said, "Tell Charlie-George-Four to get the hell out of the way if that tub moves."

Jack shouted, "There go the aft hawsers. They're free of the dock."

From his spot on deck next to the gangplank, which was groaning and beginning to sag from its mounting on the ship, the First Mate shouted, "Auf Wiedersehen, Herr Coast Guard," and disappeared into the ship again.

With that, the gangplank tore loose and clattered against the dock as the *Ammon* began backing slowly away from its mooring. I saw Charlie-George-Four scoot away through the mist to get out of the ship's path.

I think it was Robert Burns who said, "The best laid plans of mice and men often go awry." That summed up the situation in a nutshell.

I can't honestly say I anticipated this turn of events, but it did occur to me that the German steamship was probably not completely out of fuel when it put into Los Angeles Harbor. Presumably, they had sufficient fuel left to make Vancouver, British Columbia as per their original itinerary.

I said to Hutchins, "Have Charlie-George-Four follow the *Ammon* and monitor the Coast Guard's maritime emergency frequency. Tell them to listen for their mission call sign."

"Yes, but..."

"We don't have time to discuss the situation right now. I'm commandeering your staff car, Lieutenant. I'll leave it at Easy-Six. Thanks for your help."

To Jack, I said, "Come on!"

As we ran pell-mell down the dock, I pointed toward Hutchins' staff car and shouted to Pierce. "Come on, Russ."

Out of the corner of my eye, I saw the sergeant hand his M1 and helmet to the man next to him and take off in the same direction we were headed. We all piled into the staff sedan and I yelled to the driver, "Back to Easy-Six as fast as you can get there!"

I heard Russ slam the right rear passenger door just as the

sedan squealed its rear tires and tore off toward the Coast Guard base. From the backseat Jack said, "Johnny, I'm sorry. It never occurred to me the Germans would just up and leave. I'm afraid my brilliant by-the-book plan ruined our only chance to complete your mission."

"Not yet, it hasn't. I still have one card left to play."

Forty-Two

Naval Air Station San Pedro – Terminal Island

After we squeezed ourselves into the Army's Dodge business coupe at Dock Easy-Six, I pointed us in the direction of NAS San Pedro. When we arrived at Reeves Field a few minutes later, the first thing I looked for was the blimp. Even in the fog it wasn't hard to spot. ZNP-K-3 was right where I saw her last, stuck to the portable mooring mast on the north side of the field. Finding it there was the first break I needed. Now for the second.

We found the blimp's captain in the operations shack getting a weather report. He recognized Sergeant Pierce and, after they greeted each other, Pierce introduced us.

"Lieutenant Commander Gordon, I'd like you to meet Major Spicer. He's my boss at MID and he'd like a word with you if it's convenient."

Gordon, a hefty fellow with a regulation Navy beard that gave him a nautical look, shook the hand I offered and said, "Nice to meet you, Spicer. How can I help?"

I wasted no time in getting to the point. "I'm afraid we've got an emergency on our hands. Two Nazi spies made off with a prototype version of the occuscope. They're on a German passenger ship that entered LA Harbor a few days ago. Now that ship has left the harbor and is headed out to sea. We need to find it and see what we can do about recovering the occuscope."

I pulled a copy of the telegram from Cordell Hull out of my uniform jacket pocket and handed it to Gordon. "We have Department of State authorization to do whatever is necessary to capture the spies and recover the gizmo. Any chance you can help us out?"

Gordon's eyebrows went up a notch when he saw who signed the telegram. "Maybe I can." Glancing out the operations shack window, he said, "We had a familiarization flight scheduled for this morning, but there's no sense to taking passengers up if they can't see anything. Yes, I think we can help you out."

"You can fly in this pea soup?"

Gordon gave me a small smile. "Sure we can, Spicer. This overcast is dense, but relatively narrow vertically. You can already see some patches of blue off to the east. Now, do you know where this German ship is headed so we'll have an idea where to look for her?"

"Better than that. She's being shadowed by a Coast Guard motor patrol boat. They're monitoring the Coast Guard maritime emergency frequency waiting to hear from us."

"Okay then, how soon will you be ready to go?"

"We're ready right now."

Nodding, he said, "Right. I'll round up my crew and meet you at the airship in about ten minutes, but we can only take two of you because space is limited."

"Thanks, Gordon. You just made my day. Pierce, I'm afraid you'll have to be the odd man out for this trip."

"That's okay, sir. I've had all the blimp flying I need for a while."

Twenty minutes later we were riding in the sunshine above the fog on a southerly course and the blimp's radio operator was calling Charlie-George-Four while Gordon, Jack, and I studied a chart of the California coast at a small built-in navigation table on the blimp's bridge.

Jack was explaining the German ship's fuel situation. "Before we discovered the real reason the *Ammon* put into LA Harbor, the State Department authorized her to refuel in the harbor and return to Hamburg. We prevented the refueling, but she cut the hawsers and ran for it anyway. We figure she still has enough fuel aboard to reach her original destination, which was Vancouver, British Columbia, but it's a pretty safe bet she's heading in the opposite direction."

"Vancouver? Let's see." Gordon pivoted a set of dividers up the chart from LA Harbor, and then said, "That's roughly fifteen hundred miles. Assuming she's now heading south toward the Panama Canal, which is about four thousand miles, she'll have to make a fuel stop before they get there. If you're right about the fuel they have left, it looks like the *Ammon* can make it to one of the bigger ports on Mexico's west coast, maybe Mazatlán or Puerto

Vallarta."

Jack said, "That looks about right, and I doubt the Germans will have much trouble putting into a Mexican port for fuel since our good neighbors to the south aren't at war with them."

Gordon agreed and added, "They will be, though. As soon as a Jap or Nazi ship interferes with Mexico's trade, they'll get righteous in a big hurry and declare war against the evil Axis powers. Of course, their contribution to the war effort won't involve anything dangerous like actually shooting at the enemy."

The radio operator came onto the bridge and handed Gordon a note. Our skipper looked at the slip of paper and said, "We established radio contact with the Coast Guard motor patrol boat behind the German ship. So far it looks like our guesswork is pretty fair. Once she left the harbor, the *Ammon* set a course of 180 degrees, due south. At the time of this report, twelve-oh-five-hours, the *Ammon* was off Huntington Beach, still on the same course, and making 12 knots." Gordon tapped his dividers on the chart and added, "Right about here."

Jack ran his finger down the chart from the point Gordon indicated. "It looks like they're aiming to get south of Catalina and San Clemente Island, which will take them beyond the three-mile limit of our territorial waters. Then they can turn southeast and follow the Mexican coast line."

I asked, "How long will it take us to catch her?"

"No more than thirty minutes. The K-3 isn't the fastest ship in the air, but she's got more than forty knots on that old German steamship." Pointing to a spot on his chart, he added, "We should be over her about here, off Newport. Then we'll put our fancy gadget to the test and see if we can find the *Ammon*. When we pick her up, we can figure out our next step."

Unless the overcast broke up a lot faster than it had so far, the occuscope would come in handy. While we could see some patches of ground to the east, the view straight ahead was fog and more fog. I just hoped Frank Demas' miracle gizmo actually worked.

Around twelve-thirty-hours, Gordon ordered his radio operator to get another position check from Charlie-George-Four. Five minutes later Gordon had the new position and we all gathered around the navigation table again. He did some measuring and other stuff I didn't comprehend, and then said, "Right on the money! The *Ammon* is directly off Newport."

To the helmsman at the front of the bridge, Gordon said, "Helm maintain your current heading, slow to 12 knots, and descend to the top of the cloud deck, but no lower."

As we felt the airship slow and descend, Gordon turned to an ensign at a forward-facing podium near the rear bulkhead of the bridge and said, "Ensign Keller, work your magic and find us a Kraut steamship down there. The cloud deck looks to be about two hundred feet thick. The German ship is being shadowed by a Coast Guard patrol boat. That might make it easier to identify."

Ensign Keller replied, "Yes, sir," and began fooling with switches and knobs on his control panel. A few seconds later the podium sprouted what looked like an inverted submarine periscope—a vertical tube about six inches in diameter with viewing lenses and a pair of folding handles at the top. A moment after that we heard the whine of an electric motor.

Gordon explained. "That sound is the motor that raises and lowers the occuscope cable. Ensign Keller is lowering the business end of the thing a little more than two hundred feet so it hangs just below the overcast."

After that the bridge got quiet and we waited. We didn't have long to wait because Ensign Keller is very good at his job. At 1245 hours the ensign said, "Sir, I have two targets. The first is about nine hundred yards astern and looks like a Coast Guard patrol boat. The second target is eight hundred yards off our port bow. It appears to be passenger ship, but I can't make out the name at this distance. She has a dark hull, a single dark stack with two stripes, and she's flying a German flag. Both vessels are on the same course and we are paralleling that course about a hundred yards to the west."

Feeling hopeful, I said, "That description matches the *Ammon.*"

Gordon said, "Excellent work, Ensign Keller. Helm increase our speed to 20 knots until our occuscope wizard tells us we've closed within about two-hundred yards of the German ship."

The catch-up maneuver only took a few minutes, and when we were slowed down to match the *Ammon's* speed again, Gordon said, "Ensign Keller, let Lieutenant Jackson and Major Spicer take a quick look through your gizmo so they can see what all the fuss is about."

I let Jack look first, and then I peeked through the viewing lenses. It was impressive to say the least. What I saw was something like a black and white telescope view of the *Ammon* cruising along in a calm sea. While the focus seemed a little fuzzy and an occasional line of static moved from the top to the bottom of the view, the electronic image was more than clear enough for its intended purpose. Maybe Frank Demas' gadget really could help us win the war.

Ensign Keller returned to his post and proceeded to press buttons and turn dials. Suddenly and with tension in his voice, Keller announced, "Skipper, I just found a submerged target with the MAD. It's paralleling the *Ammon's* course approximately two hundred yards off her starboard bow."

Lieutenant Commander Gordon turned to me with a grim expression. "Major Spicer, I'm afraid an unexpected guest has crashed your party."

Forty-Three

US Territorial Waters – 23 Miles Due South of LA Harbor

Lieutenant Commander Gordon shouted, "Sparks, get a hold of Naval Coastal Operations and find out if they have any friendly submarines in this area. Keller, can you estimate a depth for that third target?"

"It's only a rough estimate, sir, but it's near the surface, less than one hundred feet."

I kept my mouth shut waiting for the Navy to tell us if the occuscope's magnetic anomaly detector was picking up a friendly sub, but an inner sense told me there was nothing friendly about the damned thing. That was confirmed about ten minutes later when the radio operator stuck his head into the bridge compartment and said, "Sir, NavCoastOps reports no friendly subs in the area."

Gordon turned to me and said, "Well, Spicer, we've got some decisions to make."

"It looks that way. I'm guessing the sub is here to pick up the Nazi spies and/or the occuscope prototype."

Nodding, Gordon said, "That's one possibility. It would be a lot less risky to have them aboard the sub than on the *Ammon*. On the other hand, the U-boat might just be providing escort."

I said, "Let's go with the first possibility for now. My question is when would they make the transfer?"

Gordon gave that a moment of thought. "If it were me, I'd wait until the *Ammon* is out of US territorial waters, and make the transfer after dark. That sub is taking a hell of a risk just being here. If we spot a Kraut sub in US waters, which we have just done, our orders are simple: sink the bastards."

Jack joined the conversation, saying, "There's another consideration here. We need to do something about our patrol boat. I doubt very much they're equipped with any sort of underwater detection gear, so they don't know about that sub. If we don't need them any longer, I suggest we get them out of here as soon as we can."

Gordon looked at me. "He makes a good point, Spicer. If things get hot out here, we don't want those guys to stumble into the middle of it."

Looking at the chart, I said, "On the other hand, having the patrol boat suddenly break off for no apparent reason might raise some suspicions. In another hour or so we'll be getting close to Catalina. How 'bout we tell the patrol boat to break off then, like they need fuel? That might appear less suspicious."

Gordon nodded. "Makes sense. Sound okay to you, Jackson?"

"Yes sir, but let's keep a close eye on that submarine. If she starts to fall back or makes any course changes, we need to get those guys out of there. I don't want a crew that thinks it's stalking a pussy cat to suddenly come face to face with a tiger."

Gordon agreed that was reasonable and ordered Keller to report any changes in the sub's course immediately. Then he said, "Now we're back to the big question. How do we go about picking up your spies and the occuscope?"

I said, "When I was first briefed on blimps we were told these airships carry a fifty caliber machine gun and four 350 pound depth charges. Is that what we have to work with?"

Our skipper nodded. "That's what we've got, and we have two basic options for using them. We can take action while the sub is still in US territorial waters or wait until they make the transfer. If that's what they plan to do, the transfer will probably take place after dark and in Mexican waters."

I said, "Sinking the sub after they transfer the people and occuscope has the benefit of killing several birds with one stone, but we have no authority to sink submarines or anything else in Mexican waters, so we could end up in the soup there. Sinking the sub now reduces the risk of international controversy and eliminates the likelihood of losing both ships in the dark, allowing the spies and the occuscope to slip completely out of our hands."

Gordon was standing at the navigation table looking at his chart again. He said, "That pretty well covers it, Spicer, but I'd like to suggest we wait a little longer before deciding on a plan of attack. If the *Ammon* and the sub don't change course to the southeast before long, they'll end up making a long passage through international waters before they get to Mexican waters. What they do could change our options."

"Fair enough."

The next hour passed slowly because there was nothing to do but stare at miles of nothing. Then, suddenly, there was something else to stare at. It wasn't much, but off our starboard bow the tip of a mountain was poking its peak up out of the overcast.

Jack saw it, too. "That looks like Mount Orizaba on Santa Catalina Island. It's around twenty-one-hundred feet."

Lieutenant Commander Gordon consulted his chart. "Pretty close, Jackson. The chart says two-thousand-ninety-seven."

I looked up at the big white-faced clock with large black numerals above the helm. Its hands pointed to 1340 hours. "Looks like it's time to send the Coast Guard home."

Gordon glanced out the window at the tip of Mount Orizaba again and hollered, "Sparks, call the Coast Guard patrol boat and tell them to return to their base with our gratitude for a job well done."

A moment later our radio operator reported the instructions sent and acknowledged. About fifteen minutes after that Keller got into the act. "Skipper, the patrol boat turned around as ordered, but something else is going on. The *Ammon* and the submarine are making a course change to the east. I'll have their new heading in a few minutes when they resume a straight course."

Gordon was at his navigation table again, impatiently tapping the dividers on the chart. When Keller announced a new heading of 140 degrees, Gordon gave the course change to the helmsman, and then bent close to his chart. "They just cooked their own goose."

Jack and I looked over his shoulder while Gordon explained. "It's difficult to see without territorial water boundaries shown on the chart, but the lines are essentially laid out in overlapping circles with radii of three miles around each of the Channel Islands. If the *Ammon* held her course, they would have remained in US territorial waters until they were south of San Clemente Island, by which time it would be dark, or nearly dark. By altering course toward the Mexican coast now, they will leave US territorial waters at about fifteen-hundred-hours."

I said, "I wonder what made them decide to make the course change now."

Gordon said, "I think they saw the patrol boat leave and decided to save some time and fuel by taking a short cut."

"So how does that give us an advantage?"

Gordon smiled. "Try this idea on for size. We call the patrol boat back and have them shadow the *Ammon* again, but at a greater distance—maybe two miles astern and a mile to the east—so she'll be less visible. They'll be able to see the Germans, but the Germans aren't likely to spot a vessel that small in this fog. Then, when our targets are well into international waters, the patrol boat makes a high speed dash for the steamer and takes up a firing position off the *Ammon's* port side. That position protects the patrol boat from a torpedo attack by the sub.

"The patrol boat then fires on the *Ammon*, taking care to miss hitting anything critical. Hopefully, that will make the Germans think we were just waiting for them to get into international waters before sinking the passenger ship, and since they don't know we're up here, the sub might surface for the transfer to take the heat off the *Ammon*.

"The minute the sub surfaces, the patrol boat runs away as if the sub surprised them. Once the sub is on the surface and with the patrol boat out of the immediate picture it's most likely they will go ahead and make the transfer to get their people and the occuscope to a safer place in case the patrol boat comes back or sends someone bigger after them.

"At that position they will be in fairly shallow water, so the sub can't dive very deep, leaving her more vulnerable to our depth charges. We might even be able to get some licks in with our fifty cal. before she submerges."

I said, "Got it. We sink the sub and let the *Ammon* go on her way so we don't look like the bad guys for sinking a passenger ship."

Gordon smiled. "That's it."

Jack said, "But won't the sub pick up the patrol boat on her sonar?"

"The sub is sure to be using passive sonar to prevent anyone from knowing she's there. Given that, and her position relative to the German ship, all she's hearing is the *Ammon*. She won't hear the patrol boat until they close in on their high speed run. At that point we want the sub to hear her."

I shook my head. "That plan depends on a hell of a lot of 'ifs.'"

"It does, but what are we out if it doesn't work? If the Krauts don't play along, we're right back where we are now."

Looking at Jack, I asked, "What do you think? We would be

putting the Coast Guard's patrol boat back in the line of fire so to speak."

Jack replied, "Yes, but this is different. They'd know what they were up against. That patrol boat has the advantage of being the fastest, most maneuverable vessel out there and the crew will make a good fight of it."

I nodded. "All right, if the Coast Guard and the Navy agree, far be it for a landlubber like me to argue. Let's get this show underway."

Forty-Four

International Waters – 29 Miles SE of Santa Catalina Island

Once we were over international waters the K-3's bridge got very busy. That was my cue to find a corner and stay the hell out of the way so the pros could do their stuff.

The Coast Guard patrol boat was ready to make their high speed run on the *Ammon* and we were moving to a position about two hundred yards behind and to the west of the submarine, giving the K-3 an ideal angle of attack. According to Jack, the blimp's M2 .50 caliber machine gun has an effective range of about two thousand yards, so we would be attacking the sub at nearly pointblank range.

Ensign Keller had remote firing capability through the occuscope, allowing us to accurately shoot at the sub without showing ourselves. He could also aim and drop depth charges with the scope. If we figured everything right, the German submarine, along with Si Peterson and Hilda Albrecht were dead ducks.

Gordon and Jack went over the set-up one last time to be sure all the eventualities we could think of were covered, and then Gordon said, "Ensign Keller, are we ready to go?"

"Yes, sir. I'll have the sub targeted for the gun and depth charges as soon as she surfaces."

Lieutenant Commander Gordon glanced over at me in my corner, asking an unspoken question. I gave him a nod and a thumbs up. He nodded back, and looking aft, he yelled, "Sparks, send the Coast Guard their go signal."

One minute later the radio man yelled back, "Signal sent and acknowledged, sir."

It was going to take several minutes for the patrol boat to move in and begin their mock attack on the Ammon. All eyes were on the clock over the helm as we waited.

[1634 HRS]
Sparks: "Coast guard signals they are in position."
Gordon: "Sparks, signal Coast Guard to fire at will. Ensign Keller, keep your eye on that sub. If she changes course or starts to surface, sing out."

Despite being some distance away and filtered through the fog, the next sound we heard was clearly recognizable as the chatter of a large caliber machine gun. The patrol boat fired three short bursts.

[1638 HRS]
Keller: "Sub turning toward *Ammon*, sir."
Gordon: "Keep your reports coming, Ensign."

[1642 HRS]
Keller: "Sub is surfacing and continuing toward the *Ammon*."
Gordon: "Sparks, order the Coast Guard out of the area."
I saw Gordon look at Jack and make fingers crossed gestures with both hands. We heard two more short bursts from the patrol boat's .50 cal.
Sparks: "Message sent and acknowledged, sir."

[1647 HRS]
Keller: "The patrol boat turned about and is heading east at flank speed. "The *Ammon* is lowering a boarding ladder amidships on her starboard side. I have the sub in the crosshairs of our fifty. Targeting the sub's stern section about where her engines should be."

[1650 HRS]
Keller: "Sub is turning to starboard." After a moment, he added, "It looks like she's backing her stern against the *Ammon's* hull below the boarding ladder."
Gordon: "Hold your fire, Ensign."

[1654 HRS]
Gordon: "Any sign of passengers transferring to the sub?"
Keller: "Not yet . . . yes! Two passengers starting down the boarding ladder—one woman and one man."

Gordon: "Either of them carrying anything?"

Keller: "The man has something like a canvas bag on a strap over his shoulder."

Gordon looked at me and nodded. I nodded back. If the occuscope prototype was in that bag, we were in business.

[1658 HRS]

Keller: "The woman is aboard the sub. Crewmen are taking her through a hatch in the afterdeck, sir."

Gordon: "The minute that sub moves far enough away from the *Ammon* that you can fire our fifty without hitting the passenger ship, open fire."

[1704 HRS]

Keller: "The man is aboard now and the sub is moving away, but she can't dive until that aft hatch is sealed."

The roar from K-3's fifty cal. was almost deafening due to it being directly over our heads at the front of the control gondola's upper deck. We heard one short burst followed by a long burst."

Keller: "We have hits in the rear deck and at the water line."

Gordon: "Keep after her as long as she's on the surface."

The fifty over our heads roared another long burst.

[1706 HRS]

Keller: "They're having trouble getting the aft deck hatch closed. Target is still on the surface."

There were two more short bursts from the fifty.

Gordon: "Sparks, order the Coast Guard patrol boat back in. Tell them to harass the *Ammon* so she won't stick around to pick up survivors."

[1709 HRS]

Keller: "The sub's rear deck hatch is closed now, and she is riding lower in the water. I can't tell if the target is submerging on her own or taking on water through the shell holes in her hull, sir."

Sparks: "Message sent and acknowledged, sir."

[1712 HRS]

Gordon: "Drop a depth charge right alongside her, Keller. Set it for a contact detonation."

Keller: "Changing settings. Helm, turn to two-two-five degrees and make your speed five knots."

[1718 HRS]
We felt the blimp swing sharply to starboard. A moment later one hell of a concussion jolted the bridge.

Keller: "Bull's eye! The depth charge ripped a ten foot hole in the starboard side of her hull. She's going down like a rock."

Gordon: "Hit her again!"

Keller: "Helm, dead stop."

Ensign Keller's eyes were glued to the occuscope as he pressed a button at the end of a cord from his console. At the same time we heard the patrol boat's fifty chatter again. I envied Keller his view. Just hearing the action wasn't nearly as satisfying as seeing it.

[1724 HRS]
Another burst from the patrol boat's machine gun was punctuated by the detonation of the second depth charge.

Keller: "Another direct hit. The second depth charge detonated just below the surface aft of the conning tower. Most of the target's rear deck is gone."

Gordon: "Good work, Ensign. What's the *Ammon* doing?"

Keller: "The *Ammon* appears to be under full steam, still on a course of one-four-zero, sir."

[1728 HRS]
Gordon: "Ensign Keller, let our guests take a quick look through the scope."

Again, Jack looked first and I took the second look. When I got to the scope all I could see was a lot of debris floating on the surface below us and a few men clinging to two rubber lifeboats.

Jack asked me, "You want our patrol boat to pick up the survivors?"

"Yes, and tell them to make sure all of the men they pick up are members of the sub's crew. If either the woman or the man who got aboard from the *Ammon* survived the sinking, tell the patrol boat crew to secure them and let us know."

Ensign Keller overheard my instructions to Jack and said, "I'm pretty sure the *Ammon's* passengers went down with the sub. There was no time for them to get forward, and the aft end of the sub was totally destroyed."

"Then you are to be commended, Ensign. You just helped save a lot of lives."

"Thank you, sir." He tapped the occuscope's upside-down periscope with his finger and added, "This gadget made it almost easy. I could see the men on deck looking around and trying to figure out who was doing all the shooting. The sub crew never knew what hit them."

Jack was busy writing a message for the patrol boat. When he finished it, Jack handed it to Gordon, who sent it back to the radio operator.

I said, "Jack, do you suppose the Coast Guard detachment at Terminal Island has divers available who can go down to the sub wreckage?"

"If they don't, they'll know where to find some. You want them to check the wreckage for the occuscope prototype?"

"It wouldn't hurt. I'd like to know where that thing ended up and if there's anything left of it."

Gordon heard our conversation and handed Jack a note. "Here are the longitude and latitude of the wreckage. That should make it easier to find again. She's on the bottom in less than sixteen fathoms."

"Thanks, I'll pass it along."

And that was it. The attack on the German sub took 54 minutes by the clock, and we were on our way back to Naval Air Station San Pedro.

Forty-Five

Jack Jackson and I were standing on the deck of the same motor patrol boat that took part in our operation on Wednesday. I gave optimistic reports to Major Downey at MID and to Coast Guard Lieutenant Hutchins last night, and now we were waiting to find out if my optimism was justified.

Two Coast Guard enlisted men described as "frogmen" because of their strange looking outfits with foot-flippers and underwater breathing devices were approximately a hundred feet below us surveying the wreckage of the German submarine. Specifically, they were looking for any signs of the occuscope prototype, Si Peterson, or Hilda Albrecht.

They were down there for what seemed like a long time, but it was only about 20 minutes by my wristwatch, when we saw first one frogman, and then the second, bob to the surface alongside the boat. They came up emptyhanded, except one of them had something yellow and stringy stuck in his belt. Once they were aboard and out of their cumbersome diving outfits, we got the bad news.

They found the remains of what might have been the bag carried aboard the sub by the male passenger from the *Ammon*, but it was empty and there was no sign of the occuscope prototype. They also found the body of a male in civilian clothes, although his remains were beyond recognition. The body of the female was the clincher. It turns out she wasn't a female at all, but a man in a dress and blonde wig. The yellow stringy thing brought up by one of the divers was the wig.

It took less than five minutes to deflate my optimism flatter than a blown out tire. With the patrol boat heading back to Terminal Island, I stood in the stern smoking a cigarette and cursing myself for letting the Nazis outfox me again.

Jack came over to join me. "That sure wasn't the news we were hoping for."

"No, it wasn't. The Nazis put on a hell of a show and fooled me completely."

"Hey, Johnny, it wasn't a total loss. You helped the Navy get their first confirmed sinking of a German sub by a blimp. That'll end up in the history books."

"So will my stupidity. In the meantime, Si Peterson is enjoying a cruise to Hamburg with his blonde Nazi bimbo."

Jack was thoughtful for a moment, and then said, "Has it occurred to you that this Peterson guy may not have been on the *Ammon* in the first place?"

I shook my head. "My boss at MID tried to convince me the *Ammon* was a red herring, but I thought the Germans had too much invested in the scheme for it to be that."

"Agreed, and the fact they had a rendezvous set up with a submarine indicates they expected your guy to be on the ship, but what if something went wrong and he couldn't get aboard the *Ammon*?"

I remembered Hutchins asking if Peterson and Albrecht could be waiting until the last minute to board the German ship. "Hutchins raised that possibility the other day, but it made no sense for Peterson to be hiding anywhere else. He had every reason to think he was perfectly safe aboard the *Ammon*."

"That's what I thought, but let's try out a different scenario. Let's say the Germans were afraid the Department of State or the Coast Guard might get wise to what they were pulling, just as we ultimately did, so they stashed their people somewhere else, planning to bring them aboard just before the *Ammon* sailed."

"I'm having a hard time buying that idea, but go ahead with your scenario. What happens next?"

"Then we do exactly what they were afraid we'd do and showed up preventing anyone from getting off or on the ship and threatening to lock up the whole shebang. The *Ammon's* captain realizes the jig is up, but decides to cut his losses and make a run for it, leaving us thinking your people were actually aboard.

"Making their way down the coast toward Mexico they knew the patrol boat was shadowing them, so if they went ahead with the planned transfer to the submarine using stand-ins for your people, the patrol boat would report the spies got away with the occuscope."

I saw what Jack was leading up to. "And the sub captain figured there wasn't much risk because he could hold his own against the patrol boat if it tried to interfere with the transfer. He didn't know the blimp was there."

"Exactly right. If they pulled the ruse off, the sub could hang around off the coast waiting for an opportunity to pick up your people from a different vessel. It's possible we were ahead of them all the way and just didn't know it."

"I suppose it could have happened that way. On the other hand, they could actually be on that Kraut ship and what happened yesterday with the sub was just a charade to throw us off the scent. Maybe they wanted the Coast Guard to report the submarine transfer to take the heat off the *Ammon*."

Jack shook his head. "I don't buy that. Think about what it took to get that sub all the way from Germany to the California coast. They were playing for all the marbles yesterday. If your people were actually aboard the *Ammon*, they would have transferred to the sub because it would have appeared to be the fastest and safest way to get the occuscope prototype back to Germany, especially since they didn't know we were overhead in the blimp."

"All right, if we accept your scenario with Peterson and the dame missing the boat, where does that leave us? Where the hell are they?"

Jack shook his head. "They could be anywhere. The only thing we know for sure is the *Ammon* will have reported the submarine sunk. That means Peterson has to come up with a new way out of the country, and wherever they were when the *Ammon* sailed yesterday, they've had twenty-four hours to get somewhere else by now."

"But if we knew where they were yesterday morning, it would be a place to pick up their trail. It has to be somewhere in or near the harbor."

"Maybe a hotel in Long Beach or San Pedro?"

"I hope not because it will take forever to check on all the hotels and motor courts." Then I remembered something I saw on my first trip to Terminal Island and all of a sudden I had a pretty good hunch where Peterson could be if he wasn't aboard the *Ammon*.

"I think I've got it, Jack."

"What?"

"There's a yacht club kind of place north of the Naval Air

Station."

"Yes. In fact there are a couple of marinas up there on the Cerritos Channel. Oh, I get it. You think your people were laying low aboard a private yacht in one of the marinas?"

"It would be the perfect place. They'd be close to the *Ammon*, making it fairly easy to slip aboard her in the middle of the night just before she sailed, and if they picked a yacht that could make a trip up the coast to Canada, like you originally figured they might, they would have a built in back up plan if something went wrong with their first scheme."

Nodding enthusiastically, Jack said, "You know, Johnny, you just might have something there."

"Thanks, but how do we go about finding out if it's the right something?"

Jack gave my question a moment of thought. "Well, each marina has an office, and the offices have lists of the clients renting slips for their boats. It shouldn't be too difficult to get a look at those lists, except we have no idea what we're looking for."

"There's another possibility. It's a slim chance, but based on all our conjecturing, the first thing we need to find out at each marina is if any boats seaworthy enough to make the trip to Canada have left in the last twenty-four hours."

"Good idea."

"All right, as soon as we get back to Terminal Island, let's pick Pierce up and head for those marinas, but I'll have to stop along the way to call my boss and tell him what we found or didn't find in the sub's wreckage. I'm sure as hell not looking forward to that conversation."

Forty-Six

Tides Inn Bar & Grill – Anchorage Road, LA Harbor

"I knew that German ship was a red herring. I knew it!"

"Sure you did, Downey, just like you knew there would be a German submarine lurking in US waters to take two passengers off of it.

"Don't take that tone with me, Spicer!"

"I've got work to do, Downey. I'll check in when I've got something to report."

That pretty much sums up my long-distance conversation with Downey after I informed him Peterson, Albrecht, and the occuscope prototype were not found in the German submarine wreckage. Getting sharp with him wasn't the smartest thing to do coming off of a failure, but I really didn't give much of a damn what Downey thought. Besides, I'm pretty sure General Davis will back me if the major wants to make an issue of it.

I stepped out of the telephone booth and walked across the parking lot in front of a little joint called the Tides Inn Bar and Grill on Anchorage Road. We picked the place for lunch because it's in the middle of the marinas where we hoped to find some sign of Si Peterson.

Jack and Russ Pierce were busy devouring hamburgers at a table near one of the front windows. As I approached, Jack glanced up from the thick juicy burger he was holding and said, "I can tell by the look on your face you had a pleasant conversation with your boss."

Reminding myself of the need to be diplomatic in front of an enlisted man, I just smiled and said, "Pleasant is hardly the word for it."

Jack chuckled. "Well, we got you a burger with everything on it. That should improve your disposition."

"Thanks. A little sustenance might help."

Picking up my burger, I asked, "How do you suggest handling this, Jack?"

He swallowed a bite, wiped a dribble of catsup off his chin, and said, "According to the signs we saw on the way over here there are four marinas along Anchorage Road. I think we should try showing the marina operators your pictures of Peterson and the woman first. If that doesn't get us anything useful, we ask if any vessel seaworthy enough to make it up the coast to Canada has left their marina lately."

"Okay, that's how will do it. Russ, I'd like you to find a good spot at each marina where you can see the land and water exits. If anybody takes off in a hurry, sing out. It might mean we're in the right place and we've been spotted."

"Yes, sir."

Our first stop was the East Basin Yacht Harbor on the west side of the hamburger joint. Our tires made squishing sounds as I pulled into a muddy, unpaved parking area. Sergeant Pierce quickly found a spot from which he could see all of the harbor's slips. His job was especially important because we were all in uniform, which made us stand out like sore thumbs among marina folks. If Peterson and Albrecht were there, our uniforms would immediately warn them something was up even if Si didn't recognize me from a distance.

The East Basin Yacht Harbor's office wasn't much more than a rough wood shack on a bluff above the docks. Jack opened a door that squeaked on rusty hinges and in we went. The office furnishings consisted of one desk, two chairs, and a painted plywood map of the marina nailed to the wall. A small cup hook was screwed into the map next to each slip. Hand-lettered string tags hung from the hooks of rented slips. Only about half the slips had tags.

An older fellow with a gray beard and wire-frame specs was sitting at the desk reading the December issue of Rudder Magazine. He looked up and appeared somewhat startled by our uniforms. The guy stood and said, "Yes, gentlemen, what can I do for ya?"

I flashed my MID ID and answered his question. "We're with military intelligence and we need a little information."

Squinting at my ID he said, "Happy to help if I can."

The next items I showed him were pictures of Peterson and

Hilda Albrecht. "We're looking for these people. If they've been around, it would have been in the last week. Have you seen them?"

He leaned over to look closely at both photos and shook his head. "Ain't seen neither of 'em. They spies or somethin'?"

Jack picked it up from there. "Something like that. One more question if you don't mind. Have any vessels left your marina in the past twenty-four hours that are capable of making a trip up the coast to Canada?"

The old fellow looked out a filthy window next to his desk and said, "Only got one boat here I'd want to take on a jaunt like that, and it's right there in its slip."

Strike one. We thanked the fellow and went back out to the Army's Dodge. Sergeant Pierce met us at the car. He saw no activity while we were in the office.

Our second stop was a few hundred yards east of the Tides Inn. Scott's Marina's office was a little snazzier than the one we just visited, but it, too, clearly showed the effects of being in a salt water harbor. Inside, we talked to a young man who identified himself as Ralph Scott, the owner.

We went through the same routine and got more or less the same answers. No, he hadn't seen either of the people in the photos and no boats capable of making it up the coast to Canada had left the marina recently. Strike two.

The apparent prosperity of the marinas on Anchorage Road increased the farther east we went. The Harbor Light Anchorage operated out of a modern, freshly painted white office building with blue trim. Based on what we could see from the parking lot, the boats in this marina's slips looked newer and larger than those at our first two stops. The Harbor Light Anchorage even had a receptionist in a nicely furnished lobby with lots of nautical doodads and charts decorating the walls.

We asked to see the proprietor and the young brunette in snug-fitting white bell-bottomed sailor slacks and a blue navy-style blouse with white trim led Jack and me into an office behind the lobby. There, she introduced us to a middle-aged fellow named Joe Vincente—a guy with graying curly hair and a quick smile.

I went through the ritual of flashing my MID ID, and then showed him the pictures. Vincente laid the photos on his desk and studied them closely for a long while. Then he pressed one of several buttons on the combination telephone/intercom system taking up a large corner of his desk and said, "Joanie, please come in here for a moment."

The brunette in the sailor outfit returned and Vincente pointed to the photos of Peterson and Hilda Albrecht on his desk. "Joanie, take a look at these photos. Do either the people look familiar to you?"

She glanced at the photos, took a closer look, and said, "Yes. That's Missus Peters. She and her husband were staying aboard the *Sea Wolf*, Mister Bauer's yacht."

I shot a quick glance at Jack as Vincente said, "That's what I thought, but I wanted to be sure. Thank you, Joanie."

Vincente was watching Joanie's snug-fitting sailor pants disappear through the door as he said, "Yes, gentlemen, the people you are looking for were here, at least the woman was. I never got a close look at Mister Peters."

"When did they leave?"

"Mister Bauer's boat captain took the *Sea Wolf* out early this morning. I can't say for sure the people you're looking for were aboard her, though."

As I got my notebook and a pencil out of my uniform jacket pocket, Jack took over the questioning. "Mister Vincente, what kind of vessel is the *Sea Wolf*?"

Vincente clearly knew his boats. "She's a sixty-four-foot seagoing yacht with twin diesel engines. I think she was built in 1937 or 1938 . . . a very trim ship. Mister Bauer employs a captain and a crew of three hands."

"Got any idea what her cruising speed might be?"

Vincente's brow furrowed while he gave that question some thought. "Well, she has a displacement hull and she's heavy. Even with those big diesels, I can't see her cruising at more than 18 knots."

"But you think she's seaworthy enough to make it up the coast as far as, say, Vancouver, British Columbia?"

"Oh, sure. She could handle that without any problem at all." Then Vincente cocked his head to one side and said, "You think that's where she's headed?"

Jack shrugged. "Could be. At this point we're guessing."

Vincente nodded. "I only ask because I saw her at the fuel dock across the channel when I took a Tollycraft cruiser out yesterday for a demonstration ride. But even with full tanks, the *Sea Wolf* doesn't have a range of more than, maybe, eight-hundred miles. If they're heading for Canada, they'll have to make at least one fuel stop somewhere along the way."

I was still making notes, but when I caught up, I asked,

"Mister Vincente, can you help us pin down the *Sea Wolf's* departure time this morning?"

"Well, let me think. I got here about quarter to eight. Our night watchman was still here. He pointed out the *Sea Wolf's* empty slip and said she left about an hour earlier, so that would make it somewhere between six-forty-five and seven."

While I wrote that down, Jack said, "Can you give us a physical description of the vessel?"

"Sure. She has sleek lines, a black hull, and white topsides. She also has a flying bridge, a single mast aft, and a white stripe at the waterline. The *Sea Wolf* stands out."

Figuring we had about all we were going to get, I said, "You've been very cooperative, Mister Vincente. Is there anything else you can think of that might help us track the *Sea Wolf* down?"

Vincente thought for a moment, and then shook his head. "Not off hand. Is there a number where I can reach you if I think of something?"

I considered giving him one of my MID cards with the San Francisco telephone number on it, and thought better of that. "Jack, give him Lieutenant Hutchins' number. That way he can leave a message for us without making a long-distance call to San Francisco."

Back at the car, I told Russ the story we got from Joe Vincente. Jack added, "But we still don't know whether or not Peterson and Albrecht were still on the vessel when it took off this morning and, although we think they're heading for Canada, that's mostly guesswork. I'd like answers to those questions before we launch a search for the *Sea Wolf*."

Russ took it all in, thought for a moment, and made a damned good suggestion. "Any chance we could learn something from the people at the fuel dock? They might have seen our people aboard or overheard some conversation about where the boat was going."

Jack grinned. "You know, you Army guys are smarter than you look. That's a hell of a fine idea, Pierce. The small boat fuel dock is directly across the channel from here."

Forty-Seven

Cerritos Marine Fuel Dock – Cerritos Channel, LA Harbor

Getting there involved a lot of twisting and turning past warehouses and around huge fuel tanks on streets you'd swear were dead ends, but we eventually arrived at Cerritos Marine. A faded, crudely-lettered sign next to the road promised "All Your Boating Needs—Gasoline, Diesel Fuel, Service, Supplies, & Bait." The sign overstated the facts of the matter.

Cerritos Marine consisted of a fifteen-by-twenty-foot wooden dock stuck out over the water on rotting pilings. On the dock were a small weathered shed, a fuel pump labeled "Diesel" and another pump labeled "Gasoline." Aside from a tangle of long rubber fuel hoses, the only other notable feature on the dock was the attendant—a bear of a man with stringy hair, a grease-smudged face, and filthy coveralls that looked like they hadn't been washed since Noah came by to gas up the ark. The man's feet were in rubber-soled canvas shoes that might have been blue once upon a time, but I wouldn't swear to it.

I observed all this while cautiously descending a rickety stairway from the road to the dock. At the bottom of the stairs I glanced at Sergeant Pierce. He had sized up the attendant, too, and gave me a nod that said we were thinking the same thing. The guy looked like trouble.

Jack, on the other hand, was more interested in the ramshackle condition of the dock. "Hutchins' people are getting sloppy. I can see at least a dozen maritime code violations from here."

I said, "That might be a matter you'll want to take up some other time with whoever owns this place, rather than with that kindly-looking gentleman over there."

Jack looked at the guy as if noticing him for the first time. "I see your point."

Trying not to trip over fuel hoses as I walked across the dock, I told myself I might be misjudging the attendant. He was probably the salt of the earth and overflowing with the spirit of cooperation. He wasn't.

The guy was perched atop a tall wooden stool leaned precariously against the shack. He looked up and got a silly grin on his face that displayed the few rotten teeth he had left. "What in hell is this, an invasion?" He pointed more or less west and snarled, "The war is that way, soldier boys."

Ignoring the man's somewhat limited view of current events, I flashed my MID ID. "We're with military intelligence. We have a few questions for you."

"What about?"

"You fueled the *Sea Wolf* yesterday." Holding up the photos of Peterson and Albrecht, I asked, "Did you see either of these people aboard her?"

Without bothering to look at the pictures, the attendant said, "Go to hell. I ain't helpin' you bums make no trouble for nobody. Shove off."

I gave civility one more try. "We know these people to be Nazi espionage agents smuggling a secret Navy device out of the country. If you saw them, we need to know about it."

He gave me a glare full of hate. "You got trouble with your ears, soldier boy? I said shove off."

Glancing at Pierce, I gave him a small nod, took one step forward, and kicked the leaning stool out from under the attendant. The whole dock trembled when the guy landed on it amid the splintered remains of his stool.

I have to give him credit, for a big man he was quick, but not as quick as Pierce. The attendant scrambled to his knees with intent to kill. Then he looked up into the barrel of Pierce's service forty-five. That took a little of the wind out of his sails, but not all of it."

Intending to get back to his feet, he growled, "Hey, you ain't got no right to do that!"

Pierce growled right back at him. "Stay right where you are, pal."

I said, "Actually, I do have the right to do that and anything else necessary to get the information I need, including shooting you right here and now."

Pierce punctuated my words by cocking the hammer on his Colt. It made a very convincing metallic click.

"What's it going to be, mister? Do I get answers or does the Sergeant here get some target practice?"

"The attendant looked from the barrel of Pierce's Colt to me, swallowed some spit along with his pride, and said, "Yeah, okay. The *Sea Wolf* was here yesterday. What about it?"

I held up the photos again. "Did you see either of these people aboard her?"

After staring at the photos for several seconds, he finally nodded. "Yeah, that woman was aboard for sure. There was a guy, too, but I din't see him so good 'cuz he kinda stayed out of sight, like he din't want nobody to know he was there."

This time Jack was taking the notes while I asked the questions. "Did anyone aboard the *Sea Wolf* mention they were heading out first thing this morning?"

"Nope, but they din't have to. I knowed they was goin' somewheres cuz ya don't fuel up a boat to stay tied to the dock."

"Did anyone say where they were going?"

He looked at Pierce's Colt again. "Well, kinda. Captain Paul bought a nautical chart off me. It was the San Dago to Bering Sea map. That means he's headed up north somewheres."

I glanced at Jack. He smiled what Raymond Chandler would call a "knowing smile."

Turning to the attendant, I said, "Okay, what's your name? I want it in the records so the next time a law enforcement officer has to come out here he'll know what to expect."

After another quick glance at Pierce's forty-five, which was still looking him between the eyes, the guy said, "Bateman. Fred Bateman."

"All right, Bateman. We'll be back if we need anything else."

That's when Jack spoke for the first time. "One more thing, Mister Bateman. I'll be sending a Coast Guard inspection team over here in the next week or two. You've got that long to correct all of the safety violations around this dump or you'll be shut down. I don't imagine your boss will be too happy if that happens."

Bateman nodded his shaggy head. "Yes, sir."

Leaving the fuel dock, Pierce kept his pistol in hand and his eye on Bateman. He didn't slide the forty-five back into its holster until we got to the car.

Jack said, "I guess you guys have dealt with uncooperative witnesses before."

Pierce just smiled and I said, "Yeah, a few, but did you notice he called you 'sir' when we left?"

Jack grinned. "It's the uniform."

Forty-Eight

Terminal Island Coast Guard Base – Los Angeles Harbor

Ins It only took fifteen minutes to get from the Cerritos Marine Supply fuel dock to the Terminal Island Coast Guard facility. There, we dropped Jack off at Hutchins' office to do some calculations and plotting on charts—an effort we hoped would result in a plan for catching Si Peterson aboard the *Sea Wolf*.

While Jack got busy with his charts, Sergeant Pierce and I drove over to the Temporary Personnel Quarters. There, I changed into my civvies for the sake of comfort. Then Russ and I loaded our gear, including Jack's sea bag, into the Army's Dodge and returned to see what sort of plan Jack came up with, assuming he came up with one.

We found him knee-deep in calculations well beyond my limited arithmetic skills. He was in surprisingly good humor. "Well, if we've figured Peterson's plans right, we should be able to find and catch the *Sea Wolf* without too much difficulty."

That was unexpected. "Even with the head start they've got?"

"Even with that. Don't forget they're making about eighteen knots, which is only twenty-two miles per hour." Jack glanced at his wristwatch. "Even though they left almost nine hours ago, the *Sea Wolf* has only traveled about two hundred miles.

"Here, take a look at my calculations. I converted nautical miles into statute miles to make things a little easier. One nautical mile equals one-and-an-eighth statute miles, so right now they should be just about off Lompoc, which is only about 165 miles by road, and that's the key to catching them."

Puzzled, I asked, "What is?"

"That we can travel nearly twice their speed on Highway One-

Oh-One and our route is more direct because we don't have to follow the coastline. For example, if we get moving, we can make up for their head start and arrive in San Francisco less than an hour after they pass the Golden Gate."

"Okay, I understand that, but I don't think the Army's Dodge floats. How do we catch them after we get to San Francisco?"

Jack grinned. "We borrow a Coast Guard patrol boat stationed in San Francisco. The boat I have in mind is a seventy-two-footer capable of around thirty miles per hour. It's moored at Fort Point and if we can get there in time to shove off by oh-three-hundred hours tomorrow morning, for example, we'll catch the *Sea Wolf* around oh-eight-hundred hours along the coast off Humboldt Bay."

"Tell me, how far is Vancouver from here?"

"Around fifteen-hundred miles, but we can catch them long before they get that far."

"I understand, but according to the guy at the Marina, the *Sea Wolf* only has a range of eight hundred miles. What if they stop somewhere for fuel? Wouldn't that throw your calculations off?"

"It would, but Eureka—Humboldt Bay—is only about seven hundred miles from here, less than halfway to Vancouver. If they hope to make it on only one fuel stop, they won't be putting in before they get there. Now, if it were me, I would make at least two fuel stops instead of cutting it too close with a small fuel reserve.

"I've covered that eventuality by sending out an alert to all Coast Guard stations between here and San Francisco on the district teletype network. The alert includes the vessel's description and instructions to be on the lookout for her. If the *Sea Wolf* is seen, the information is to be sent immediately to my attention at Station Fort Point, so if she puts in somewhere between here and San Francisco, we should know about it before we shove off from Fort Point."

As usual, Russ Pierce was standing off to one side following the conversation, and what he heard raised a question in his mind. "If the *Sea Wolf* is spotted by a Coast Guard station, why not just have them pick her up? Wouldn't that be safer than risking losing her again?"

It was a good question, and I gave him the best answer I could. "It might be, Russ, but remember who we're dealing with here. Si Peterson knows me and he knows damned well I'll eventually figure out what he's up to. He's sure to have an alternate plan in the event he suspects we're getting too close, and that plan could be dangerous for whoever tries to take him, or it might be clever enough to let him slip away. I'd much rather have him stick with what we're pretty sure he's doing until we're face-to-face. I don't know that we can do a better job of catching him than anyone else, but we have the advantage of knowing him and how desperate he is to get away with the occuscope."

Russ nodded. "I see your point."

Turning to Jack, I said, "I think your plan is about the only feasible way to handle this, but how about saving ourselves an all-night drive by flying up to San Francisco?"

Jack held up a sheet of teletype paper. "The answer to that is weather. A large storm is expected to hit the San Francisco Bay Area anytime now. It's a slow moving front that's not generating much wind, so predictions are it will stick around in the area well into tomorrow. The clouds behind the front, however, are loaded with precipitation. That makes them dense. If we fly up there, we are very likely to find the local airfields socked in, leaving us with nothing to do but turn around and head back."

"Okay, that pretty well settles it. Let's get on the road."

Jack said, "All right. I need to call Station Fort Point and make sure they have our patrol vessel ready to launch when we get there. I'll meet you out front."

The Army's Dodge undercover car has a couple of unique features that are handy in situations where you actually want to be noticed. For one, there is a red plastic lens in the glove compartment that snaps onto the driver's side spotlight. Snap it on and you have an instant cop car. In addition, the rear package shelf has a red light that tilts up to show through the rear window. There is also a switch on the dash I was told turns on a siren. Making San Francisco in less than eleven hours could require breaking some speed limits, so the red lights and siren might be useful in the event we encounter a cop or two along the way.

I started the Dodge while Russ squeezed onto the backseat. Being a club coupe, the space back there was cramped to say the least. "Don't worry, Russ. We'll take turns back there so you don't end up permanently bent into a pretzel."

"Thank you, sir. I think this seat is intended for kids."

Jack showed up a few minutes later. Climbing onto the passenger side of the front seat, he said, "All set. Station Fort Point will have everything ready for us when we get there. Ah . . . I hope this mission still has the Department of State's blessing."

Smiling, I said, "I haven't gotten any telephone calls from Cordell Hull to the contrary, so we'll assume that's the case."

"Good. I used that detail to avoid a lot of time-consuming paperwork. The Coast Guard is picky about who they let borrow their vessels."

"I can understand that. I still have a carbon copy of Cordell Hull's telegram in my pocket in case we need it."

Once out of the Los Angeles Harbor area, we made a gasoline stop in Wilmington. Then, with a full tank and cardboard cups of coffee purchased at a café next to the gas station, I turned north onto Pacific Coast Highway. Not long after joining US 101 in Ventura we passed a sign listing the towns ahead. One of them was Santa Barbara.

"I wish we had time to make a stop in Santa Barbara."

Grinning, Jack said, "I can see why you might want to do that. By the way, I haven't said anything to Susan about us working together, have you?"

"Yeah. I talked to her on the telephone night before last—the day you came down to NAS San Pedro. She mentioned you were headed down to LA on a last minute assignment. Just to put her mind at ease, I told her I'd seen you and all was well."

"Thanks. This war business has her pretty upset, primarily because of us. You being at Pearl Harbor on the seventh really shook her up."

"I know. I could have kept my mouth shut about that, but I was afraid I'd let something slip and Susan would be upset because I didn't tell her." As an afterthought, I added, "Women."

Jack said, "Sisters."

Forty-Nine

Coast Guard Station Fort Point – San Francisco Bay

We made darn good time getting to San Francisco despite stopping every two hours to swap seats and switch drivers. Our good time was partly due to the fact we didn't see a single highway patrol cruiser all night. There I was, finally in a position to speed and get away with it, and there wasn't a cop in sight.

Coast Guard Station Fort Point is located on a tiny strip of beach alongside Crissy Field just east of the Golden Gate Bridge's southern anchorage. In a rainstorm at two-thirty in the morning, however, there wasn't much to see besides a scattering of light colored wood-sided buildings and a pier jutting out into the bay. After checking in at a two-story headquarters building, Jack led us out to the end of the pier, where we found *CG-439*, a 72-foot Fast Patrol Boat wearing a Navy gray paint job.

During the trip north Jack gave us the lowdown on *CG-439*. She has a wooden hull and is powered by a pair of 800 horsepower gasoline marine engines. Her primary armament is a 37-millimeter rapid-fire pom-pom gun, sometimes called a "one pounder." *CG-439* also carries a .30-caliber light machine gun. Her crew, counting the captain, includes fourteen men.

Jack explained that *CG-439* is something of an oddball—one of three speedy 72-footers built specifically to chase down rumrunners during prohibition. Now she is used to pursue other types of seagoing lawbreakers—in this instance, a pair of Nazi spies.

Seeing her in person, I was struck by *CG-439's* sleek shape. She rides low in the water with a streamlined bridge. Even tied to the dock she gives the impression of speed.

Aboard *CG-439* we were hustled into the enclosed bridge to escape the rain. Despite the torrential downpour pounding the wooden decks, we could still hear the burbling exhausts of the powerful gasoline marine engines in the stern.

Jack introduced himself, and then Russ and me, to the vessel's skipper, Ensign Pete Meredith. Meredith, a young fellow with blonde hair and a deep tan, impressed me as a capable, no-nonsense officer. "Good to meet you all. Who's commanding this mission? Major Spicer?"

I said, "Technically, yes, but for now, I'll defer to Lieutenant Jackson."

Turning to Jack, Ensign Meredith said, "Okay, Lieutenant Jackson, where are we headed?"

"Out the Golden Gate and up the coast. We're looking for a 64-foot motor yacht called *Sea Wolf*. We think she's heading up the coast at a speed of roughly eighteen knots. The *Sea Wolf* has a distinctive paint scheme that should make her easy to identify. Her hull is black and her topsides are white. She has a single mast aft and a white stripe at the water line.

"The vessel left LA Harbor yesterday around oh-seven-hundred hours and her ultimate destination is probably in the Vancouver, British Columbia area. We believe she is carrying two passengers, a man and a woman—both Nazi spies—attempting to smuggle a top secret Navy device out of the country. We are authorized by the US Army Military Intelligence Division and the Department of State to use whatever force necessary to capture the vessel and its passengers, including sinking her with all hands."

Ensign Meredith whistled softly. "You fellows mean business. All right, Major Spicer, are you ready to cast off?"

I nodded. "Let's go."

"Yes, sir." Gesturing to a hatch on the port side of the forward bridge bulkhead, Meredith said, "You gentlemen are welcome to go below decks or stay up here on the bridge."

One glance down the ladder at the cramped quarters and the stench of an atmosphere heavy with gasoline fumes convinced me the bridge was the better place to be. Jack and Sergeant Pierce came to the same conclusion.

The central feature of the bridge was a podium mounted against the forward bulkhead and centered behind *CG-439's* windshield. The ship's wheel mounted on the podium was bright metal with eight spokes. In addition to various switches and engine instruments, the podium sprouted two pairs of gray levers with black knobs. The levers on the right side of the podium were the throttles, one for each of *CG-439's* two marine engines. The pair of levers on the left served a function similar to an automobile gearshift, shifting the drivetrains transmitting power to the propellers into forward, reverse, or neutral.

The section of the forward bulkhead to the left of the podium was taken up by the hatch leading below decks, and the area to the right was occupied by a gray metal swivel chair mounted atop a pedestal bolted to the deck. The word "captain" was stenciled across the back of the chair in black letters. Both sides of the bridge and its aft bulkhead were fitted with windows offering an unrestricted 360-degree view around the vessel. There was also a hatch in the rear bulkhead opening onto *CG-439's* deck.

A Chief Warrant Officer stood at the helm awaiting his orders. Ensign Meredith gave them to him. "Okay, Mister Perez, take us out through the Gate."

The Chief acknowledged his orders and opened a sliding window on the port side of the bridge. Getting a face full of rain in the process, he shouted, "Cast off breast and stern lines!"

A moment later, "Breast and stern lines clear," came back to us out of the storm.

Perez turned helm's wheel to port and waited a moment as if feeling what the vessel wanted to do. Then, as the stern swung slowly to starboard, he nudged the port transmission into reverse. Even though the engines were still at idle, *CG-439* slowly inched away from the dock. When we felt the bow line go tight, the Chief shifted the port engine back into neutral and yelled, "Let go the bow line!"

Ten seconds later we heard, "Free of the dock!"

Chief Perez turned and looked aft, then shifted both transmission levers into reverse. We backed away until the bow was a hundred feet or so from the dock. The Chief closed his throttles, shifted both engines into neutral, and swung the wheel to starboard. Finally, he shifted the engines into forward and gradually opened the throttles again.

We were on our way. It was all very skillfully done and *CG-439* had a solid, stable feel about her, much more so than the smaller patrol boat we took out of LA Harbor this . . . make that yesterday . . . morning.

Ahead, ghostly glimpses of the towers and span of the Golden Gate Bridge appeared out of the murk. From our perspective, the bridge looked huge, towering more than seven hundred feet above our heads in the darkness.

I noticed Jack looking at his wristwatch, so I checked mine. It was five minutes after three a.m. We were right on schedule.

As we passed under the Golden Gate Bridge, Chief Perez gradually opened the throttles until we were running along at what seemed like a pretty good clip. Speeds on water always seem faster than they do in a car.

Ensign Meredith calmly gave the helmsman his next instructions. "Mister Perez, after clearing Point Bonita, make your heading 345 degrees."

"Aye, sir."

We were still pointed west when I spotted a bright beam of light cutting through the storm on our starboard side. Ensign Meredith noticed me looking at it and said, "That's the Point Bonita Light. Once we're past it we'll turn northwest to follow the coastline. Say, would you like some coffee? We've got a pot on in the galley." I nodded, and turning to Jack and Russ, Meredith asked, "How 'bout you gentlemen? Coffee?"

Sounding a little like a diner waitress, Meredith yelled down through the bridge hatch for four javas, and a few minutes later a seaman appeared through the hatch carrying four steaming tin mugs of coffee by the handles, two in each hand. I was quite impressed with the young man's ability to carry the mugs without spilling a drop despite the chopping motion of *CG-439* as we began our turn to the northwest. The coffee was strong and hot.

Ensign Meredith spent a few minutes studying a chart he spread out on an ingenious fold-up chart table hinged to the bulkhead in front of his seat on the bridge. Returning the chart to a cabinet below the chart table, Meredith said, "We should make Humboldt Bay in a little under five hours." Glancing at a large clock mounted in the top of the helmsman's podium, he added, "That will be around oh-eight-hundred hours. I'm expecting to leave this storm behind in about three hours, and sunrise along the coast here happens at oh-seven-twenty hours today, so we should have good visibility for spotting our target, assuming your estimate of its speed is accurate. Until then, we're keeping a double watch in case the *Sea Wolf* is behind your estimate and we encounter her earlier than expected. Under these conditions, though, we could pass within a half mile of the vessel and never see her."

Fifty

Aboard Fast Patrol Boat CG-439 – Off Humboldt Bay

According to Jack, Humboldt Bay went undiscovered for a hundred years or more. The 17th and 18th Century European explorers who sailed up and down the California coast discovering stuff kept going right past the entrance without ever knowing the bay was there. When we arrived, I saw why.

Humboldt Bay is a narrow lagoon paralleling the California coast a hundred miles or so south of the Oregon border and from the ocean it's practically invisible. The land separating the bay from the ocean is a low sand bar that looks just like a hundred other beaches along the California coast. The bay's entrance doesn't appear to be anything more exciting than the outlet of a small river, so nobody bothered to explore it until the early 1800s.

When the Russian-American timber company finally got curious enough to take a closer look, they found a bay about fifteen miles long and four-and-a-half miles across at its widest point. The only way in or out—the entrance everyone kept missing—is about five miles north of the bay's southern end.

The largest town on Humboldt Bay, Eureka, is four miles north of the entrance on the east shore. A smaller town called Arcata sits at the northern tip of the bay. Today US Highway 101 skirts Humboldt Bay's eastern shoreline.

By the time we reached a point roughly three miles west of Humboldt Bay's entrance the sun was out in all its glory and celebrating the occasion by scattering a dazzling confetti of sparkles across the blue Pacific. It was a few minutes before eight, Friday morning, which meant Jack's time estimates were right on the money . . . except for one detail. We were there, but the *Sea*

Wolf wasn't.

Jack, Ensign Meredith, and two crew members were on deck scanning the horizon with binoculars, but they weren't seeing much besides a lot of ocean. As I approached Jack, he said, "Damn it, Johnny, it looks like I've let you down again."

"Let's not give up quite yet, Jack." Turning to Meredith, I asked, "The Coast Guard maintains a station in Humboldt Bay, don't they?"

"We sure do."

"Do they have a radio?"

Nodding, Meredith said, "Affirmative."

"How 'bout giving them a call and asking someone to take a quick look around the bay for the *Sea Wolf*, especially alongside any fuel docks?"

"Will do. What are your orders if they see her?"

"Just to keep us informed of her movements and try not to appear interested in her. Nothing else."

"Roger."

Meredith hustled below decks to the radio room. Returning ten minutes later, he said, "They're sending a harbor motor launch out with a portable radio aboard. If they spot the vessel they'll give us a call. It'll take 'em about forty-five minutes to cruise the bay."

"Good. In the meantime, let's stick around here and assign a crew member to watch the bay's entrance just in case the *Sea Wolf* is in there and decides to leave."

"We already have it covered. I sure hope this isn't a wild goose chase; for your sake, I mean."

I knew what he really meant, but kept my thoughts to myself. Instead, I strolled to the stern and gave Jack a pat on the back and said, "Cheer up. Even if we figured it wrong, we took our best shot. Nobody can ask for anything more than that."

Having done my bit for team morale, I lit a Lucky and kept my fingers crossed. About fifteen minutes later a crewman stuck his head outside the bridge and said, "Skipper, Station Humboldt Bay calling on the wireless."

From amidships, Meredith shouted, "What's the message?"

"They have our target in sight. She's at the Eureka Slough marina fuel dock where the Samoa and Eureka channels split."

Meredith had a genuine look of surprise on his face as he said, "Tell Station Humboldt Bay to keep the *Sea Wolf* in sight and let us know as soon as she leaves the fuel dock. Tell them they are not to approach the vessel under any circumstances."

Jack and I followed Meredith to the bridge, where he opened

a chart of Humboldt Bay on his snazzy fold-up chart table. Pointing to a spot on the map, he said, "They're right here, about five miles from the entrance. How do you want to proceed, Major?"

"It looks like they've bottled themselves up in a natural trap. Let's take advantage of that. Put us in the middle of the entrance channel and bring your guns to bear on the spot where we expect the target to appear when they attempt to leave the bay. Tell the launch in the bay we may have to fire on the *Sea Wolf* so they'll know to stay out of the way."

Meredith relayed my instructions to the helmsman and his deck crew. He then told his radio operator to let Station Humboldt Bay in on our plans. *CG-439's* decks got busy as we moved toward the bay's entrance and the crew readied their guns.

"Ensign, do you have a loudhailer aboard?"

"Yes. It's that black box with a microphone on the bulkhead above the windshield. I'll switch it on so the tubes will warm up."

The .30-cal machine gun was in the stern and the 37-millimeter pom-pom gun was mounted amidships aft of the bridge. These mounting positions meant that, for both guns to be effective, Meredith had to position the boat perpendicular to the entrance channel.

As *CG-439* maneuvered into position across the channel with our bow pointed south, I said, "Jack, you handle the loudhailer. When the *Sea Wolf* shows up, make it clear she has one minute to heave to and prepare to be boarded or we'll open fire. We're going to do this quickly without giving Peterson another opportunity to slip out of our grasp."

Jack nodded and asked, "Where will you be?"

"Back by the big gun. If we have to fire on the *Sea Wolf*, I want to give the orders so I can take full responsibility for whatever happens. In fact, I think I'll go back there now and tell the crew what they're in for."

Ensign Meredith walked back to the gun position with me and gathered the four members of the gun crews around us. Without preamble, Meredith said, "This is Major Spicer. He is with Army Military Intelligence and this is his party. Our orders are to follow his orders to the letter . . . ," the Ensign paused to look each of the gun crew members in the eye, ". . . even if those orders include the sinking of an unarmed civilian vessel. Do you all understand that?"

Four crisp "yes sirs" followed immediately, and I said, "This is an extremely unusual situation and we will handle it without bloodshed if that's possible. However, hundreds, perhaps thousands, of lives depend on our success, so we will do whatever is necessary. I'll be giving the gun orders and I'll try to make them as clear as possible. Okay?"

Again the men responded with a chorus of "yes sirs."

Next I gestured to Sergeant Pierce who was standing calmly by the bridge taking everything in. "Russ, we'll need to board the *Sea Wolf*. You'll head the boarding party." Turning to Meredith, I said, "Assign three crew members and equip them with side arms to form the rest of Sergeant Pierce's boarding party."

"Roger. I know just the men for the job. I'll also get a lifeboat ready to lower and take the boarding party across to the *Sea Wolf*."

Turning back to Pierce, I said, "You know what we're looking for. If possible, we need to take Simon Peterson and Hilda Albrecht into custody, but our primary objective is the occuscope prototype. Understood?"

"Understood. What about the *Sea Wolf* and her crew, sir?"

"Good question. Any suggestions, Ensign?"

Meredith put on a thoughtful expression. "Well, we can put a prize crew aboard the vessel to take her back to San Francisco. As for the *Sea Wolf's* crew, we can either detain them aboard *439* or aboard their own vessel for the trip back. Putting them about *439* would be my preference."

"Then that's what we'll do."

The ensign nodded. "Okay, I'll make the arrangements."

While Meredith and Pierce went off to take care of their preparations, I stood amidships and looked out at Humboldt Bay. Before long I would be face-to-face with Si Peterson for the first time since he blew up the Optitronics plant. He led me on a wild goose chase all over heck and gone, and he made saps out of me and everyone else at MID. Now I was going to make damn sure he got his comeuppance.

Fifty-One

Aboard Fast Patrol Boat CG-439 – Humboldt Bay Entrance Channel

CG-439's radio operator popped up on deck a few minutes after nine to tell us Station Humboldt Bay reported *Sea Wolf* leaving the fuel dock. That piece of news had the effect of elevating the tension aboard *CG-439* several notches.

Even though we knew it would take *Sea Wolf* fifteen minutes or longer to reach us, Chief Fernando Perez stood at his helm staring intently at the bay end of the entrance channel. The one pounder and .30-cal crews double checked the readiness of their guns. Standing on the bridge next to Perez, Ensign Meredith was frowning in concentration, although I had no idea what he was concentrating on. Also on the bridge, Jack fussed with the loudhailer microphone cord while he watched for the *Sea Wolf*. The only man aboard *CG-439* who appeared calm and relaxed was Sergeant Pierce. That was one big reason I'd picked him for my team.

As for my state of mind, I was wondering what the hell I was doing preparing for battle aboard a Coast Guard boat a long way from Hollywood Boulevard. The mental image of a fish out of water swam through my mind.

Suddenly the waiting was over. The low black bow of the *Sea Wolf* slid into view at the channel entrance like the snout of a sinister sea serpent. Her crew spotted us a moment later and the *Sea Wolf's* skipper immediately throttled back, letting his vessel coast to a stop.

The channel was more than a thousand feet wide, and *CG439* only filled seventy feet of that width. I imagined the man at the *Sea Wolf's* helm weighing his chances of successfully making a run past us to one side or the other. I wasn't too concerned about that, though, because even if he tried it, the *Sea Wolf* would still be well within the range of our guns.

Our target was now dead in the water about two hundred yards to the east waiting for us to make the next move, so I made it, signaling Jack to give the warning we arranged. A moment later, Jack's amplified voice crackled across the space between *CG-439* and *Sea Wolf*.

"Ahoy, *Sea Wolf*. This is the United States Coast Guard. Your vessel, crew and passengers are under arrest. You have exactly one minute to surrender and prepare to be boarded. If you fail to comply, we will open fire."

I automatically glanced at the sweep second hand on my wristwatch. It was passing "2" on the dial.

To the one-pounder crew, I said, "If I give the order to fire, put a few rounds into her bow at the waterline."

The man at the trigger adjusted the one-pounder's aim slightly. "Aye, sir."

"5"

There was no visible activity aboard the *Sea Wolf*. She was still just sitting dead in the water and slowly drifting toward us. I wondered if the skipper was conferring with his passengers about what they wanted to do. Or maybe he was calling our bluff, waiting to see if we really intended to fire on them.

"7"

Our engines rumbled for a few seconds and I took a quick glance toward *CG-439's* bridge. Chief Perez was making a slight adjustment in our position to correct for the current. Jack and Ensign Meredith both had their eyes glued to binoculars aimed at *Sea Wolf*.

"9"

I had to look twice to be sure of what I was seeing, but *Sea Wolf* was definitely underway again. A disturbance in the water at her stern confirmed that her engines were engaged. I yelled, "She's moving! Keep her in your sights!"

"12"

Sea Wolf suddenly lunged forward and I realized what her skipper was up to. He was making a dash across the channel entrance like a duck in a shooting gallery. If he could elude us for a few minutes while *CG-439* turned into the bay, he might be able put his passengers ashore, giving them an opportunity to escape by land. Si Peterson was seriously underestimating my resolve.

"One pounder, FIRE!"

The pom-pom gun made a hell of racket—a rapid, mechanical "CHUGGA . . . CHUGGA . . . CHUGGA" as rounds left the muzzle. During a period that couldn't have more than three seconds, the gun spit at least a dozen rounds at its target.

The impact on *Sea Wolf* was spectacular in the extreme. Her bow literally exploded, rising out of the water for a split second, and then dropping back with an enormous splash. Within a matter of seconds, she was sinking by the bow.

Turning to the *CG-439's* bridge, I made a "let's go" gesture toward the sinking vessel. Chief Perez reacted immediately, opening his throttles and swinging our bow toward *Sea Wolf*. He maintained a position slightly aft of her so our guns could remain on target.

I jogged to the bridge and said, "Okay, gentlemen it's in your hands now."

Jack nodded once and yelled through the open bridge window. "Boarding party to your boat."

Pierce and his team of three crew members trotted to the lifeboat hanging over the gunwale by two davits and swung themselves aboard. Less than a hundred yards from *Sea Wolf*, Perez slowed *CG-439* and Jack yelled, "Away the boat!"

At the same time a lot was happening aboard *Sea Wolf*. Two crew members were struggling to shove a large black inflatable rubber life raft over the side. A third crew member remained on the bridge, seemingly attempting to steer the vessel toward the shore, although her twin screws and rudder were now out of the water and the momentum she had a few moments earlier was gone. Her skipper was on deck near the bridge yelling orders to a crew that didn't seem at all interested in what he had to say. And two muffled pops spaced about ten seconds apart came from somewhere inside *Sea Wolf*.

To no one in particular, I said, "Damn it, Peterson got away again!"

Jack looked bewildered. "Huh? If he's aboard the *Sea Wolf*, we got him, Johnny."

Shaking my head, I said, "Five will get you ten what we have his dead body."

I watched the boarding party row alongside the *Sea Wolf*. One crew member kept the lifeboat snubbed up against *Sea Wolf's* black hull while Pierce and the other members of his boarding party hopped aboard.

When he realized what was happening, *Sea Wolf's* skipper spun in their direction, reaching for something in the waistband of his pants. Pierce's forty-five barked and the man dropped to the deck. The two men who were trying to launch the rubber life raft stopped and raised their hands. The guy on the bridge quickly joined them.

While the rest of the boarding party herded the *Sea Wolf's* remaining crew aboard the lifeboat alongside her, Pierce disappeared below deck. A few minutes later he reappeared with his pistol holstered and a canvas bag in his hand. He dropped into the lifeboat and the boarding party began their return trip to *CG-439.*

I met Pierce at the gunwale, and while the boarding party secured the *Sea Wolf* crew members, Pierce showed me what was in the canvas bag. I breathed a sigh of relief when I saw the damaged occuscope prototype again. At least we had that much.

Pierce gave me the answer to the obvious question before I asked it. "Colonel Peterson and a woman are both dead, each from a single gunshot wound the head. Peterson did the shooting. A thirty-eight caliber revolver is still in his hand."

Nodding, I said, "When I heard the shots while you were rowing over, I figured that's what you'd find. He figured suicide was preferable to standing trial and being executed as a spy."

"At least he took another Nazi spy with him when he went, sir. I'll take the boarding party back to recover the bodies. Anything else you want from the *Sea Wolf*?"

I thought for a moment. "If there's time before the vessel sinks completely, you might take a look through Peterson's stuff to see if there's any additional evidence we can use."

"Yes, sir, but I don't think we have to worry about the *Sea Wolf* sinking any further. She's in shallow water. I felt the bow hit bottom while I was aboard. I expect it will stay just about where it is until someone hauls the hulk away."

While Pierce and his boarding party headed back to perform their unpleasant task of recovering three bodies, I asked Meredith a question Pierce brought to my mind. "Ensign, can you arrange with the Coast Guard station here to have the *Sea Wolf* salvaged, or whatever you call it?"

He nodded. "Yes, sir. There isn't much left of the vessel to salvage, but it's a navigational hazard where it is, so I'll ask Station Humboldt Bay to get it out of the way or to arrange for someone else to do it. Is there anything else aboard her you want?"

"Sergeant Pierce will take another look around while they recover the bodies. Unless he says there is more evidence aboard, I think we have everything we need." After a pause to clear my thoughts, I added, "Speaking of bodies, autopsies will be required. I imagine the nearest county hospital has a morgue where that can be done. We'll need to make arrangements and transport the bodies."

By the time all the details concerning *Sea Wolf*, her crew, and the deceased were worked out, everyone was pretty fatigued. Meredith put into Station Humboldt Bay for the night, planning to begin the return trip to San Francisco in the morning.

Jack, Sergeant Pierce and I, however, would not be aboard *CG-439* when she departed. That was decided during a long distance telephone conversation with Major Downey at the Presidio.

With irritation in his voice, Downey said, "Well, Major Spicer. Good to finally hear from you. Where the hell are you?"

"At Coast Guard Station Humboldt Bay near Eureka. The good news is we have recovered the occuscope prototype Colonel Peterson stole."

After a moment's pause, Downey said, "Okay. I take it you have bad news, also?"

"Yes, I'm afraid I do. Colonel Peterson committed suicide rather than surrendering. He also killed Hilda Albrecht, the suspected Nazi spy."

Several seconds of long distance static came down the line before Downey said, "What's your current situation there?"

I wasn't expecting a standing ovation for recovering the occuscope yet again, but Downey didn't even sound appreciative. I said, "Peterson was heading for Canada by boat. This is where we caught up with him.

"I'm going to be here a few days. We need to get autopsies reports for Peterson, Albrecht, and the captain of the boat on which Peterson was attempting to escape. I was forced to sink it. And I have three prisoners—members of Peterson's boat crew—to transport wherever you want them."

Yet again there were several seconds of long distance silence. "Is there an airfield nearby?"

"Yes, there's a field at Eureka."

"Okay. I want you and your people back here. I'll send a plane up there tomorrow morning with a team aboard to clean up the mess you made. After you've briefed the new people, get your team and the occuscope on the plane and get back here pronto."

A few choice words about the "mess" I'd made while recovering the occuscope were going through my mind, but I was too damned tired to make an issue of it. I simply said, "See you tomorrow, Major," and ended the call.

After writing up my report for Downey while everything was still fresh in my mind, I hit a bunk in the Coast Guard dormitory like a ton of bricks. It had been one very long day.

Fifty-Two

Crissy Field – Presidio, San Francisco

Stu Irvin brought us in low over the Golden Gate Bridge, made a U-turn over Alcatraz Island, and pointed his AT-7 at Crissy Field's southeast-northwest runway. As we turned for our final approach I noticed two Army staff cars and one Navy or Coast Guard sedan parked at the northwest end of the strip. Several officers in olive drab and navy blue were gathered around the cars. We had a welcoming committee, but I doubted I was going to enjoy the kind of welcome they planned for us.

When the ship rolled to a stop, Stu came back to open the hatch, saying, "With all that brass out there, I think I'll hang around the cockpit a while."

Climbing down from the ship with Jack and Sergeant Pierce behind me, I wished I could join Stu in the AT-7's cockpit. Major Fred Downey was part of the welcoming committee. I expected him to be on hand, but I did not expect to see Major General Chester Davis, head of MID, standing alongside the major. It didn't seem likely the top man flew in from Washington, D.C. to pin a medal on my chest.

We stopped a few feet from Davis and, despite the fact I was in civvies, we snapped to attention and saluted. I said, "Reporting as ordered, sir."

Downey, Davis, and a Coast Guard officer wearing the silver oak leaves of a commander returned our salutes and Davis, pointing to the canvas bag I was carrying in my left hand, asked, "Is that the Navy's missing gizmo?"

I offered him the bag. "Yes, sir."

Davis turned to Downey and said, "You take charge of it,

Major, and try not to lose it again."

General Davis' comment was my first clue that maybe things
weren't as bad as I thought. He turned back to me and said,
"Come with me, Major Spicer. I need to hear exactly what the hell
you've been up to. The rest of you can wait for us in the MID
conference room."

On that note, Davis turned and began walking up the hill
toward the Presidio. I quickly caught up and walked alongside
him. "Okay, Johnny, tell me the story."

Not sure where to begin, I started with our detective work
back in LA Harbor when we discovered Si Peterson was aboard the
Sea Wolf. I was just getting to the point where we arrived at Coast
Guard Station Fort Point when one of the Army staff cars and the
Coast Guard car passed us on their way to Building 100. General
Davis' car followed slowly along behind us like a well-trained
puppy.

At the top of the hill, we crossed Doyle Drive and entered the
Presidio grounds. Davis gestured to a bench overlooking the bay
and we sat. There, I reported the events at Humboldt Bay in
considerable detail. I thought about adding a comment or two
explaining some of my decisions, but decided to stick with the
facts. When Davis had the details, he would draw his own
conclusions.

After several moments of silence, Davis turned to me and
said, "Good job, Johnny. We threw you a lousy detail and you
pulled it off with better results than any of us had a right to
expect."

I'm sure the General detected the relief in my voice as I said,
"Thank you, sir. I couldn't have done it without Sergeant Pierce
and the Coast Guard guys. It was a total team effort."

Davis nodded. "Of course, I'll need your written report for the
records."

Pulling the hand-written three page report from my inside
jacket pocket, I handed it to Davis, saying, "I wrote my report last
night while everything was still fresh in my mind."

The general accepted the report with a nod and said, "Thanks,
Johnny. Now that I've heard what really happened up there, I see
no evidence of misconduct."

That surprised me. "Misconduct, sir?"

Smiling, Davis said, "Yes. Our Major Downey's version of the
story was a little different than yours. He was ready to convene a
court martial the moment you stepped off that aircraft. I think his
nose is out of joint because you jumped the chain of command

when you called me directly to contact the State Department. You did what needed to done, but Downey seems more concerned about protocol than results."

"I see."

"Don't worry, Johnny. I've got Downey's number. I'm transferring him to a new assignment in Washington. He'll be pushing papers for the duration, which is apparently what he does best. If Peterson had been honest with me about Downey, I'd have pulled him out of here long ago."

I said, "Forgive me for saying so, sir, but Si chose his subordinates, including Downey, to suit his ultimate purpose and he chose well."

"That's my sense of the situation, too. I was tempted to give you Downey's job just to rub salt in the wound, but that would be a waste of manpower. I need you out in the front lines doing what you do best."

"Thank you for that, sir."

Smiling again, Davis said, "I thought you'd feel that way." Davis looked thoughtful for a moment, and then continued in a philosophical tone, "Johnny, you and I are actually a lot alike. By that I mean we're both professionals. Even though you aren't enamored with the uniforms and military ritual, you know your job and do it well. You always give it your best, regardless of the odds against you. I'll take one man like that over ten by-the-book guys like Downey anytime."

"Thank you, sir. Coming from you those words mean a lot."

"You're welcome, son. Now, anything else on your mind before we go?"

"Yes, sir. I would like to put Lieutenant Jackson, Ensign Meredith, and Sergeant Pierce in for commendations. I realize our mission was classified, but they deserve more recognition than a verbal well done."

Nodding, the General said, "I'll have my adjutant write the commendations. He's good at saying nice things without giving away the farm. Also, I get the idea you'd like Pierce assigned as your aide-de-camp on a permanent basis. Am I right?"

"Yes, sir. I would consider that a big favor."

"Done. Anything else?"

"A new assignment, sir?"

Davis chuckled. "Can't stand sitting around on your hands, huh? Well, I've got something coming up for you, but it's a week or two off yet. Tell you what, you and Pierce take some leave time and report back here a week from Monday. You can meet

Downey's replacement then and he'll give you the details of your new assignment. I'll have orders for your leave cut immediately so you can get started. Pick them up from Colonel Peterson's former secretary."

"Thank you, sir."

Standing, Davis said, "You're welcome, son. Now let's get back to work." With a grin he added, "All this lollygagging isn't winning the war."

General Davis climbed into the back of his staff car and I hiked back down the hill to where I left the Army's Dodge very early yesterday morning at the Coast Guard station. I actually had to stop and think about when I parked the Dodge there. It seemed a very long time ago.

At Building 100 I found everyone in the conference room listening to Davis who was quoting from my report. I didn't think my presence was required, so I walked down the hall to Si Peterson's old office and asked Sylvia Eckert if Davis instructed her to type up leave orders for Pierce and myself. Miss Eckert handed me the forms ordering our leaves. They were already signed by General Davis.

That chore completed, I settled into a chair outside the conference room and thought about the week off Davis gave me. I already had a pretty good idea how I was going to spend it.

The meeting broke up a few minutes after three and the first man out of the conference room was Downey. He glared at me, but said nothing. Next, Sergeant Pierce joined me in the hall.

He looked pleased and said, "Thank you for recommending me for a commendation, sir."

"You deserve it, Sergeant. Did Davis also tell you he's assigning you to be a permanent member of my team?"

"Yes, sir. I'll do my best to live up to your expectations."

"I have no doubt about that, Sergeant. And did Davis tell you we have a week's leave coming before we're expected back here?'

Smiling, Pierce said, "No, sir, he didn't mention that."

Handing him his leave papers, I said, "Here are your orders, Russ. I'll see you back here a week from Monday."

"That's swell, sir. Thank you. This gives me a chance to see my mom and sister up in Portland. It's been a while."

"Good, and don't thank me, this was General Davis' idea. By the way, I think your bag is still in the trunk of my car out front. Come on out with me and I'll get it for you."

While unloading Pierce's bag from the Dodge's trunk, I saw Jack leave Building 100 with the Coast Guard commander who met us at the airfield. They spoke for a few minutes, and when their conversation ended, Jack headed in my direction.

"Everything okay, Jack?"

"Everything's fine, Johnny. That's my boss out here in the California district. After talking to General Davis, he commended me for a job well done."

"Davis is also working on official commendations for you and Ensign Meredith. They'll be a while coming, but you'll get them."

"Thanks, Johnny."

"Are you about ready to head for home?"

Nodding, Jack said, "Yeah, I'm more than ready, although I haven't figured out exactly how I'm going to get there yet."

"Well, it so happens I'm just about to get into this Dodge here and point it toward Santa Barbara, where I plan to spend the week's leave I've got coming. Would you like a lift?"

"I sure as hell would. In fact, I think my sea bag is still in your trunk. Are you leaving now?"

"I am."

"Then we better get a move on. We've got a seven-hour trip ahead of us." Grinning, Jack added, "And we have to stop for a telephone call so Mister Whiskers will wait up to let you in."

THE END

MEET H. P. OLIVER

H. P. Oliver began his career with a degree in journalism from San Jose State University and spent the next twenty-some years writing award-winning entertainment and educational media. Now he applies his creativity and imagination to writing historical mysteries.

About mystery writing, Oliver says, "To be truly engrossing, a mystery needs a little meat on its bones—something more than just figuring out who done the evil deed. Taking a story back in time or even basing it on actual historical events is a great way to endow a good yarn with even more color and depth. Historical periods and locations give the writer an opportunity to take most readers where they've never been before."

H. P. Oliver lives in northern California and spends much of his time working on projects throughout the western states. In addition to his love of history, Oliver's interests range from vintage film to restoring classic cars.

For information about H. P. Oliver's books, including synopses, previews, video trailers, and purchase links, visit his fan site at www.HPOliver.com, where you will also find illustrated history articles and other fascinating features. Plan to stay a while.

BOOKS BY H. P. OLIVER

◆ CLASSIC MYSTERIES IN HISTORY ◆

THE TRUTH BE TOLD
(E-Book)

AND THE ANGELS SING
(E-Book)

SILENTS!
(E-Book & Paperback)

WINGING IT
(E-Book & Paperback)

GOODNIGHT, SAN FRANCISCO
(E-Book & Paperback)

SO LONG, L A
(E-Book & Paperback)

◆ JOHNNY SPICER CAPERS ◆

JOHNNY SPICER: THE FIRST CAPERS
(E-Book)

PACIFICA
(E-Book & Paperback)

REVOLVER
(E-Book & Paperback)

TEMBO
(E-Book & Paperback)

S. N. A. F. U.
(E-Book & Paperback)

H. P. Oliver's books are available at Amazon.com